Shadows Fate

(Book 3 of the Ruadhán Sidhe Novels)

By Aiki Flinthart

2018

To all the authors out there – both published and aspiring – don't give up.

Thank you to my husband for his unfailing support and willing services as beta-reader. Thanks also to everyone who has encouraged and assisted me along this very challenging journey called authorship. Often, it sucks, and only the kindness of friends and strangers keeps you going.

Shadows Fate

Cover artwork by Harper by Design

A Cataloging-in-Publications entry for this title is available from the National Library of Australia.

ISBN-13: 978-0-6482878-4-1 (Trade Paperback)
ISBN-13: 978-0-6482878-3-4 (e-book)
Computing Advantages & Training P/L
PO Box 3388, Darra
QLD 4076, Australia

NOTE: This book is written with AUSTRALIAN SPELLINGS, not USA spellings.

Discover other titles by Aiki Flinthart at: **www.aikiflinthart.com**
Including:

The Ruadhan Sidhe Novels (YA Urban Fantasy)
Shadows Wake (#1)
Shadows Bane (#2)
Shadows Fate (#3)

The 80AD series (YA Adventure/Fantasy)
80AD Book 1: *The Jewel of Asgard*
80AD Book 2: *The Hammer of Thor*
80AD Book 3: *The Tekhen of Anuket*
80AD Book 4: *The Sudarshana*
80AD Book 5: *The Yu Dragon*

The Kalima Chronicles (YA Adventure/Fantasy)
IRON (#1)
FIRE (#2)
STEEL (#3)

Sold! (Contemporary Romance/Adventure)

Short Story Anthologies
Return
Like a Woman

Shadows Fate

Book 3 of the Ruadhán Sidhe Novels

Aiki Flinthart 2018

ONE

The plane juddered and bounced in an airpocket. Oxygen masks fell from the ceiling and dangled, swaying.

Logan gripped my hand. 'Alright, Rowan?'

'Fabulous,' I muttered. 'I hate flying. And crashing is worse. Tell me again why we're doing this?'

'You and Michael need to die,' he said.

'Stunning idea.'

'Not mine, yours.'

'Shut up,' I growled.

-Prithee, hold fast. My father's terse instruction slid into my mind. *We approach stall speed. This will get bumpy. Maeve, Jennifer, now would be a good time to slow us.-*

<We're trying, Calain.> Maeve's hysteria-edged reply thrust into my head. *<We just don't have enough connection to the* sianfath

to control something this big and heavy. We're too far from shore and the forests.>

-Apologies. The Italian tracking systems are more efficient than we suspected. We had to go further offshore to evade detection. But I'd prefer not to truly crash, so please, slow our descent.-

Jennifer burst into tears. 'I can't do it, Mother. I just can't!'

'You *can* and you *will*,' Maeve snapped. Only her sharp profile was visible across the aisle but even I could tell she was lying.

Logan turned stoic grey eyes my way. His fingers crushed mine. The left engine coughed and sputtered. In the cockpit, something popped. Calain swore aloud, struggling with the controls. The acrid scent of electrical-fire smoke wafted through the small cabin. An alarm sounded, strident and piercing. Below, the sparkling Mediterranean looked like diamond-tipped concrete.

Maeve twisted and looked back at me, fearful.

'Shit.' I closed my eyes and tried to calm my heart's hammering. I clutched my armrests until the leather tore. The hard plastic underneath broke and crumbled into shards.

'Five minutes to impact,' Calain shouted over his shoulder. 'Ladies, focus yourselves or we all may perish here.'

The left engine coughed again and died.

Calain swore. 'We are committed, now. The plane must crash if the world is to believe Michael's death. But I would lief as not die in truth.'

I distanced myself from the chaos around and sought the *sianfath*, the life-connection binding all of us to the natural world. I should be able to act as a conduit and feed its power to Maeve and Jennifer to bolster their telekinesis.

But Maeve was right: the forests so integral to the sidhe's connection to the Earth were too distant. While there was life in the ocean, it was too scattered for me to draw on.

The sianfath *out here is weak. I—*

<*Go beyond, Rowan,* Maeve cut in. *The block in your mind is gone. You have the ability to extend much further than you've done before. You could reach around the whole world if you needed to. The coast isn't far. Draw from there.*>

But you'll need massive amounts of energy. People could die if I'm not careful.

<We *will die if you don't try!*>

I swore.

<*Join with Jennifer and I in the* lorntinn, she added. *Being connected in the unity with us will make it easier to control the flow and anticipate our needs.*>

I hesitated. Joining with others in the *lorntinn* meant opening my deepest shields, exposing my heart and fears to Maeve. It might make things a little easier, but it would also give her too much knowledge she could use to manipulate me, later.

I can do it without the lorntinn, I returned.

Her fingers whitened on the seat arm as the plane jolted again. <*Fine. But remember, you* must *hold back a little power for yourself. Without that regulator organ, releasing all the energy to us could leave you with a shortfall.*>

Shut up and let me concentrate. I shut her out and focussed.

Logan squeezed my hand. I tugged free to better keep him from harm. Blowing a thick breath, I stretched further, past the silent depths of water, west to the coast of Italy. Further than I'd ever tried before. I attenuated myself into the *sianfath*, stretching thin the anchor that held me to my body; risking losing myself in the rush to save my family. There, at the edges of my extension, the flare of orange non-light indicating humans. A brilliance, a seductive temptation of concentrated energy, drawing me like a moth.

'Three minutes to impact!' Calain's voice had lost its calm. Beside him, in the copilot's seat, my mother called my name in tones of desperation. The right engine's roar sputtered to a halt. Now the only sounds were the shrill alarm, the groaning of metal, and the wind whistling outside. The plane's juddering increased as it bounced through the thick ocean air. Calain fought to keep the nose up.

There was no time to seek further. I skimmed off the fierce essence of human life from the city. The orange brilliance dimmed. The power of thousands of bodies swelled in mine, pricking beneath my skin, tasting of ozone and clouds. I was energy, life, potential. I could do anything.

'Maeve,' I shouted over the din, 'get ready. I've got more than I can handle so we have to do this fast.'

Two silver-green tendrils poured from me, into Maeve and Jennifer. The sidhe women stiffened in their seats. Maeve gasped and Jennifer let out a terrified scream. The energy roiled around their bodies, finding ways in, filling them until they glowed with it. Wisps of smoke coiled up from their clothing. The second smoke detector in the cabin added its ear-piercing alarm to the chaos.

'Control it, Jennifer,' Maeve commanded. 'Or it will burn you inside and out. Use it to power your telekinesis.'

'It's too much!' her daughter cried. 'I don't know how to—'

'One minute!' Calain's roar cut across her.

Jen! I threw the thought at her, pushing it through her mental shields. *Remember the training we did in Brisbane. This is no different. Your go-to move was to push in front and behind at the same time – to balance. Remember Newton's law? Do the same thing: some down against the ocean, some up against the plane.*

Jen's fear-filled thoughts settled into clarity. She thrust and the plane jolted upward, tilting to one side. For a moment the ocean loomed in my window, white-capped waves just fifty or sixty metres beneath the wingtip. Calain swore and twisted at the controls, trying to compensate for Jen's uneven push.

Maeve's jaw clenched and the plane righted itself. I fed both women more energy. Our descent slowed. Maeve's lips drew back from her teeth in an animal snarl. Sweat beaded on her smooth forehead. Jen whimpered.

The plane lurched and dropped a sickening few feet.

I drew more energy. The city's orange reservoir of life dimmed further, blackening to death in a few specks. I groaned but fed Maeve and Jen, regardless. The plane levelled again, slowing until we moved at no more than the speed of a car; then a walk.

Calain leapt from his seat, bending to exit the cockpit. His head brushed the ceiling when he straightened in the cabin. His broad shoulders filled the door. He tugged at the external door control mechanism.

'Everyone ready? Maeve, release us. We'll only have a few minutes to evacuate once we hit water so keep calm.'

Maeve nodded, the muscles on her neck and forearms corded.

Calain braced himself. 'Go.'

The plane dropped the last few feet onto the water. The crash broke my concentration and I released my connection to the city. Logan reached for me.

'Don't!' I panted. 'There's still too much in me. Get out.'

Maeve groaned and whispered a plea for help. She and Jen both still had too much energy as well. I could hold more. They could only channel it. Without anything to expend it on, the power would backlash and destroy them. It would do the same to me, just a little slower. I pulled it back from their bodies and squirrelled it away inside myself. Maeve slumped in her seat, her ridiculous yellow lifejacket rucked up around her neck.

'Mother?' Jen shook her.

My mother, Anna Gilmore, emerged from the cockpit. I gestured urgently at Calain and the door. He yanked it open and hurled it out. He activated the self-inflating life raft and threw that out, too.

Water lapped at the door, splashing into the cabin.

'Logan,' I said, 'get Maeve and Jen out.'

He hesitated then scrambled out of his seat.

Water sloshed over the door frame as the weight balance changed. Anna gasped and retreated. Calain picked her up and hurled her out. Her scream ended in a splash.

Two seats forward, Erin Fairchild stood and rushed to the door, leaping past Calain without hesitation.

'Hey!' Tied to the seat in front of me, Michael Eisen's efforts to free himself shook the chair. 'What about me? Get me out of here!'

Calain gave him a sardonic look. 'I'd far rather let you drown with your plane, Eisen. But we need you for the moment. Cease your caterwauling and hold still.' He drew a knife from his pocket, flicked it open, and slashed the bonds holding Eisen to his seat. Calain jerked his head at the door.

'Out.'

Michael complied, glaring at Calain as he edged past.

Logan, carrying Maeve over his shoulder, jumped into the ocean. Jen followed, staggering as a wave surged beneath the plane. One wing dug into the water and the craft listed dangerously.

Once she was gone, only Calain stood by the door. 'Come, daughter,' he urged me.

I stood in the aisle, clutching at the seat backs and clinging to the ragged edges of self-control. Power pulsed through my body. Too much to manage and my connection to the *sianfath* was lost so I couldn't feed it back to the city. It had to be released, but how?

'Go,' I managed, through gritted teeth. 'I can't hold the energy any longer. At least I can use it to destroy the plane.'

If search parties found the plane intact the accident would be suspicious and our death announcements even more so. If our activities in Italy were to succeed, I needed to be invisible. Dying was the best way.

Calain stepped towards me, brow furrowing over intense grey eyes.

'Do it from outside. You can't stay in here.' The plane rocked violently and he staggered. 'Hurry!' Water poured into the door and the nose tilted, plunging into the cobalt depths.

'I have to be touching it to feed the energy,' I said. My legs trembled with the effort of holding myself up against the incline. 'Otherwise it'll go into the water and be wasted. You need to get clear.'

'God's blood!' Calain growled. From outside, Anna's voice screamed our names. Calain dived into the water and I was alone.

I staggered towards the door as the cabin creaked and shook around me. Water poured in and the nose tilted further. My feet slipped. I hit the floor and slid, catching at a seat frame in desperation. The metal cut cruelly into my skin. Muscles in my shoulder tore and burned like the power within me.

The plane was almost vertical in the ocean, the front windscreen looking into the abyss, the exit in clear air. Water boiled, rising up through the cabin towards me. I sucked three long, deep breaths and jack-knifed my body, flinging myself towards the door. My fingers caught the edge. Saltwater poured over the lip, blinding me. I fought the urge to gasp for air and held what I had in my lungs.

The door submerged and the plane hung, suspended by the air bubble trapped in the tail. I wriggled into the clear water, my body heavy with the personal items I carried strapped to my waist. I grabbed the doorframe again, this time from the outside.

For a moment the plane and I hung in gentle accord with the icy water, floating. Creaks and groans of twisting metal echoed through the liquid grey-blue. Sunlight shimmered past me in flickering beams that softened the aircraft's sharp lines and vanished into hungry darkness.

My lungs ached. My body and mind burned from within. I couldn't wait any longer. Hopefully the others were out of the water.

Silver-green energy poured through me into the metal. The aircraft's unliving body resisted energy meant for the organic. The aluminium glowed red. Water bubbled. Agonising pain lanced through my hands and air cascaded from my lips. I held on grimly, changing the energy's shape, seeking a way to drive it between atomic bonds. There. The silver-green shifted to a dull grey and drove into the metal. The heat spread. Energy flashed through the frame, breaking seams and tearing bolts. The life-force of thousands of humans ripped apart the jet's body with the crackling shriek of rending metal, and broke it into a dozen pieces.

The doorframe tore from my grip and slipped into darkness. With barely enough strength left to move my arms, I struck out for the surface. The sun's shimmering-white disc overhead seemed an impossible distance. Too far. Lethargy weighted my limbs. I'd expended too much energy; forgotten to keep any for my body. I hadn't the strength to get to the surface.

My mouth opened. I had to breathe.

TWO

<Logan! She's going to drown.>

I didn't think that would bother you.

<Don't be childish. We need her, still. She's the only sidhe with the shadow-thought ability and we need her help to defeat the Mors Ferrum.>

Ah. Of course.

Something dragged at my hair, hauling me up. My head broke free of the water. I gasped, coughing and choking, spitting saltwater. Logan shifted his grip, rolling me onto my back and sliding an arm across my chest. He towed me to the life raft that bobbed close by, brilliant orange against the ocean's soft blue-grey.

Calain dragged us both into the flapping, tent-like shelter. I huddled on the rubber floor, coughing and trying not to vomit, my limbs leaden.

'Rowan!' Anna pushed my sodden hair aside.

I blinked blearily. 'I'm ok.'

She gathered me into her arms and held me as I shivered. 'Get her a blanket. Maeve, how far away is that boat?'

There came a ripping and crinkling noise and someone tucked a shiny space-blanket around my shoulders.

Maeve said stiffly, 'My son, Dante, is in Rome. Out of my range. So I can't ask him where the boat is. It was supposed to meet us, but we landed off course.'

'Why were we so far from shore?' my mother asked, glaring fiercely at Maeve. 'The plan was for you to lower the plane gently, then break the fuselage – not force Rowan to do it.'

'We were too far from the *sianfath*.' Maeve raised her chin. 'Apparently Dante's information about the Italian government's ability to detect us was incorrect. But I can't tell you why.'

Erin pulled her phone out of the sealed plastic bag around her waist. 'I could call him.'

Calain laid a hand over hers. 'Nay. We should all leave our telephones disconnected. They are trackable and we do not wish to be found by the Coast Guard, remember?'

'So, what then?' Erin snapped. 'We just wait?'

I tried to shut her out. Shut it all out. But dozens of voices whispered and screamed, deep in my mind, louder than the blanket.

'How are we supposed to get to shore?' Anna said.

'Fret not, Anna,' Calain said calmly. 'Once Maeve's sufficiently recovered, she has the telepathic range to find the captain and direct him to our whereabouts. Rowan, is the plane destroyed?' Calain peered out the raft's flapping door. 'And the homing beacon? We don't want the Coast Guard finding it too soon, either.'

I nodded.

'Destroyed? How? What the hell did you do?' Erin's sharp questions brought me out of my mother's safe embrace.

I lifted my heavy head and regarded her bleakly. 'I murdered a hundred people in Ravenna to save you.'

She gaped at me, her usual acerbity silenced for once.

'Oh, Rowan.' My mother's voice was full of regret and tinged with horror.

I couldn't bear their condemnation, so I huddled in the blanket and tried to blank out the terrified whispers of the dying that echoed in my skull. The black abyss of exhaustion dragged at my mind and body. I had no strength left to rejuvenate myself.

'She did what she had to,' Maeve stated, squeezing water from her long, dark braid. 'What was necessary to get us to land. If the Mors Ferrum get that parcel containing our DNA and information they will use it to expose and kill every sidhe on the planet.' She pinned Michael with an arrogant glare.

He lifted his chin and returned a sneer.

'But,' Maeve continued, keeping eye contact with him, 'you *humans* have no idea what that would mean for the world.'

Michael's jaw clenched. 'It would mean,' he said, 'an end to your manipulations and power-mongering. Once Alexander Dyson gets that information, you are finished. As the Mors Ferrum's leader, Dyson will have what he needs to find you and wipe you out once and for all. You people are responsible for all the worst holocausts of history. Every brutal leader this world has ever experienced has been a sidhe.'

Maeve's chin came up. Her dark-rimmed grey eyes flashed. 'Yes, but—'

'He's right, Maeve.' Calain's deep, calm voice cut across hers. She glared at him. Calain forestalled her retort. 'From the human point of view, he's right and you know it. The Mors Ferrum doesn't know the difference between Light sidhe and Dark. We can't change their minds because it's true that sidhe are responsible. What they don't understand is how vital a role the Light play in the world's ecology. They don't realise that wiping us out would wipe humanity out as well.'

His flat words fell into a shocked silence. Michael opened his mouth, then closed it and looked away.

For a while all I heard was the splash and slosh of waves against the side of the orange inflatable raft, and Jen's sobbing breaths. The raft spun and rocked in a sickening motion, increasing the queasiness that churned along with seawater in my stomach. I rested my head on my knees, hoping it would help. Someone stroked my wet hair. I shuddered as Anna's worried thoughts bled through her touch. It took a moment to refocus and strengthen my mental shields enough to keep her out.

In the trauma of the plane crash I'd lost concentration and let my mind-castle walls falter. How much of my thoughts had the other sidhe read? Was it obvious to them how sickened I was by the deaths I'd caused? How much I hated myself for making the choice between the sidhe and the humans so easily; so quickly. None of my companions said anything.

Logan studied me, his thoughts worried and tinged with fear. For me or for himself? Did he think I was still going to lose control and suck the essence out of everyone? I smiled bleakly. With the corruption of Calain's guardian gone from my mind I was totally in control of my gifts, now.

That was the problem. I no longer had anything else to blame for my choices. I had chosen to kill those people and no amount of justification from Maeve could make that right.

The worst part was: I'd do it again.

Nausea swelled in my throat, pouring saliva into my mouth. I swallowed hard and pushed past Erin to the flapping plastic door of the tented roof. Thrusting my head outside, I vomited seawater and self-contempt into the ocean's uncaring emptiness. Tears burned my cheeks, mingling with water from my hair. I lay over the raft's bulging side and watched the sparkling water carry away my guilt.

Behind me, Erin made a noise of disgust. Anna and Logan both called my name, questioning.

'I'm fine.' I stayed in the clear, cold air, unwilling to return to the atmosphere of anger and distrust inside.

The winter wind rose and blew sharp across the water, turning the gentle swell into choppy whitecaps. I squinted up at the sun, trying to work out which direction we were floating. The morning was well-advanced, but the sun gave little warmth at this time of year in the northern hemisphere. We'd ditched the plane off the east coast of Italy, but the empty horizon said we had definitely landed further out than we'd intended. It could take days for my half-brother's rescue ship to find us.

We'd all brought water and food. But we had to intercept the parcel Michael had sent; the parcel containing all the DNA samples and information about the sidhe and our powers. Paul Eisen, Michael's son, had requested the courier hold the delivery, but there was no guarantee his request would make it to the right people in time. We didn't have days to bob around in the ocean. Hours were more than we could afford. We needed to get hold of that boat captain and get to shore.

I pulled a water bottle from the belt around my waist and rinsed my mouth. As I spat into the ocean, a smooth, grey form surged forth from the waves. With a yelp, I fell back.

'What is it?' Logan appeared at my side, pushing aside the orange flapping canvas.

'There's something in the water.' I pointed. Waves curled and splashed.

'I don't see—'

A rounded snout emerged and a black eye rolled clear of the waves to fix on us with uncanny intelligence.

'Dolphin.' I laughed, relieved.

Jen squeaked and shoved between us, her fears apparently forgotten in the delight of a close encounter.

The grey snout jerked back and forward a few times, emitting high-pitched squeals and clicks that drove straight through my skull. I covered my ears but it didn't help.

Inside the raft, Erin gasped and cried out. I twisted to look back at her.

'What is it?' Maeve asked her.

'I can hear her. The dolphin, I mean.'

'We all can, Erin,' Maeve said. The dolphin admitted another series of squeals and Maeve flinched.

Erin glowered. 'No, I mean I can *understand* her.'

My jaw dropped.

'Ask her what she wants, then,' Logan advised. He seemed unsurprised, just watching the creature, amusement softening his solemnity. Maybe I was the only one who found it a bit surreal, though Erin appeared almost as stunned.

'How come *she* can understand the dolphin?' Jen muttered.

Logan shrugged again. 'No-one's ever been able to work that out. Some sidhe have an affinity for animals and others don't. Sorry, Jen. Not fair, huh?'

Erin pushed between us, reaching out and touching the dolphin's smooth dome. Her smugness shifted into amazement as the animal squealed and turned its eye on us again.

'Slow down.' Erin pressed her palms against her temples and groaned. 'I don't understand.'

On impulse, I slipped the tiniest thread of myself through the *sianfath* and through Erin's shields, hearing what she heard. Hopefully, she wouldn't notice me.

For a moment all was chaos and strangeness; a way of thinking I couldn't begin to comprehend. Then our mutual bond to the *sianfath* surfaced and the dolphin's thoughts shifted into something more coherent. Still strangely-formed, but understandable; images and ideas, emerging and vanishing too fast for me to grasp.

As if sensing Erin's confusion, the images slowed and simplified. I got a sense of barely-curbed impatience, like a mother speaking to a toddler.

'She says there's a boat that way.' Erin pointed southwest then looked back at the dolphin.

The dolphin spoke again, squealing and clicking, her snout throwing sparkling drops of water in the air.

I released a breath. 'Wow.'

Erin laughed, her face alight and easy for once. We exchanged tentative smiles, bonded by our astonishment and delight.

'What did the dolphin say?' Calain asked.

'In a nutshell,' I said, 'something along the lines of "you're welcome".'

With a gasp, Erin scrambled back from the door, lightness falling away, our brief connection shattered by anger and fear again. 'How *dare* you? You were inside my shields without invitation. Listening to *my* private conversation. And you wonder why I don't trust you.'

'Erin!' Logan's voice whipcracked across her tirade.

Erin shut her mouth with a snap, glaring at both of us. 'You'd better teach her some basic manners, Logan,' she said stiffly. 'I don't care how new she is to this. She needs to know what's acceptable.'

'I'm sorry.' I ground out the apology, guilt weighting my tongue.

She swept me with a scornful glare. 'No, you aren't. You never stop and think. You just do whatever you think's best, regardless. Well, one of these days it'll get you killed, Rowan. Or all of us.' She turned away with a choked sob.

In the uncomfortable silence that followed, Maeve contacted the sidhe boat captain. Before long, Dante's sleek pleasure craft glided into view. When Erin scrambled to the raft door, Calain held her back.

'We'll bide here for the trip,' he said. Her angry protests left him unmoved. 'The fewer folk see us and Michael, the better. The captain will tow us to shore.'

Erin retreated, swearing under her breath.

The boat idled, rocking in the choppy water. The smell of diesel made me ill all over again. One of the boat crew tossed ropes to us. Calain caught one, but the other two fell short. Logan, and I slipped into the ocean to retrieve them. Seawater splashed in my mouth and I sputtered. Shivering, I struggled through the icy water, back to the raft, rope in hand. Logan and Calain each grasped an arm and hauled me in. Calain tied the ropes to the raft while Anna wrapped me once more in the space-blanket, scolding.

'G-give it a rest, Anna,' I managed. 'I'm f-fine.'

The raft lurched forward, throwing everyone to one side. Crushed beneath Michael and Logan, I groaned. I righted myself and clung to a handhold, but the shivering deepened, taking such a hold that I forgot what it felt like to be warm and dry. Anna eyed me worriedly.

'We have to get you dry. You'll catch your death.'

Maeve said coolly, 'She can dry herself, if she cares to. It takes almost no energy.'

I bared my teeth at her, too cold and exhausted to be diplomatic. 'Shall I t-take it from the crew who are rescuing us, or you?'

'You depleted yourself? I did warn you to watch your levels.'

When I didn't reply, Maeve sniffed and stared out the opening towards the hazy horizon. Jen, after one defiant look at her mother's back, scooted closer and wedged her slender body against mine, adding her warmth.

'You can take from me, if you need to,' she murmured, her expression a conflict of fear and trust.

I gave a shaky laugh. 'Thanks k-kiddo. I think the heat is fine, though. You can do something else, though. Switch off the GPS locater?'

'What?'

'There's bound to be one built into the raft somewhere,' I said. 'Just go micro-scale telekinesis and blow a fuse.'

Her confusion cleared. After a moment, a faint smell of burning electronics reached me.

Logan slid closer to us and lifted the blanket, wrapping his arms around me and pulling my back against his broad chest. Sandwiched between him and Jen, my shivering eased and I slipped into a restless, dream-haunted sleep.

THREE

<The captain will tow us to shore, but not to a marina or port.>

–Yes.–

<Calain, you seem displeased. You should be happy. Your memories are returned, you're restored to your daughter and wife. Now we're on a path that could well result in the achievement of all your dreams for peace between the sidhe and humans.>

–Maeve, there is much I wish to say to thee, but now is not the time or place.–

<Whatever you think, Calain, you must know my actions have always been for the good of the sidhe as a species.>

–As I said: Not the time or place. Thou hast much to answer for. Thy treatment of me is but one of many. Thy treatment of my daughter is unforgivable.–

<You've worked for over five hundred years to get to this point, Calain. You've known the whole time she would be the one to help you achieve our goals. She's a weapon and a tool. You must remember that or you'll falter at the time when she needs you most to be strong.>

–When you need me most, you mean. We both know what she may have to do if we can't stop this parcel getting to the Mors Ferrum. And we both know what that might do to her.–

<Yes. And you must be the ocair – the key –, not her father, when the moment comes.>

'Ruadhán.' Calain's soft call woke me.

I opened sticky eyes to find I'd fallen sideways across Logan's lap. Logan lay stretched out beneath me, asleep. Jen's tousled, dark head rested on my thigh. Maeve was curled up, her head pillowed on the raft's inflated side, graceful and contained even in sleep. Erin lay on her side, a fist under her cheek. She drew a deep sobbing breath in her sleep. Only Calain and Michael remained alert; Michael staring darkly at Calain, who ignored him and watched over us.

Calain repeated my name then shook Erin awake.

'What?' I nudged Logan and Jen. They groaned and moved aside, letting me get to the entrance, where Calain pointed at the sea. The sun flared on the western horizon, peeking from behind low clouds. The boat had brought us close to a beach.

'We've arrived. I've untied us and the boat is heading back to sea. We'll have to swim the rest of the way and pull the raft.'

We reached the shore undetected, just on dusk, and landed on a deserted stretch of beach. There, we punctured the raft and buried it deep in the coarse sand. Sandy, exhausted and with frayed tempers, we then trudged into the beachside town of Lido Adriano. Erin, the only one who'd had the forethought to put her phone on roaming before we left Australia, found an Airbnb house there and booked it while we dug in the sand. She led the way with an irritating air of smugness that made me want to slap her. By the time we reached the house and fell inside, though, all I wanted was a shower and a bed. My legs were rubber and Logan half-carried me up the weathered steel and timber steps to the front door.

It took a while for all eight of us to cycle through the two bathrooms. While I was showering, Maeve and Anna went out and found the one small store still open, and a restaurant. They returned with huge amounts of food and a pile of grocery essentials. The only thing we all lacked was a change of clothing. I'd tucked a tshirt and change of underwear into the sealed plastic bag holding my other things, so I wore those and a towel until the overloaded washing machine and drier were done. The others were similarly attired.

A beachy-looking group gathered around the enormous faux-marble dining table and inhaled rich Italian food. But there was little conversation beyond requests to pass containers and condiments. What could be said, really? Officially, Michael Eisen and my current identity, Meghan Greene, were now dead. The others on this trip had never existed on the passenger list. Nobody seemed to want to talk about our next move. The tracking on the parcel showed it stuck in Customs in Rome. Being after hours, there wasn't a lot we could do.

Erin switched on the tv and flicked channels until she found a newscast subtitled in English. I understood Italian, but there was no point in telling her. After the headline of a minor earth tremor in the central mountains, the story switched to us and everyone turned to watch the screen.

Billionaire fitness industry businessman, Michael Eisen, has been reported lost in the Adriatic Sea this afternoon. Mr Eisen's plane vanished off the radar around eleven AM this morning. No distress signal was received, and air searches have found no wreckage. Mr Eisen was coming to Italy to set up a series of health spas, gyms and health research facilities that would have created thousands of jobs for Italian workers. His son, Paul, was unavailable for comment. The search will restart at first light tomorrow.

Michael swore and glared at me. I ignored him, and the dagger-look Calain sent him. The TV talking head continued.

Medical authorities are concerned over the deaths of more than eighty people today in Ravenna and nearby villages of Punta Marina and Lido Adriano. Most were elderly or ill, but reports indicate all of them died at approximately the same time. A hospital spokesman said there was no apparent connection between any of the deaths and no current theories about why they all happened at once. Investigations are ongoing as the death toll continues to rise.

I rose from the table, the rich food heavy in my stomach.

'Rowan?' Anna threw her arms around me. I bore it for a few seconds, then prised myself free.

'Don't. There's no forgiveness for what I did.' I wrapped my arms around my waist. 'I can still hear them, in my head. Every. Damned. Voice.'

All the faces around the table turned to me; some scornful, some horrified, some curious.

'What do you mean?' Maeve's question was fraught with worry.

I inspected my bare toes, cold on the cracked beige linoleum floor. 'One was a war veteran. His mind was full of death and despair. One was a teacher. Hers was seventy years of love for children. And one was an environmental specialist.' I laughed disbelievingly. 'I have his knowledge. He was on the verge of a breakthrough in understanding how to protect key species. He was one of us. Partly. He didn't know it.' I dug my fingers into my hair and groaned, no longer able to suppress the whispers. The voices became a babble, then a roar drumming on the inside of my shields, begging for release.

A chair scraped and Maeve stood before me.

'Leave her alone.' Anna pushed between us.

'Don't be stupid,' Maeve snapped. 'I'm not going to hurt her. She has to release them or she'll go insane. No-one can hold that many for long and stay in their right mind.'

'Release what?' Anna frowned at her.

Calain gripped Anna's wrist and drew her aside. 'Their souls,' he said quietly.

'That's ridiculous,' Anna scoffed. 'You don't believe in religion. You told me yourself.'

'True,' Calain said. 'But all living things are connected to the *sianfath*. It's their connection, their individuality, that's caught in Ruadhán's mind. A soul isn't the right word, but it's the closest English equivalent. In the sidhe language it's *enath*, the essence. Holding onto them is one of the difficulties in using the *skath-sheel* gift Ruadhán bears. Aeona, my mother, struggled with it, too.'

'And Rowan has them inside her somehow?' Anna said.

Calain nodded. 'Most of us can't see or sense them. Aeona could, and it seems Ruadhán can. Aeona told me she'd been forced to draw life from thousands of soldiers in her time as a weapon for Tordal Ivaldison and his son, Kieran, in the 1300's. When she finally ran away, she kept one soul locked in her mind. She called it a piece of grit in her conscience to remind her what she'd done.'

I put my back against the blue-painted plasterboard wall and slid to the floor, curling into a protective ball.

'Maeve's right,' Calain said. 'Holding so many will drive you utterly mad. Let them go.'

Maeve touched my forehead. I pushed her arm aside.

'Don't even *think* about trying to get into my mind again, Maeve. Not after last time.'

'I was just going to help you—'

'I don't need your help. I know what to do,' I said.

'Then do it.' She watched me for a few seconds then made a noise of frustration and stalked away, head high and shoulders back.

Anna crouched in front of me, her vivid blue eyes dark with worry. Logan joined her, his mind brushing against my shields.

'You stay out too, Logan,' I warned.

'I know you're still angry with Maeve,' he said, 'and with reason. But she's right about this. You can't hang onto them.' He gripped my shoulder, the warmth of his skin an anchor for me as I fought the tide of humanity threatening to drown my thoughts from within.

'But they'll be *gone.*'

Logan shrugged. 'That's the point. You can't keep them, Rowan.' He sighed. 'If they escape you they'll go searching for their bodies. While a lost *enath* can return to a living body, these people are dead. They would just be tormented and lost forever. You have to let them go.'

'You don't understand.' I rested my forehead on my fists. 'Who am I to play God this way and decide their lives are worth less than mine? I killed their bodies to save myself and all of you. How can I obliterate their souls, too?'

'Oh, Rowan.' Anna held me close again. 'I'm sorry. I'm sorry we put you in such a horrible position. I know it's not easy. I know you tried so hard for so long not to kill anyone.'

'Oh, please.' Erin's sharp voice intruded. 'I think I'm going to be ill. Stop whinging and do what needs to be done.'

'Erin.' Logan's tone was loaded with reproof.

A chair scraped. 'What?' she retorted. 'She had no problem letting my father die, or digging into my head. But now she's all worked up about some sick old people she didn't even know?'

'She's saved your life at least four times, Erin,' Logan said. 'So, shut up.'

'My life wouldn't have *needed* saving if you hadn't brought her into it, Logan, so don't give me any holier-than-thou bullshit.' Erin's voice broke. 'I'm only here to make sure she does the right thing and destroys the Mors Ferrum. I'm not here to be her friend. Or yours, for that matter. Not after what you did to my father.'

Logan flinched, his expression haunted, stricken. 'Erin, please...stop.'

'Whatever. If you can't see she's just attention-seeking then I'm wasting my time. I'm going to bed.' Her footsteps faded down the hall and a door slammed.

'Happy families, I see,' Michael drawled. He leaned back in his chair, one elbow hooked over the white-painted straight back, his legs crossed at the ankles.

'Don't you start.' Anna shot to her feet, her red hair curling wildly, hectic spots of colour in her cheeks. 'She saved your son's life. You should be grateful, but all you do is snipe at us. This is all your fault, Michael Eisen. You keep your mouth shut and stay away from my daughter.'

He rose, sneering as he towered over her. 'Or what, Anna?' He flung his arms wide. 'What else can you do to me? Paul might be alive, but you've turned him against me. Taken my business away and now my life, too. I don't exist. You can't hurt me.'

A steak knife rose from the table and sliced through the air, stopping just an inch short of his jugular. He stiffened, eyes wide. Across from him, Jen rose as well, her slender thirteen-year-old body quivering and indignation sparking from her mind.

'She might not be able to,' she said, her voice low and gritty, 'but I'll bet I can.' The knife point touched his skin. Michael stepped back. The knife followed him. He grabbed the handle and hauled at it, his face flushing red with effort. Jen gave him a nasty little smile. The knife stayed where it was, drawing a bead of blood from his corded neck.

'Enough, Jen,' Logan said. 'He gets the message. Why don't you show him to his room? The sedative Maeve gave him should be taking effect about now.'

Jen nodded, her grin stretching as Michael glanced back and forth between her and his empty wineglass in horror. He blinked slowly several times before listing sideways. Jen let the knife clatter to the table and caught him telekinetically before he fell. His head smacked the table as she lifted him, but her scornful expression didn't change. She floated him along the hall to the small room he'd been allocated in the middle of the house. Its only window was too tiny for a grown man to squeeze through, and the door could be locked from the outside.

Logan, Anna and Calain refocussed on me.

I sighed and scrubbed the tears from my skin. 'I know.'

I closed my eyes. Tethering myself to my body, I stepped free of it and drew all but one of the unhappy souls with me into the *sianfath*. The environmentalist I kept tucked away in one of my castle-rooms for various reasons, only one of which made any logical sense. One by one the brilliant orange *enaths* trailed after me, coming into focus as their connection with the *sianfath* strengthened. Regretfully, I cut the almost-invisible orange lines tying them to me and to their old lives. With wails and laughter, one-hundred-and-three souls slipped into the silver-green of the *sianfath* and were absorbed by it. In turn, the *sianfath* brightened a little.

I slumped against the wall, empty and lost.

Logan scooped me up and, with a nod to my parents, carried me to the room he'd chosen. Calain's brow darkened and he took a step towards us. Anna restrained him with a word and a head-shake. I didn't need parental protection. Tonight, I needed someone to hold me and to fill the void that had just been ripped in my heart.

With the door closed behind us, Logan tucked me under the hideous crocheted blankets and slid in beside me. He pushed an auburn curl away from my eyes and pulled me close against his side. I sighed and rested my head on his shoulder.

'That's our real job, isn't it?' I murmured.

'You mean the cycling?' he asked. 'Yes.' A hint of sadness coloured his voice. 'Most of us do it unconsciously. I'm sorry it's harder for you. It's what the humans don't understand. The sidhe are responsible for the movement of energy through the Earth's ecosystems. Not the physical energy of matter conversion. The psychic energy that keeps the *sianfath's* connection between all living things functioning.'

'The gene allowing us to feel the energy,' I said, frowning, 'is also the one that's folded in human DNA, isn't it? So they can't see or feel what we do.'

'Yes,' he repeated. 'They only see the physical ecosystems. They don't understand how intertwined it is. The physical and psychic are two sides to the same coin. Without one – without us to manage the *sianfath* – the Earth dies. Slowly, painfully and incurably.'

'So,' I said, rolling onto my back and staring up at the popcorn-plastered ceiling, 'how is preventing the package getting to the Mors Ferrum going to help? I know we have to stop them using our genetic information to find other sidhe, but that's only a short-term solution. I'm sure Michael's not the only one working on our DNA. And Erin's just one geneticist on our side. She can delay our DNA being sequenced.' I studied Logan's profile. 'But they'll find us eventually.'

'I know,' Logan said heavily. 'You're right. But stopping them now might buy us enough time to come up with a longer-term solution. A way of hiding the sidhe forever so we can continue our role undiscovered.'

'That seems...' I wasn't sure how to say it without offending him. 'Naïve.'

He chuckled, low in his chest. 'I prefer optimistic.'

'Not your normal thing.'

'No,' he admitted, stroking my cheek, 'it wasn't before I met you. Now, corny as it sounds, I have hope.'

'Hope for what?' I whispered, my heart thudding as he caressed my neck.

'The world. The destruction of the Mors Ferrum. Hope for us; that I've found someone I can trust and be happy with,' he murmured. 'You never gave up on me, even when I betrayed you.' He swallowed and his jaw muscles jumped.

'It wasn't you, Logan.' I touched his mouth, hating the pain that shadowed him. 'With that Dark gene switched on, you weren't you.'

'I was,' he grated. 'I made the choices. I killed Ian and hurt everyone I love. I'll never forgive myself for that.'

'I guess,' I said, kissing his cheek, 'I'll keep forgiving you – over and over until you get the message.'

His grip tightened around my shoulder. 'I don't deserve you.'

'Hmmm.' I kissed him again, hiding a smile 'I suppose there's always Erin, then. But I'm not sure anyone deserves her.'

His lips curved. 'She's just scared. She's not this snarky, normally.'

'Just around me, huh?'

He laughed and trailed his fingers lightly down my arm. 'You two do rub each other the wrong way. But I think it's a case of jealousy for her.'

'Ha! Jealous of what?'

'Well,' he whispered, kissing my neck, 'you do have me?'

'True.' I rolled onto my side so I could see him. 'Speaking of you, there's something else we should talk about.'

He stopped kissing me and leaned back. 'Sounds ominous.'

'In Brisbane, when Erin mentioned the parcel was coming to Dyson, the leader of the Mors Ferrum...' I drew a slow breath. 'It occurred to me that...'

Logan stilled. 'What?'

I laid my palm gently on his cheek, fingers entwined in his dark hair. 'If we can get into their headquarters, maybe they'll have a database she can hack. Maybe we can find out where they took your father.'

His body stiffened and he gripped my wrist. I flinched and he relaxed his hold.

'Sorry. I...' His jaw worked. 'I had considered that. But I don't think...He murdered my mother, Rowan. He's Dark sidhe. What the hell would I say to him?'

I leaned up on one elbow and gazed at him. Light from the window threw sharp shadows under his cheekbones and jaw. His eyes were in darkness. 'We can correct the Dark gene,' I offered hesitantly.

'But you can't undo what he did.' His mouth pressed into a bitter line. 'Or whatever he's done since being recruited into the Mors, if that's what happened.'

'No,' I agreed, my heart sinking. 'I'm sorry. I shouldn't have mentioned it. I was just afraid you might meet him unexpectedly and...well...'

He gave a mirthless chuckle. 'Get distracted at the wrong moment and wreak bloody vengeance on him?' He shifted and light fell on eyes hardened to flint. 'Hardly. I want Dyson. I want Dyson and the whole damned organisation. Personal vendettas will have to take a back seat. For now, anyway. Ask me again after this is all done.'

'Well,' I said, 'right now we have better things to do.'

His expression softened.

My heart full of fear and uncertainty, I kissed him in the hopes of making it all go away for just a little while.

FOUR

<So you'll help us?>

Of course, Madre. When your plane went missing and my captain reported you off course, I travelled to Bologna to be at hand. I'll be with you in the morning. I have my assistant out shopping for you now.

<What of your search?>

...no progress. I haven't given up hope yet, though.

<I'm so sorry, Dante. I'm sure you'll find her. And perhaps we can help.>

How?

<We have a Mors Ferrum cell leader as our prisoner.>

Oh? Interesting. How did you manage that?

<Long story. Your father's here too. With his wife, Anna, and your half-sister, Rowan.>

I foresee a delightful family gathering.

<Behave, Dante.>

Don't I always?

The morning brought cold rain and bad news. At six-thirty, unable to sleep, we gathered around the scarred table and ate scrambled eggs and bacon in silence. There was no central heating, just a radiator that clunked and groaned but didn't warm the room. The autumn weather had turned chilly, so most of us were rugged in a strange assortment of multi-coloured, crocheted blankets, and tasteless floral duvets. My feet were bare, my toes icy on the beige linoleum. I'd lost my shoes in the ocean.

At least I hadn't lost my favourite karambit knife. That lay in its hidden sheath, stitched into the underside of my bra, along with a set of lockpicks. A girl could never be too careful.

Halfway through the meal, Erin swore. She looked up from her phone and glared at me.

'Your stupid package has cleared customs. It's showing as In Transit.' She touched the screen. 'It's coming from Rome and the delivery address is in Florence, so there's a chance it won't get delivered until tomorrow. Which means we have one day to intercept it.'

A smirk curled Michael's lips as he sipped on instant mud-coffee out of a cracked red mug.

'Can Dante help?' Logan asked Maeve. 'He's in Rome, isn't he?'

'He was.' Maeve shook her head. 'We discussed options when I spoke with him about arranging the boat, before we left Australia. He didn't have any way of reaching the right people in Customs without exposing himself to the wrong ones. The Mors have a secondary office in Rome and their people are planted throughout Customs. They've been trying to apprehend known sidhe through facial recognition software when they enter or leave the country.'

'What *can* he do?' That was Erin again, sarcastic as usual.

Maeve sent her a condescending look. 'He's a Hunter, remember? He's spent the last hundred years recovering sidhe abducted by the Mors Ferrum. He'll know how we can intercept the parcel. He's on his way now.' She checked her watch. 'He should be here in less than an hour.'

'What will happen if we can't stop the parcel?' Jennifer's plaintive question fell into a tense silence.

'I can tell you what,' Michael said, sneering. 'Once Dyson has the information about you, he'll transmit it to every Ferrum outpost.' He lifted his cup in a toast and grinned nastily. 'And once they know how to detect your DNA, and how to neutralise your powers, we win. I give you less than a year before your parasitic damned species is erased and your abilities are gene-spliced into humans, for the betterment of mankind.'

A chair scraped. Calain shoved Michael against the wall so hard a print of the Madonna bounced off and smashed. Michael's coffee cup hit the floor and shattered, spraying brown liquid across the lino. Calain held Michael against the plasterboard, his shoulders tense.

'You misbegotten, doghearted whoreson! That's my family, my *people*, you threaten.'

Michael's face purpled but he continued to grin. 'Go ahead. Kill me. You killed my parents. Finish the job.'

'Calain!' Maeve and Anna spoke together. I held my breath, half-hopeful Calain would do what I hadn't had the courage to – kill Michael Eisen. But then, I'd promised Paul his father would be kept safe.

Calain hesitated, the anger draining from him, replaced with pity. He released Michael. 'Seek not to raise my ire, Eisen. And seek elsewhere for your revenge. Your parents did not die at my hand.' He sighed and rubbed the back of his neck.

'Oh, really?' Michael shot back, disbelief writ large in his expression. 'And I suppose you're going to deny being at my house that night? I've seen the photograph of you standing there, watching my house burn.'

'No,' Calain said. 'I'll not deny I was there. But I came at the request of your father.' He drew his shoulders back, towering half a head over Michael. 'Henry Eisen wanted my help to get out of the Mors Ferrum. I was to escort your family into hiding. The Mors found out. Alexander Dyson sent a team. Your parents were dead before I arrived. Dyson had taken you already. Your uncle, who raised you, was a committed Mors member.'

'Dyson?' Michael scoffed. 'That's not possible. My parents died forty years ago. Dyson's only in his fifties. He'd have to...' He paled and slumped against the wall. 'No!'

Calain smiled thinly. 'Dyson is Dark sidhe. Did you not know?'

'You're lying, damn you.' Michael started forward, then stopped when Calain simply raised a brow at him.

'Actually, I've long suspected your parents were used as bait to try and draw me out of hiding.' Regret coloured Calain's tone. 'Dyson has been hunting me for over a hundred years – ever since he took over the Mors leadership in eighteen seventy-three. Of course, then he was called by another name. I've tried to stay off their radar for the last five hundred years, but Dyson...knows me.'

Michael seemed to recover his scorn. 'What a load of crap. You can't prove any of this.'

'No,' Calain said, 'but it's true, nonetheless.'

Something in the way he said it seemed to shake Michael, for he swallowed and sank into a chair.

'Have you ever met Dyson?' Calain asked, seating himself.

'Yes,' Michael's answer was surly. 'In Vienna two years ago.'

'I haven't met him in his current guise,' Calain continued, pity in his expression. 'But I'll wager he wears contact lenses, is around six foot and extremely thin. And you may have noticed, if you were observant, a burn scar on his right hand. Am I right?'

Michael rubbed the back of his own hand, but didn't nod or agree. He simply stared, stone-faced, at Calain.

'Dyson got that burn in eighteen ninety-six.' Calain returned, unflinching. 'When I tried to raze his London establishment to the ground with him in it. Fire is one of the few things that will kill us quickly. It destroys our cells faster than we can draw from the *sianfath* to heal.' He pressed his mouth thin.

I shivered at the memory – his memory – of his aunt, Mairi Silverblade, and her death at the stake so many centuries before.

Michael rose. 'You're lying.' His tone held less conviction. 'There's no way the Mors Ferrum is run by a goddamned sidhe. What would he gain by it? We've been hunting you bastards for a thousand years and we've caught more in the last thirty than ever. Dyson seems to know instinctively where…'

Calain's smile slipped into ironic but he only said, 'I don't understand Dyson's motivations, either, but that has no bearing on the truth of who he is.'

With a low growl, Michael stalked from the table and slammed the door on his tiny cupboard-room. Jennifer narrowed her eyes and the lock and bolt on his door clicked audibly into place.

Calain's shoulders slumped and tension in the room eased. Anna rubbed his back and he sighed.

'I had hoped, perchance, to reason with him. To persuade him to help us.'

'He's not a reasonable man,' she said bitterly.

'But we still need him to get us into the Mors receiving office to retrieve that parcel,' Erin put in. 'So there's no point in alienating him more.'

'If we wait until the parcel is delivered we might miss our chance,' Anna said. 'We need to intercept it before it gets delivered.'

'There is no "we",' Calain said, laying a hand over Anna's. 'I won't risk you again. And Maeve wants Jennifer out of this as well. You two will fly to Ireland this afternoon. There's a driver coming to take you to Marco Polo airport in Venice.'

'What?' Anna snatched her hand away, a scowl carving furrows in her forehead. 'I don't *think* so. I'm not leaving my daughter and you have no right to tell me what to do, Calain Gilmore. Rowan?'

I studied the half-eaten eggs on my plate, pushing them around with my fork.

'Anna.' Calain's deep voice was calm and reasonable. 'You and Jennifer are the most vulnerable ones. We need you out of danger. Erin,' he added, 'you should go, too. This will be dangerous and you have no warrior skills.'

Erin didn't even glance up from her phone. 'Not going. Don't bother.'

'*I* don't want to go, either,' Jen said, folding her arms and glaring at her mother. 'I helped in Brisbane. I helped save Logan. I did the thing with the gun magazines and stopped those men shooting us. I have my throwing spikes. I'm *not* vulnerable. Tell them, Rowan.'

'I'm...' I encountered Maeve's gaze, thick with fear and resentment. 'Anna, can I speak with you in the other room?' My mother hesitated then nodded. We retreated to my room and I sat on the bed while she took the chair.

She opened her mouth and I interrupted.

'Hang on.' I drew energy from the wooded park nearby and touched her forehead. I frowned in concentration, for this was new work to me. I'd read the method in Aeona Silverblade's book "*Mod an Meonn*" – *Method of the Mind* – but theory and practice were vastly different in psychic work. Brick by brick, I built a shield for her thoughts. A copy of the three bedroom Georgian cottage where she'd grown up in a backwoods village of Lancashire. She wouldn't feel it or see it, but the cottage was the place she'd felt most secure and loved in her childhood. And I wanted that for her. It also served the practical purpose of protecting her thoughts and our conversation from the roomful of sidhe outside.

Finished, I gusted a sigh and rotated my neck, exhausted again. Anna patted her head.

'What'd you do? I don't feel any different?'

'Just built a shield for you so the others can't read your thoughts. You had one before – Calain must have put it in place when he left us fourteen years ago – but someone dismantled it. Probably Maeve. She won't be able to, this time.'

Anna paled. 'I hadn't even considered that. Oh my God. What would they have heard already?' She flushed bright red.

I laughed. 'Don't worry, Logan tells me they have a relaxed attitude to sex. I'm sure they weren't embarrassed by anything you and Dad did.'

Anna gave an uncomfortable chuckle and pressed a palm to her scarlet cheek. 'It's so strange having him back. His eyes are the same. The way he speaks. The way he holds me. But the plastic surgery...he doesn't *look* like my Calain and I'm having trouble getting used to it.' Irritation flickered. 'Plus, I'd forgotten how dictatorial he can be.'

'He is a bit heavy-handed,' I said. 'But you were only together for eight years. You've fended for yourself for the last fourteen. You're not the twenty-year-old he met.'

'Yes,' she replied, thoughtful. 'I was a lot younger and starry-eyed about marriage and roles. I was happy to let him run our lives because I'd always wanted to be a stay at home mother. Then...'

I huffed. 'He did rather screw that up by leaving and dying, didn't he? D'you think you two will be able to work things out?' Part of me ached for normality, family, home, stability – the things I'd never had growing up and always envied. Part of me resented losing her undivided affection and resented my father for trying to run my life.

Anna screwed up her nose. 'I don't know. Early days and we have a lot on our plates at the moment. Speaking of which – what did you want to talk about? I'm not leaving you here, if that's it.'

I stood and stared out the window. Cars swooshed past, spraying water off the wet road, their drivers intent, glancing off my life as they focussed on their destination, their children, their shopping, their work. If I let my shields relax, I heard every one of them. So I kept my shields firmly up.

I leaned on the windowsill, my forehead on the cool glass. My father's gold signet ring glinted in the morning sunlight. I turned it on my finger, absently admiring the way the emerald caught the light.

'What if we just ran, Mum? Just got the hell out of here and left this to Maeve and her son, Dante?'

'Really? You'd to that?' Anna lit with hope for a moment, then crashed into resignation. 'No, you know we can't.'

'Why not?' I flung my arms wide and paced the small room. 'We've done it my whole life. Every time people found out about my strength and speed, we'd go. It served us pretty well. We're both alive.' I hugged myself. 'We have Dad back. Let's just go.'

Anna stood and rubbed my arms. 'And you always complained about moving, remember? You hated running away, even when you were little. You wanted to stand up to whoever was chasing us.' She laughed. 'Remember when you were eight we had to pack up and leave Singapore in the middle of the night? You were so angry. You wanted to *make* the bad men leave us alone. You had your throwing knives ready and everything.'

I chuckled. 'I remember. I had a teacher I really liked at school, we'd just redecorated my room in a Star Wars theme, and I'd made friends. I thought it was perfect. Then I had to leave it all behind – again.'

Anna stroked my cheek, her eyes soft with knowing sympathy. 'And you stopped trying to make friends because it hurt so much.'

I hunched a shoulder.

'Now you have friends,' she said. 'And a wonderful young man who clearly adores you. Are you willing to give it all up because you're scared of losing it? Can you say irony?'

With a groan, I sank on to the bed. 'I just… I don't want…'

She sat beside me, an arm over my shoulders. 'I know, sweetheart. You're scared. We all are. I'm terrified of losing you – and losing Calain again. I'm frightened of what these Mors Ferrum people will do to all of us – especially to the sidhe.' She lifted my chin. 'Do you want that? Do you want to be responsible for the death of a whole species?'

I shoved her hand aside, glaring. 'Not fair. The Mors have been chasing the sidhe for a thousand years. Logan said Dante has spent the last hundred years rescuing kidnapped sidhe. And it's not my fault Michael got so much information about us. You can't put the responsibility of saving the whole damned race on me.'

'No. You're right. But…' She sighed and shook her head. 'I've never been a big believer in destiny. You know I've always said you make your own fate.'

I nodded.

'But I think you have to accept your part in this, Rowan, as much as it terrifies both of us.'

'But Mairi's prophecy says: "In the embrace of the *sianfath* and the *lorntinn,* the *ocair* may be the deliverance of those that dispossess the sidhe." How does that relate to me?' I buried my head in my hands. 'Calain is the *ocair* – the key. But the *sianfath* is already everywhere and *lorntinn* just means something like "group-mind" or "the unity". Neither of those things is me, so why I can't I just leave it to Calain and the others? They know what they're doing and they don't trust me, anyway. This...' I gestured wildly at the window. 'This is too much. I just murdered a hundred people! They need someone...better than me.'

'Oh, Rowan.' Her eyes were huge. 'You're a good person. You're just having to make horrible choices.'

'No, you don't know...' I couldn't continue. How could I tell my own mother about the resentment, the anger, simmering in me? Everyone wanted to use me for something. Everyone was sure their cause was so noble, so just. A sense of duty and responsibility carried me with them, but my uneasiness grew with each passing hour.

That proved I wasn't a hero. Heroes didn't think like that. Heroes rushed into battle, borne on the wings of righteousness and justice.

I was just afraid and angry.

'I didn't sign up for this,' I said. 'I just wanted to get the Mors Ferrum off our backs so we could settle down.'

Anna sighed. 'And that's the problem. If Michael is any indication, his organisation will live up to their name: The Iron Death. The Mors will *never* leave us alone, especially once they have the package. The DNA samples and the information about your powers will lead them right to every sidhe on the planet. It will be a massacre. You won't be able to live with yourself. You've been lonely your whole life and these are your people. You have to help Calain, Rowan, you know you do.'

I swore and she laughed. 'I agree wholeheartedly, sweetheart, but life's about making the right-thing choices more often than the wrong-thing ones. And this is one helluva right-thing choice.' She stood and tugged her shirt straight. 'Tell you what. If it will make things easier for you, I'll take Jen to Ireland.'

I lifted my head. 'Really? You'd do that? I can't bear the thought of anything happening to either of you.' She nodded. I jumped up, threw my arms around her and squeezed, letting go when she gasped. 'Thank you,' I said. 'I'll stay and try not to get myself killed. Deal?'

I stuck out my hand and she shook it. As hard as I tried to keep a straight face, she regarded me narrowly and groaned.

'I can't believe I fell for that.' She thumped me on the arm. 'You never had any intention of leaving, did you?'

'Ow,' I said mildly, rubbing my arm. I kissed her on the forehead. 'I did seriously consider it for a few minutes last night. But you're right.' I smiled to cover the sinking in my stomach. Yes, I'd manipulated her into choosing to leave, but at least a small part of me wanted to be convinced to go with her. 'This all started when I decided to make a stand in Cairns. This is my fight. I just didn't want you and Jen to be caught in the middle. You'll keep your promise?'

Anna glared. 'Yes, but you'd better keep me in the loop. I want hourly updates.' She cast a darkling look at the door. 'I don't trust them to take care of you properly.'

I managed a chuckle. 'Not even my own father? Not even Logan?'

She sighed and her shoulders slumped. She caught me into a close hug, her breast soft against mine, her hair tickling my nose. 'I'm afraid, Rowan.'

'Me too,' I whispered. 'But it was too hard in Brisbane. I don't want you to be used against me again.'

She let me go and sniffed, shaking her red hair back defiantly. 'Just promise me you'll look after yourself and your father. I want both of you back in one piece.'

I nodded and opened the door. 'Send Jen in for me, will you?'

'I won't go,' Jen said as she closed the door. She stood in the middle of the room arms folded, jaw sharp with determination. Her straight dark hair was scraped back, utilitarian, to convince me she'd left all softness behind. 'Tell them I don't have to. You need me.'

I shoved a hand through my hair, trying to pull the right words from my brain. I trusted her more than Maeve or Erin. I didn't want her to go, but too many people owned pieces of my heart. If I lost control of my gift; if I made the wrong choice at a crucial moment...at least Jen and Anna would be out of my reach, unharmed. It was my only comfort.

'I do need you, Jen,' I assured her.

She beamed and reached for the door handle. I gripped her arm and dragged her to sit on the bed with me. She pouted.

'But you still want me to go,' she said.

'I don't want you to, but I need you to.'

'But why?' Her dark-rimmed, dove-grey eyes swam in tears of frustration. 'You know I can help.'

'Yes, and that's why I need you to go.'

'Huh?' She recoiled in confused anger. 'That makes no sense at all.'

I pressed my palms to my temples, wishing I could think of another way, hoping I'd never have to put this idea into action.

'I have a plan, Jen.' I drew a deep breath. 'I haven't told anyone about it because I'm hoping I won't have to use it. So shield well. But it's a contingency if everything else we try to get this package goes wrong.'

'What is it?' Spots of colour in her cheeks flushed her nut-brown skin darker. Her eyes sparkled.

'I can't tell you, either. Not yet. But I will need you in Ireland to help me make it work. I'll also need you to get a message to Tom Fairchild and Harry, in Brisbane.'

'Tom? Why?' Jen frowned. 'They don't have any special skills. They're men. All they can do is telepathy.'

'Nevermind.' I waved aside her questions. 'Just trust me on this. I'll need them and any other sidhe you know, especially any of Maeve's daughters, so make a list and have it ready. We'll get new phone sims today, so give me your email and I'll send you the new number when I get it. I'll keep you updated.'

'And when you need me, what will I have to do?' She leaned forward, eager.

'Jen,' I said wearily, 'don't wish for it. I hope we don't have to take that path, because it could kill both of us.'

FIVE

Madre, it's almost time. Be ready.

<Are you sure this is wise? It's dangerous. We don't know how she'll react.>

That's the point.

When we re-joined the others, Logan sent me a quizzical look and brushed his mind against mine. I held my shields against him.

'Jen's agreed to go to Ireland,' I said.

Maeve gave a little gasp and covered her mouth.

I spoke to my mother. 'Take her to Lothien castle and be safe, both of you.' I caught Anna into a hug.

She gave a broken laugh. 'Just make sure you come home to me.' She grabbed Calain's hand and held it to her cheek. 'Both of you.'

On impulse, I touched her forearm and steeled myself as I opened the path to my precognitive ability. Nothing. I opened wider, seeking forward as far as I could. I hadn't yet mastered the ability to control how far into the future I saw but, as far as I could tell, nothing bad was going to happen to her in the next few days.

Outside, a horn beeped twice, startling me out of my semi-trance.

'That'll be your driver,' Calain said. 'I'll walk you out.'

I hugged Jen and whispered into her ear, 'Keep a thought-window open for me.'

'Can you reach all the way to Ireland?'

I shrugged. 'You heard Maeve – evidently I can reach around the world. I hope she's right. Go.' She headed for the door and I called out, 'By the way, you might want to check out the secret passage between the master bedroom and the library. The estate managers don't know about it and I stashed a few…useful things in there when I was there a few months ago.'

Jen's downcast expression segued into excited anticipation and she practically skipped out the door.

Anna hugged me. 'That was well done. I love you, sweetheart. Look after yourself, ok?'

I nodded and turned away, unable to watch her walk out of my life, perhaps forever. Maeve and Calain followed them out to the car, leaving Erin to watch over Michael.

I stood at the back window, staring blindly out at the dead grass and ugly ceramic pots in the small backyard. Logan put an arm around my waist and I leaned my head on his shoulder.

'They'll be ok,' he murmured, kissing my forehead.

'I know.' I gave him a rueful half-smile. 'I checked ahead. Sometimes only being able to see disasters is a blessing.'

'Nothing?' His gaze softened.

'Not for the next few days, anyway.'

'I'm glad. Maeve will be, too. Jen's a good kid.'

I pulled away. 'I didn't send her away to make Maeve happy.'

'Hey.' Logan tugged me back against his hip. 'On your side, remember? I don't agree with what she did to you or Calain. But she is Jen's mother. She does love her daughter.'

'Really?' I said. 'Because all I've seen her do is criticise Jen.'

He shrugged. 'She's hard on all her kids, and me. It's tough being a Hunter. She wants to equip us to survive.'

'How can you have any sympathy for her after what she's put all of us through? She didn't tell you about carrying the Dark gene, or about your father killing your mother. How can you forgive her?'

His lips thinned. 'Not easily, I admit. But I also remember all the care she lavished on me after she took me in.'

'That was just so she could train up another Hunter.'

'Stop it, Rowan.' He gripped my arms, hard. 'This antagonism between you has to stop. Maeve has spent the last two hundred and eighty years trying to protect the sidhe. She's had twelve children of her own and adopted five other orphaned sidhe – and watched three of her own offspring murdered by the Mors Ferrum.' He released me, pain pulling at his mouth. 'So, yes, she's had to harden herself. A lesser woman would have gone mad with grief. She threw herself into trying to save her people from extinction. No, I don't agree with all her methods. But I *understand* her motivations.'

There was an uncomfortable silence between us as I swallowed anger.

'I'm sorry,' I said quietly. 'I just can't help feeling resentful. She used me and she's still trying to.'

He sighed. 'I know. We'll work it out – together. I won't let her force you into anything. You just need to trust me, and yourself, a little more.'

I shivered. 'That's what I'm worried about, Logan. She won't have to force me and I can't trust myself. We both know I'll do whatever it takes to protect you and Calain. It just terrifies me how easily I slip into that. How little I weigh up the consequences. Erin was right: I rush into things; make the choice to save what's important to me.'

'And?' He frowned. 'I don't see the problem.'

'What if, one time, I choose wrong? What if I choose what I want over what's important in the bigger scheme of things? I'm not the right person for this. I'm not the self-sacrificing hero-type, Logan. Erin's right not to trust me. None of you should.'

Logan gripped my arms again. 'Stop it, Rowan. It won't come to that. You're a good person. Yes, sometimes you need to slow down and think a little. But on the big things you've always made the right choices and you will again.'

I shook my head. He made a sound of frustration and pulled me close against his chest, stroking my back.

'You may not have faith in yourself, Rowan, but I do. I wish you could see yourself as I do. Let me help. Please?' He leaned back and studied me. 'Let me into your inner shields. Let me show you what I really mean by trust.'

'What, exactly?' I frowned.

He stroked my cheek. 'It's a sidhe thing. The people you love and trust most, you let inside your inner shield; into the core of who you are. A deep *lorntinn* – the unity – is an important part of a relationship. It's how we help each other through tough times.' He hesitated and cleared his throat. 'I know I could probably use your help dealing with what I did in Brisbane.'

I pulled away, uneasy. 'I—'

The clatter of dishes and splash of water interrupted us and we both glanced around, me with a twinge of relief. I wasn't ready for the level of intimacy Logan seemed to be proposing. I'd spent my life hiding myself from people. It would be a difficult habit to break.

And what if he didn't like what he found? What if he realised I wasn't as good as he thought? Or I couldn't help him the way he wanted? What did I know about psychology? I couldn't even comprehend what he'd been through when his Dark gene was switched on…let alone help.

Dishes clattered again. Michael Eisen stood at the kitchen sink, up to his elbows in suds. There was something odd about the way he moved. His body was still, only his arms and hands moving in robotic fashion as he picked up and methodically scrubbed each plate before standing them in the dish drying rack. He barely blinked.

Erin sat at the dining table, engrossed in something on her phone.

'Erin?' Logan strode over, snatching her phone when she ignored him.

'Hey!'

'What have you done to Michael? He doesn't strike me as the type to voluntarily do the dishes.'

Erin shrugged and grabbed the phone back. 'Calain dismantled the shields he'd put around Michael's mind. I implanted a geas. Why should I do the dishes? I'm a geneticist, not a cleaner.'

'A geas as in an obligation to do a certain thing?' I strolled over to the sink and waved in front of Michael. He didn't flinch or move except to grab another plate. 'I thought that was some sort of fairy tale magical thing.'

'Hello.' Erin pointed to herself. 'Elves, remember? All those Irish stories of the sidhe did have some basis in truth.'

The glimmerings of an idea teased me. 'Why did we bother locking him into his room or tying him to the plane seat?'

She gave me a cool look. 'Because a geas is a temporary redirection of neural pathways. Eventually the original energy and chemistry re-establishes itself and the geas gets wiped. If you try and make it permanent it causes brain damage and memory loss.'

I studied Michael. 'How long will it last?'

Erin shrugged. 'Depends on the person. They don't work on sidhe. With him, I'd say no more than half an hour, probably less. He's pretty arrogant and strongminded.'

'These are not the droids you're looking for,' I muttered, my lips twitching.

'What?' she said sharply.

'Nothing. This could be handy, that's all.'

Logan tilted his head. 'I don't see how. Dante told me all Mors Ferrum are shielded.'

'You're forgetting: I can walk through shields when I'm in the *sianfath*.'

'But you're vulnerable when you leave your body behind,' he said.

I smiled at him. 'I'll be relying on you two to protect me.'

'Like you protected my father,' Erin snapped, her chair scraping as she got up from the table. 'No, that's right – you didn't. He died. I don't owe you anything, Rowan.'

'Erin!'

Erin rounded on Logan. 'Or you. You're the one who shot him, and she just stood by and *let* him die!'

I sank into a chair, my knees weak. 'I'm sorry, Erin. I had no choice, nor did Logan.'

'Crap. You did have a choice and you *chose* to let Ian die so you could save yourself. He might have been a know-it-all jerk sometimes, but he was my father.'

Her words broke on a breathy sob. To my horror, her eyes drowned in tears. She dropped into a chair again, crying unrestrainedly. Logan stood beside me, ashen, fingers clenching and unclenching. He'd been under Michael's influence at the time, but he remembered everything he'd done – and how sensible it had seemed when he'd done it. He'd known Erin and Ian since he was a child.

There was nothing I could say. She knew the story. We'd explained it in great detail. She was right: I had chosen. I'd chosen my own survival, yes, but I'd also chosen not to release the corrupted version of Calain trapped in my mind. He would have drained every human and sidhe for miles around on a whim. To keep Calain under control I'd had to let Ian die, and I would live with that choice for a long time. As would Logan.

I touched his wrist. He pulled free and scrubbed at his face.

Erin continued to weep, her shoulders shaking, breath coming in ragged sobs. I sat across from her, not sure how to approach her, or even if I should.

'Is this a bad time?' A smooth, faintly amused baritone voice sounded from the back door. The three of us jumped. I shot to my feet. Logan and I raised our hands in automatic self-defence. Erin wiped her cheeks and sniffed.

'Who the hell are you?' she demanded.

'Dante!' Logan strode forward and engulfed the stranger in a rough hug.

I hung back, studying my half-brother. Only a little taller than me, and dark-haired, he was much like my memories of my father before the plastic surgery Maeve had inflicted on him. Dante had a sidhe's characteristic black-rimmed grey eyes and nut-brown skin. Wiry rather than bulky like Calain, he carried himself with easy grace and wore an exquisitely-tailored dark grey suit with a narrow, mid-blue tie and a crisp white shirt.

'Logan, you're looking well for someone who just died in a plane crash.' He stepped into the room, leaned on a thick walking stick, and surveyed us with quick intelligence. His sympathetic gaze returned to Logan. 'And Maeve told me about your father's part in your mother's death. I'm sorry. I didn't know.'

Anger clouded Logan's brow then vanished, replaced by regret. He clasped Dante's arm. 'Thankyou. I'm doing my best to forget what's unchangeable.'

Dante bowed. 'Wise man. Revenge is a cold mistress.' His jaw hardened and he seemed to stare through Logan.

'Yes,' Logan replied. 'How's Nesrin?'

The half-smile that curved Dante's lips didn't reach his eyes. 'She's away at the moment.'

Logan frowned. 'Everything ok?'

'But of course.' Dante extended a hand and strolled over to me. On his little finger, a ruby signet ring glinted in the grey morning light. 'You must be Rowan.' His English was lightly accented, carrying overtones of expensive English boarding schools and European charm. 'I'm delighted to meet you.'

I hesitated, debated, then shook his hand and opened my mind. *An explosion of shop-windows; glass sparkling on black paving stones; blood on a lean male hand, extended towards me; screams; fear, pain.* I released Dante, gritting my teeth to stop myself blurting out the vision.

Staring at me, he cocked his head and tossed the walking stick high, catching it dexterously. Twin bands of silver spiralled partway down the timber length and back to the top, like a Celtic knot. An iron cap protected the bottom tip. He caressed the gleaming golden wood and slapped the silver curled-fern head into his open palm.

'That was most interesting,' he said, pointing the knob at me. 'The shop was somewhere in Firenze, I believe.' He held up his hand, inspecting it curiously. 'The bloody hand was mine. I see I shall have to be careful. What's your forward range?'

I gaped at him. 'You saw my precog vision? How? I thought only women had gifts other than telepathy.'

Dante shrugged. 'It's still a form of telepathy. Your range?'

'I don't know,' I admitted. 'Sometimes a few minutes; sometimes days or weeks.'

He sauntered over to the table. 'Well, we shall just have to be careful.' His white teeth flashed and he pulled out a cracked wooden chair. He dusted it off, and sat, crossing one leg over the other. Across the table, Erin straightened and tugged at her wrinkled red blouse.

'Erin Fairchild.' She flicked back her bobbed black hair, smiling flirtatiously as she extended a hand.

Dante kissed her knuckles with old-fashioned flair.

'Ciao bella,' he murmured. 'Dante Moschello, Conte di Lucca, al tuo servizio.'

She dimpled, sneaking a coy look beneath her lashes.

'So, how did you see what I saw?' I asked, ignoring their little interchange. Erin sent me an irritated look.

Dante, his focus lingering on Erin's chiselled cheekbones and perfect mouth, replied to me, 'Indeed. I have no gift for precognition.' He switched his mischievous look to me. 'I can merely step through shields and see what you do.'

'You can get through shields,' I repeated, dumbfounded. It was my own skill, but I could only do it when I was stretched out in the *sianfath*.

'Only when I'm touching someone, of course,' he said. 'Which is a bit of a nuisance. But mitigated by how useful the ability is in my line of work.' He tugged at the white cuffs of his shirt and brushed imaginary dust off his lapel. 'Takes the guesswork out of knowing who to trust, you understand.' His eyes slid back to Erin and his grin broadened.

She gazed at him in horror, stiffened and rose from the table. 'You're a jerk. I should have known, being *her* brother. I'm going to take a shower. Tell me when you decide what we're doing next.' She levelled a finger at me. 'And don't think you can leave me behind, Rowan.' Without waiting for my answer, she stalked down the hall.

Dante watched her leave, his smile quirking to one side. 'Charming.'

'You didn't exactly play nice, Dante,' Logan said. 'She's been through a rough time. Cut her some slack.'

'I'm not here to play nice, Logan. As you know, well.' Dante inclined his head. 'And who is this industrious fellow, if I may ask.' He pointed the cane at Michael, who continued to wash dishes with robotic efficiency.

I wanted to ask if he'd been trying to tell me Erin wasn't trustworthy, but she was probably listening in.

'Michael Eisen,' Logan supplied. 'Erin's got him under a geas.'

'Ah.' Dante rose and approached Michael. 'Fascinating.' He touched Michael's bared wrist and grimaced. 'Her geas is strong. It's obliterating any thoughts he might have about his intentions or the Mors Ferrum. We shall have to wait until it wears off. How inconvenient.'

'We already tried Reading him,' Logan said. 'But someone has put the strongest shield any of us has ever seen around his innermost thoughts. Not even Maeve could get through.'

'And what about you?' Dante's shrewd scrutiny fell on me.

I shrugged. 'I haven't tried.' I didn't want to admit my hesitation was due to fear of what I might find in his intentions. Back in Australia, the anger at Michael Eisen had been to raw, too strong. I'd been afraid if I found out what the Mors Ferrum was going to do, I'd just drain him, without compunction. I needed time to calm myself enough to read his thoughts without emotion.

'Well, I'm certain I shall be able to,' Dante said. 'E il mio cavallo di battaglia.' Which translated to something incomprehensible about his battle horse, so I suspected it must be slang. He opened his arms wide. 'I am irresistible – so I'm told.'

Logan chuckled. It was the first genuine amusement in him I'd seen for several days.

'Dante your old-world charm is a little overwhelming. Your sister is looking stunned.'

'Che cavolo! Scusi per favore sorellina.' Dante bowed extravagantly, a wicked gleam in his eyes.

'Dante, you promised to behave.' Maeve's dry interjection made me edge closer to Logan. He slipped his arm around my waist.

Unruffled, Dante sauntered to his mother's side and kissed both her cheeks. He inspected her. 'Madre, you're pale. What ails you? Not this idiota, surely?' He indicated Michael Eisen.

Maeve sent Michael a darkling look. 'Don't underestimate him. We did and it almost got us killed.'

'So I hear,' Dante replied. 'Most careless of you.'

'Maeve did you—' Calain entered from the hall to the front door and paused. 'God's blood!'

Dante wrinkled his nose and swept his father an elaborate bow. 'Such an ugly phrase these days. So oldfashioned, much as we both are, I suppose. Mio Padre, Lord Gilmore, Earl of Lothien, I presume?' He studied Calain, eyes twinkling.

Calain's mouth twitched. He extended a hand. 'Conte di Lucca, I presume?'

Dante inclined his head. 'By title, if not actual bloodline.'

My father's smile broadened. 'I swear you are the spit of me at your age, in face if not form.' He touched his cheek. 'No more, though. But I see you carry my rowan-wood cane. I wondered where that went. Maeve?'

She had the grace to blush and shrug one shoulder. 'I wanted a souvenir when we parted.'

'*Your* cane!' Dante's fingers tightened on the curled-leaf knob.

'Tis naught,' Calain said, dismissive. 'Twas given me by my mother, Aeona Silverblade. Rowan-wood, silver and iron. All meant to be good defences against fae folk.' His mouth twitched. 'Aeona's sense of humour. Since you clearly are my son, 'tis fair it passes to you. Use it well.'

I twisted Calain's signet ring and dismissed a faint surge of jealousy. He had as much right to Calain's attention as I. It was just strange to suddenly have a sibling.

Dante bowed stiffly. 'I do use it well...Father.'

Calain pressed his lips together. 'I'm sorry, I knew naught of your existence.' His gaze flicked to Maeve. 'Your mother never told me.'

With a shrug, Dante wandered away, methodically straightening the tasteless ceramic ornaments littering every surface. 'I did not lack a father, my lord, unpleasant through he was. I discovered your existence when he died and mio Madre was obliged to tell me why I'd stopped aging like a human.' His mouth stretched in a quick smile but a hint of old pain lurked in it.

He sucked a breath. 'But our broken family is hardly the conversation we should be having.' He yanked out a chair at the table and sat. 'This parcel you are so desperate to regain. What is the nature of the contents? Why is it so important?'

Calain drew up a chair opposite. 'Didn't Maeve tell you?'

'The basics only,' Dante said. 'I wish to hear everything about how you've all come to be here. I understand you were working for the Mors Ferrum?'

Calain stiffened. 'Not by choice.'

'Indeed,' Dante's tone hinted at scorn. 'One always has choices. Especially when it comes to bettering our chances of survival as a species.' He leaned back and waved languidly. 'But then, you've had so many more years of experience and so many more opportunities to help our people. I'm sure you've never let any slip by.'

Annoyance flickered through Calain's eyes. I echoed it. Was that some sort of dig at Calain? What for? Had Calain done something in the past that Dante disapproved of?

'I had no memory of who I was,' Calain grated. 'Maeve sent me in to Michael's cell as a spy. Ruadhán restored my memories. I had given them to her when she was but a child.'

Dante glanced at me. 'Accidenti! And she held six hundred years of your memories without losing her mind? I am impressed.'

I flushed and moved to the window, not wishing to hear my own praises sung when I didn't deserve them. I'd done more wrong than I had right. I still held a copy of Calain's memories locked away, deep in my mind. And Aeona Silverblade's nested within those. How much of their years of war and bloody slaughter affected me and my thinking? How much influence would my father and grandmother have on me, without my knowing?

I stared out the window, unseeing, half-listening to the ongoing conversation.

'So, what do you recommend we do to regain the parcel,' Dante said, cool. 'Or shall we just sit back and see what happens?'

'No,' Calain replied, his voice tight. 'With Ruadhán ready, the time has come to act. We need to stop the Mors and do what is needful.'

'Ah. So Rowan's the reason you've been waiting so patiently, so idly, all these years?' There was no mistaking the scorn in Dante's tone now. 'Have you wasted a thousand opportunities to help our people in the hopes she will fix everything? How, exactly?'

I hunched my shoulders, blocking out their words as Calain, with stiff politeness, repeated the prophecy of Mairi Silverblade. I didn't want to hear it, even though I already knew my father had been waiting for my birth for centuries. It was too much pressure. I stared out the window, concentrating on the *sianfath's* peaceful influence. Under the silver-green balm of its power, the roaring of blood in my ears settled and I relaxed my death-grip on the windowsill.

'You're pinning your hopes on a vague prophecy from a woman six hundred years dead?' Dante said. 'Do you even know how to make it come about? You might be the *ocair,* but who – or what – are the others?'

'I don't yet know,' Calain said stiffly. 'But I trust Mairi's vision. She was never wrong.'

'Well,' Dante said, standing and checking his watch, 'perhaps it is my more modern upbringing, but I prefer to find a more certain path to success.' His chin lifted and he swept the room with cool hauteur. 'We need to find the Mors headquarters and retrieve your parcel. And there will be added benefits to accessing their headquarters.' His jaw worked.

'Dante,' Maeve said, 'I know you want to—'

'Madre,' Dante replied, 'don't presume to know what I want. Come.' He brushed at his suit, his cheerful charm restored. 'It's almost time to depart. Gather your things. I shall watch our industrious friend at his washing. I find it most amusing.'

Logan left my side and went to our room to pack. I stayed by the window, gazing blankly out.

Maeve took up a position near me, her slim hands twisting together until the knuckles were white. She cleared her throat.

'Thank you,' she said. 'I know I've done the wrong thing by you and I'm not asking you to forgive me. I just wanted you to know I appreciate you looking after Jen. Convincing her to go with your mother to Ireland, I mean.'

I sent her a bleak look. 'I did it for her, not you, Maeve, but you're welcome.'

She put out a hand. 'Can we, perhaps, put aside our differences for the moment and work together on this problem?

I debated my feelings for her. Logan reappeared from our room and watched us, his grave expression holding a hint of hope. She had used and manipulated me, Logan and my father. But I understood Logan's point about needing to work with her on this journey. Being at odds with her and Erin was exhausting for all of us. Reluctantly, I grasped her hand. Logan smiled and vanished back into our room.

On impulse, I opened my precognitive ability. Her block against my skill no longer worked, courtesy of a counter I'd learned from Aeona's book. But I didn't think it necessary to tell Maeve. At least, not yet.

The zip of a bullet. A cry of pain. Maeve, crumpled onto a beige floor, blood matting her dark hair and seeping scarlet onto a cheap blue and green rug. Another scream – Erin's – cut off in a sickening gurgle. A crash of glass. Five men clad in black military gear and masks.

SIX

<Dante, don't alienate her. She won't listen to me. We need her to listen to you. If we can't control her this will fail.>

Madre, for an intelligent woman you have handled this girl ill. She doesn't need controlling, she needs...the correct motivation.

<And I suppose you know what will motivate her?>

Indeed. As I said before, just be ready.

<We have tried—>

Just trust me, Madre.

I snatched my hand back, bile rising in my throat. Dizzy and gasping for air, I bent down, trying to get blood back into my head. The images lingered, their clarity and power forcing logical thought aside, possessing my whole mind.

'Rowan?' Maeve touched my shoulder.

I shuddered and shifted away, opening my eyes.

Under my feet: a blue and green rug on a beige floor.

Somewhere close by, a gate squeaked.

'Shit. Logan!'

I leapt. A bullet zipped through the window as I tackled Maeve to the floor. Something smashed in the kitchen. Maeve and I hit the ground together, knocking the wind out of me. She sagged in my arms.

'Get down.' I yelled over my shoulder at Logan as he sprinted into the room.

How many? Logan's terse question appeared in my mind and I broadcast the answer, hoping everyone had opened their shields to me. I wasn't used to this form of communication by default; they were. It made sense.

At least five, I replied. *Erin will be hit next. Get her. They'll come in through the window and the back door, here. Someone needs to protect Michael.*

And Maeve? That was Dante, his mental voice clipped and direct. Somehow, entwined with his thoughts, were Calain, Logan and Erin as well, giving his words a choral effect.

I checked Maeve. Her eyelids fluttered and she stared vaguely at me. No blood stained the floor beneath her.

The bullet missed her. Just dazed by the fall. We have to get out of here.

No time. They're already coming in. Everyone take an entrance. I'll get Erin.

I'll get Michael, Logan added.

A shadow darkened the window above me. I thrust Maeve's limp body underneath a spindle-legged couch and rolled aside. A bullet slapped into the tiles near my hip. Chips of ceramic sprayed, slicing into my leg.

I jumped to my feet and snapped a kick, driving the edge of my foot into a knee. The joint crunched and the black-clad man dropped to the floor, a stifled scream escaping his lips. I lifted my bare toes and kicked at his temple. He sprawled on the tiles.

I yanked my karambit blade out of its sheath under my bra and held it in my fist.

Across the room, Calain engaged in close combat with a large man wielding a black knife. Logan had Michael pushed into a corner and protected him against two more attackers, one swinging a truncheon and one with a knife. Erin appeared in the hall doorway, wearing only a white t-shirt and underwear, her hair dripping. She struggled in the grip of yet another black-clad intruder. Her nails raked blood on his wrist. He held a wicked knife to her throat. I snatched a throwing-knife from the belt of the unconscious man at my feet and hefted it in my left hand. Heavier than my knives. I flipped it through the air. The blade stabbed deep into the shoulder of Erin's captor. He grunted and tore the blade free but didn't release Erin.

I grabbed another knife.

Five more soldiers burst through the door, and spread out, black sub-machine guns in full view. One close to me took a bead on Logan. I sliced with the karambit and opened a deep gouge in his forearm. He swore, fumbled the gun and recovered. He took a step back, out of my reach. In the hall, Erin screamed, blood-curdling and terrified.

Shit. Too many.

I stilled and anchored myself. I slid into the hazy, welcoming world of the *sianfath* and stabbed tendrils of myself into the ten soldiers. Their silver-green life forces pulsed and tempted me. Such power. Such…

Wait, silver-green? I hesitated.

'Cessare! Stop!' Dante's voice cut through the chaos. *Cessare Rowan.*

A shadowy image of his body appeared before me in the *sianfath.* He held a slim, straight sword which appeared to be made of pure light. He sliced it through the threads connecting me to the soldiers. Ice needles of pain splintered through my skull. I retreated to my body and slumped against the wall, panting. My head throbbed and exhaustion stole strength from my legs. I collapsed onto a tattered blue mock-suede chair.

The nine standing soldiers lowered weapons. Five spread out to cover the entrances and windows. Four moved into the centre of the room. There they stood, guarding each other's backs and watching us. I struggled to my feet, drew back my left arm, knife poised to throw at the four men in ski-masks.

'I said, stop,' Dante said, stepping into the room from the hall. He fiddled with the knob on his cane and sauntered into the middle of the room. With a nod for the four men there, he paused and swept me, Calain and Logan with an amused look.

I hesitated and glanced at Logan. He nursed his left arm, holding it against his chest. A bruise darkened his forearm and he winced every time he moved it. Behind him, Michael shoved himself up the rose-wallpapered kitchen wall, shaking his head and blinking.

Under the couch, Maeve groaned. I dragged her out. She scrambled to her feet, dusty and red-faced. She touched the back of her head and winced. Apparently oblivious to the tension in the room, she brushed dust from her wrinkled grey silk pants and blue shirt.

Dante nodded at the still-alert men in the centre of the room. They straightened, put away their weapons and dragged off their ski-masks. Revealed were two men and two woman, all intense, fit and watchful. All with grey or blue, black-rimmed eyes and golden skin. All sidhe.

The man at my feet groaned. The shortest woman hurried over, watching me warily as she approached. She knelt beside the injured man and laid hands on his twisted knee. Around her, the *sianfath* shimmered as she drew power and used it to heal him. With a word of thanks, he joined his team and now ten of them confronted us.

'What in God's name is going on?' Calain demanded. 'Are you unharmed, Rowan?'

'Fine,' I said, though my knees still shook.

'Apologies,' Dante said, sweeping us all a low bow. 'These are my men.'

'What?' I kept a grip on the throwing knife and karambit, uncertainty staying my hand.

'I was testing you,' Dante replied patiently. 'Thank you, men. Wait for us in the cars. Take Mr Eisen with you. We'll be leaving in a moment.' He saluted them lazily. They snapped off sharp return salutes. Michael protested as the soldiers man-handled him out the side door, leaving the rest of us in astonished silence.

I started forward, anger boiling to the surface. 'Why the hell—'

'Let him explain,' Logan said, low and quiet.

'They were using live rounds!'

'He knows what he's doing, Rowan.'

'Thank you, my friend,' Dante said, smiling. 'Your faith brings me such joy.'

'Enough,' Calain snapped. 'Explain.'

'Very well,' Dante replied. 'Teams are my speciality. I bring sidhe together and weld them into teams that function as one unit, trusting each other.' He studied each of us, cool and faintly amused. 'Since we have only today to do this, I needed to know how you would all respond under stress. Whether you can be trusted and whether I can work with you to do what must be done.'

'And?' I grated, sheathing the karambit and leaning against the wall.

Maeve sat on the couch, one hand to her head. Erin sank into a chair at the kitchen table, her face pale.

Dante spread his hands. 'And, given your rather strained personal relationships, you did well.' He pointed at me and Logan.

'Your first thoughts were to protect those less skilled or more valuable than yourselves. And you communicated.' He grimaced. 'Though I note, Rowan, you fall back onto your physical training and verbal communication. Why did you wait to use your *skath-sheel?* It would have been quick and effective end to the threat.'

I unfolded my arms and glowered at him. 'Because I'd rather not, thanks.' I wanted to ask him what he'd done to me, in the *sianfath,* but hesitated to admit his power over my skill in front of Maeve and Erin. Whatever he'd done, I still felt the after-effects and that was frightening.

He gave me a wintry look. 'I'm afraid you don't have the luxury of choice, sister. We need every advantage if we're going to get that parcel back. You are a weapon. You must act without hesitation.'

'I'm not a weapon,' I growled. 'I've already told Maeve and Michael. I'm not going to be used like some pawn in this game. I'll decide when, and if, the *skath-sheel* is used. And I will not use it just because it's the easy way out of a difficult situation.'

'Why?' Dante asked, cocking his head at me.

Blood burned in my cheeks. 'It's…wrong.'

Dante snorted. 'You sound like a six-year-old, Rowan. This is bigger than right and wrong; greyer than black and white. There are no absolutes and no guarantees of victory. You…' He strolled closer. 'You are our first chance, in over six hundred years, of winning this game and I'm damned if I'll let you throw it away on your childishness.'

'Childish!' I glared at him, drawing my shoulders back. 'How is it childish to not kill? Not to stoop to their level?'

He sighed. 'That thinking is, in itself, childish, Rowan. We're not posting memes on social media. We're facing an organisation that has – for over a thousand years – hunted our kind with a view to extinction. There's no room for doubt or hesitation. No room for schoolyard morality. Only their lives, or ours.' He laid a slim hand on my shoulder, his mouth twisting. 'You need to decide now whose are more important because there won't be time, later.'

I thrust his arm away. The environmentalist's essence, his voice, his thoughts, plucked at my mind.

'Leave her, Dante.' Logan's low warning sliced through the tension. 'She's not a Hunter. She hasn't had our training for this.'

Dante's smiling charm fell away. 'She is now, Logan.'

'Enough.' Calain broke in. 'It will be her choice. No-one will force her, no matter what's at stake.'

'So,' Dante said, sneering, 'having waited patiently this last half a millennium, you'll be content to let her decide whether the Mors lives or dies? I think not, Padre. Don't be hypocritical.'

'*She* is right here,' I snapped. 'And *she* doesn't need either of you to make decisions for her. I'll use the *skath sheel* if it becomes absolutely necessary. Not before.'

All three men turned to me, Logan troubled, Calain penitent, and Dante condescendingly amused.

'Just so,' he said softly. 'But you must decide, ahead of time, what is your point of no return, Rowan. When the moment comes, if you wait too long – as you did today – our people will die. Decide now and be prepared to cross that threshold or our task is doomed from the start.'

I said nothing, merely clenched my teeth to hold back another hot retort. He was right, of course. I just didn't want to think about the sort of situations that would require that kind of commitment from me. But I also couldn't lose anyone I cared about, which meant more killing was inevitable.

Dante's scorn softened to sympathy I couldn't bear so I turned away.

'You ok?' Logan's concern brushed against my shields.

I nodded. 'We should go, I guess. We have to stop that parcel.'

After a shrewd look at me, Calain escorted Maeve and Erin out, leaving Logan, Dante and I in the house alone.

'What did you do to me?' I confronted Dante. 'In the *sianfath?*'

He slapped his cane across one palm. 'I merely severed your connections to my men to prevent you draining them.'

Logan gaped and stared back and forth between us. 'You can do that?'

Dante shrugged. 'I've never come across someone with Rowan's skill – so I didn't know I could. I did it by instinct. Probably affiliated with the skill of walking through shields. Useful, though.' He sent me a knowing look, tinged with pity, beneath his long lashes. 'At least you know I can stop you...should you need me to.'

'Yes,' I said, breathless. I wasn't sure what to think. Something about his skill made me uneasy. We were relying on my ability and here was someone I barely knew who could counter it and render me almost helpless. On one hand, I was grateful. On the other, worried. He was Maeve's son. Her agendas were his.

Was he a friend or another uneasy ally?

We left Lido Adriano in a ridiculous convoy of four tiny Fiats, all the same model but in different colours. Dante's team had split us up so there were two of my people in each car. Squashed into the rear seat, I sat against one window, Logan against the other. A broadshouldered sidhe sat between, taking up space and saying nothing.

I could have spoken to Logan telepathically, but there was little to say. I was also afraid he'd read too much of my self-doubt and fear. I didn't want to be talked out of it. Part of me needed to be afraid of what was coming.

We stopped in an Autogrill service station by the freeway southwest of Bologna. Just long enough to refuel, change into fresh clothing and throw down an espresso. Dante's people provided us with clothing and accompanied us everywhere, even into the bathroom. The jeans, boots, black shirt and black leather jacket fit perfectly. Maeve must have told him my sizes. Gratitude and resentment rubbed elbows in my thoughts as I emerged from the bathroom. The short female sidhe shadowed me.

When I emerged, Logan passed me a brioche and take away cappuccino. 'Okay?'

I nodded, studying the busy shop out of habit as I sipped. At eight in the morning, not many Italians were out and about. There were a few American tourists, their strident accents jarring through the service staff's liquid Italian. A young Australian couple bickered lightheartedly over the vast selection of chocolates on display. Their broad accents and blond hair reminded me of Paul Eisen. For one, homesick, moment, I wished I was back in Cairns, before all of this started. Wished I'd made different choices; not let Logan influence my decisions; run away when I'd had the chance.

In the dining area, Michael Eisen slouched in an orange plastic chair, glaring out through the huge glass windows that overlooked the carpark. Outside, cars zoomed past on the autostrada, weaving, never indicating, yet never seeming to endanger each other. I'd heard terrifying things about driving on Italian roads, but so far it seemed a lot more polite and sensible than in Australia. Here they let people in, even without indicators.

Beside Michael, Erin scowled at her phone. She sighed, shoved it aside and sipped at her coffee.

'Ready?' Logan nudged me.

'Guess so.' We headed out, followed by the soft footsteps of our minders.

I paused and faced the two sidhe. I considered my next words and chose to speak in English – partly to see if they understood, and partly to hide the fact I understood Italian. 'What're your names, anyway?'

A wry smile stretched the woman's thin lips. 'Mia.' She jerked a thumb at her massive companion. 'Angelo.'

'Right,' I said. 'Shall we go?'

Mia gestured at the three sidhe minding Erin and Michael in the dining area. Not far away, Dante, in silent conversation with one of his men, saluted in acknowledgment. As Erin rose from her seat, Michael bent and collected something from the floor. He passed it to her. She hesitated, said a few words, and stuffed the item into her pocket.

I strode out into the crisp autumn morning and headed for our silver Fiat.

'Logan,' I said, glancing back at Dante, still visible through the plate glass shop window, 'who's Nesrin?'

'Why?'

'You asked Dante about her, back at the house,' I said. 'He hesitated when he answered. I just had a feeling…I don't know.'

'Nesrin Kaya's his wife. I know what you mean, though. He normally talks people to death about how wonderful she is.' His smile softened. 'She is blindingly intelligent. And the only full sidhe I've met with green eyes.' He shrugged. 'Maybe they're going through a tough time. I know he's been pretty obsessed with hitting Mors facilities over the last six months or so. Travelling all over the world. It must take a toll on their relationship.'

I made a non-committal noise and continued towards the car. Calain and Maeve stood nearby, Calain leaning on one of the cars with his arms folded.

'Dante says it's about an hour and a half to Florence from here,' Logan said aloud as we neared Calain. 'He's waiting on a call-back from the Florence freight depot with an eta for delivery. It'll be close, I think.'

'And what happens if we don't get there in time?' Maeve said. 'What do we do?'

Dante sauntered up and touched my arm. I flinched away by reflex.

'We send your friend Michael in to collect it for us,' he said.

'He's not going to be thrilled with that idea,' Logan said.

Dante fixed his focus on me. 'Then we'll have to find some way of convincing him.'

'Don't look at me,' I said. 'I have no influence on him. Erin can lay another geas on him.'

'He's too strong-minded.' Dante shook his head. 'He'd fight this instruction harder than washing dishes – especially now he knows what it feels like. If she established the command, it would only last a short time. Not long enough to get him in and out. We'd also have to send someone with him because he would behave oddly and that could alert people.'

'What did you have in mind, then?' I asked, suspicious.

'We may have to change him, permanently.'

'But Erin said that could lead to brain damage,' I protested. As much as I disliked Michael, I wasn't prepared to turn him into a vegetable. I'd promised Paul he would come to no harm.

'That's not what I meant,' Dante said, sympathy in his cool gaze. 'We'll discuss it later. We need to go, now.'

In the car I opened a thought-window to Logan.

Do you know what he meant?

...No...at least, I don't think...

You're hiding something, Logan. You once told me we couldn't lie to each other like this. Tell me what you think he meant.

On the opposite side of the car, Logan grimaced. Dante sat in the passenger seat and Mia drove. She'd slipped into the left lane, travelling far faster than the speed limit, weaving in and out of traffic. Behind us, the other four cars in our convoy did the same. I clung to the seat, swallowing the urge to shout a warning as she missed a van by inches.

I think, Logan's reluctant thought came at last, *he may be suggesting you try to unfold Michael's DNA – to reactivate the gene allowing humans to sense the sianfath.*

What? Why would I do that? We have no idea what effect it might have.

I know, but it does make a kind of sense. If we can convince Michael – by showing him – how we're essential to the world's survival, then he might help us voluntarily.

A lot of 'ifs' and 'mights' in there, Logan. If unfolding his DNA has some horrible side effect, like death, then what do we do?

I don't know. I'm honestly not sure what to do at the moment, Rowan.

Are you alright? It's not like you to be so...unsure.

There was a long silence and I glanced past Angelo's bulk. Logan stared blindly out the window.

Logan?

I'm...you're right. After what I did in Brisbane I'm doubting every thought I have. I used to be so certain I knew what was right. Who was right. But in Brisbane everything I did...it all felt right too. How the hell do I know what to do?

That was the Dark gene's influence on your brain chemistry, Logan. It's suppressed now. You're ok. As my mother said: life's about making the right-thing decisions more often than the wrong. Like you said before, maybe I can help you for once.

I seem to remember you saving my life a couple time. Does that constitute help? A wry smile curved across his lips.

You know what I mean. I'm not sure I'm ready for that deep lorntinn *thing, but I'm sure we can work this out together.*

I'll try, Rowan. But deciding what's right will be tricky. There are just too many things at play and I have a feeling we're only privy to half the story.

Tell me about it. That's how I've felt for the last month.

I know. I'm sorry. At least consider the idea of working on Michael's DNA. It may be our only option.

I shut the thought-window and gazed out the real one. Outside, autumn-shaded hills slipped by, sometimes topped by small, medieval hill-villages of crumbling stone walls, sometimes bare, and sometimes with just a few remnants of history overpowered by garish Lego-block modernity.

There had to be another way to convince Michael to help. If we took him into Mors headquarters as a hostage he would find a way of betraying us. So, what, then?

SEVEN

<And what if she refuses to do it, Dante?>

    Madre, you underestimate my persuasiveness

    <You don't know this girl. She's...headstrong; intractable>

    You mean she hasn't been brought up to heed your every word as law? She's a modern woman, Madre. Not a little miss propriety born two hundred years ago

    <Believe me, I know. But we need her co-operation.>

    Take your hand off the rein for once. I have this under control.

I knocked on Dante's thought-house. It was – unsurprisingly – an Italian medieval hill-top fortress, complete with battlements, a moat, and holes to pour boiling oil onto his enemies.

    Sister? To what do I owe the pleasure?

    The parcel. It's not addressed to the Mors Ferrum headquarters, is it?

    No indeed. It's to a receiving office just outside the city centre. We still have no idea where their headquarters are. Somewhere in Firenze, we believe.

    Let me guess, in a palace?

His mental laugh echoed. **One would think so, especially since they tend to be theatrical and the Palazzo Vecchio was a de Medici residence. The de Medici's were of the Mors, that we know. But no, it will be something more innocuous and easier to protect. Too many tourists in the Vecchio.**

The receiving office is an easier target?

*Definitely. However the freight company tells me the driver is due there in approximately an hour.

We may not make it in time?

As you can see by the crazed look Mia wears, we are doing our best. But we may be too late.

Can we storm the office? There are at least fourteen of us who are trained.

We could, of course, but it is poor tactics to rush into a building with no planning. I've stayed alive a long time by not using poor tactics. I am attempting to get blueprints for the receiving office. It's part of a large corporate building. One of many Mors Ferrum shell companies. We have no idea how many staff or what their security is like.

And if we blow it we lose both men and the element of surprise. I understand. What do we do if we miss the parcel?

We beat a strategic retreat to my Firenze safehouse and plan an infiltration of Mors Headquarters. After all, this is about more than just that parcel. With Michael Eisen, we have an opportunity to cut off the dragon's head, so to speak. If we kill Dyson we can remove the Mors as a threat to our kind forever.

Somehow, I doubt this is their only base, Dante. I'm sure they'd pop up again under a different leader, even if we managed to take out this Dyson person.

*Possibly, but we would have a great deal of intelligence which would help us find...others of our kind. Taking this base would cripple them. And, if you put your mind to it, you could do much worse, sister. You could destroy them all.'

I won't. Don't ask me again. You have no idea what that would entail.

I closed my mental shields against him and leaned my head on the cold window. I disliked the feeling of being whisked along by other people's agendas. It was bad enough when it was just Maeve calling the shots. Now I had her, Calain, and Dante all pulling me in different directions. Add Erin's angst over her father, and Michael's overt hatred and I was starting to feel like everyone's emotional piñata.

'Che palle!' Mia's angry exclamation woke me with a start.

I grabbed at the door handle as the car swerved and Mia shouted another profanity at a slow-moving Mazda. I rubbed sleep away and squinted at the buildings zipping past. We were deep in an urban environment, presumably Florence. Ugly square apartment blocks, with peeling paint, and tiny balconies cluttered with dead pot plants and kids' broken toys, lined the roads and blotted out the surrounding hills. Hardly the medieval city I'd been expecting.

'We're about ten minutes from the city centre,' Dante called over his shoulder. 'And the receiving office is four blocks away.'

'Has the parcel been delivered?' I asked.

'Yes,' Dante replied. 'At ten fifteen; about five minutes ago.'

I swore in fluent Italian. Angelo, squeezed between Logan and I, chuckled faintly.

'Indeed,' Dante said.

'What's the plan?' Logan asked.

'We haven't time to ensure Michael's co-operation so I'll go in and ask for the package,' Dante said, shrugging.

'Just like that?' I said.

Dante shrugged. 'They'll be expecting someone from Mors to collect it. I'll pick the password from their thoughts. It's the most likely scenario to give us success.'

'It sounds too easy,' I muttered.

'Is she always this cynical?' Dante smiled at Logan

Logan's mouth twisted into wry amusement. 'Pretty much. But she does have a point. What if they realise you're not Mors Ferrum?'

'How?' Dante said. 'It's a receiving office catering to many different businesses. According to my sources there are no Mors Ferrum staff there. Just a receptionist and security staff.'

'What about backup?' Logan put in.

'My people will surround the building,' Dante replied. 'But I'm sure I can manage.'

'You said you didn't want to go in without information and a plan,' I said.

Dante smiled. 'You slept. I received information and planned. I have been doing this a very long time, sister.'

'How the hell have you survived this long being so blasé?' I snapped, folding my arms.

'It's a gift,' he said, chuckling. 'But if you are so concerned, eavesdrop. Logan knows my signal for trouble – a flash-image of a skull and crossbones pirate flag.'

I laughed in spite of my irritation. 'The Mors aren't the only ones who tend to be the theatrical.'

Dante shrugged. 'One does one's best to keep things amusing in this industry.'

Here's the building. Angelo, make sure all the exits are covered. His thoughts dropped into mine through the window I'd left open. Along with him came the strange choral effect of many-minds entwined. This time the sensation was heightened because he'd gathered in his ten people, along with my group, so there were fifteen sidhe enmeshed with Dante's words. All of them crowded into the great hall of my thought-castle.

Too close. The effect was both uncomfortable and soothing – like being wrapped in the too-smothering embrace of a loving family with no-where to get away and hide. But there was only one person in the group-mind I trusted, Logan. Even my father I didn't know well enough to be comfortable with in such close mental proximity. And Erin's presence grated like a thorn, her anger and pain pricking my conscience.

I struggled against the psychic connection. I untangled myself, wrenching my thoughts free from the promised warmth, pushing them all out of my mind and slamming the door.

Next to me, Angelo blinked.

Dante twisted in the front seat, a scowl marring his smooth brow. 'How did you...? No, never mind. We're here.'

Mia pulled the car into a tiny parking space with impressive deftness. She stayed behind the wheel and kept the engine running.

'You know what to do.' Dante nodded to Angelo. 'Rowan, I think it's best if you and Logan stay here.'

'No! Why?' I had my hand on the door. Angelo reached over and held it closed.

'Because,' Dante said, 'the success of my missions depends on the *lorntinn*. I hold the team together. We trust each other. You just broke out of my connection. The last time the unity failed I lost...' He paused and cleared his throat. Mia sent him a sympathetic look and Angelo shifted uncomfortably.

Dante frowned. 'The point is: I can't co-ordinate or trust a team that won't listen and won't work together. You're a liability.'

Stunned, I sank back against the seat and fought for breath. Had he punched me in the stomach I could not have felt more winded. Angelo climbed out of Logan's side and Logan slid back in next to me.

Dante leaned into Mia's window and spoke, but he looked at me. 'Mia, if something goes wrong your orders are to take these two to the safehouse. Don't try to help us. Rowan is our best chance at stopping the Mors. Don't let her risk herself. If you fail I'll hold you personally responsible. Understood?'

Mia nodded and swallowed. I said nothing. He could have given that order telepathically. Dante and Angelo walked to the other cars and gathered the rest of the team, leaving one man to guard Michael and Maeve in the last car. I could do nothing but wait and fume as Dante's people and mine spread out to surround the building. Erin didn't make an appearance. She stayed in her seat in the car behind ours, glowering at me through the windscreen.

Logan craned forward, watching the others approach the steel and glass office block.

'Go, Logan,' I muttered. 'You don't need to stay with me. I don't need a babysitter.'

'No,' he said, after a long pause. 'I'm still in the *lorntinn*. Dante will call if he needs me.'

'How can you stand it?'

Logan switched his attention to me. 'What?'

I wrapped my arms around myself. 'The…intrusiveness of what he does. He brings all of them right inside your head. It makes me feel…claustrophobic.'

Logan sighed and pulled me against his side. I curled into his chest, grateful for once to have someone to lean on.

'I keep forgetting how new you are to all this,' he murmured, kissing my forehead. 'We're all used to allowing people into our minds – at least, into the public spaces, if you will. But most of us can usually only do it with one or two at once. To the rest of us, the *lorntinn* is a privilege and a joy. To be so closely woven with so many other minds – especially in a deep-level *lorntinn* – is the nearest we can get to being one with the *sianfath*.'

He raised my chin, searching my face.

'You know that feeling you told me about? The sense of belonging you have when you stretch yourself into the *sianfath?*'

I nodded, half-reluctantly.

'That's what the *lorntinn* feels like to the sidhe. The more you care for them, the deeper you allow them. It's a beautiful thing. People fight tooth and nail to be in Dante's teams because he's so good at it. It's the closest thing we have to what our people had thousands of years ago, when there were more of us and we lived in villages, in harmony with the *sianfath.*'

I dropped my head onto his shoulder, ashamed of my childish rejection of something Logan and the rest of my people valued. But the thought of opening my innermost shield – the only thing protecting the core of who I was – made me deeply uncomfortable.

'Mia?' Logan addressed the sidhe. 'What's your take?'

She considered then responded, 'I just know it took me thirty years to get a place on this team and I wouldn't give it up for anything. So Miss Rowan is staying here, because that's what the Count meant by "personally responsible". If I let you out, I'll be off the team.'

I sighed and rubbed at the tightening band of tension around my skull. Pressure built, along with a too-familiar sense of unease, indicating impending trouble.

'Dammit. Logan, I think—'

Logan stiffened and he stared past me, at the building. Mia's head snapped around to follow his gaze.

'—something's about to happen,' I finished.

'Too late,' Logan growled.

'What is it?' I peered out the window, almost tempted to rejoin the collective, but reluctant to as well.

'Shit!' Logan reached for the door. I grabbed his arm.

'What?'

He shook me off. 'Stay here. Mia, if anything happens to me, get her away. I'm going to help.'

'No!' I started to slide after him. A metallic click near my ear made me freeze in disbelief. In the front seat, Mia had a nine-mil cocked and aimed at my left shoulder. There was no hint of humour in her.

Logan slammed the door and sprinted towards the building. One of Dante's men met him near the front entrance and the two of them ran around the side.

'This is ridiculous.' I tried for calm and failed. Mia stayed out of easy reach, her focus fixed on me with unwavering intent.

'You have to let me help, Mia.'

She jerked her chin. 'Go ahead. You can help without leaving the car, so I hear.'

I wavered. No. I had no idea what was happening. I could drain people who were innocent bystanders and I wasn't going any further down that path.

'At least tell me what's happened,' I snapped.

'Someone warned them. There was a greeting party,' she said grimly. Her focus switched to the building and she sucked a quick breath. 'Lucio!' She groaned. 'Bianca, no!'

I lunged, wrenching the gun from her lax grip and turning it back on her. Keeping her steady in the sights, I climbed out of the car.

'When you come to,' I said, 'go take care of Erin. She'll be having hysterics and she has no way of defending herself if anyone finds her. Sorry about this.' I stretched just a single filament into the *sianfath* and drained just enough of her life force to put her to sleep. She slumped sideways in her seat. I tucked her gun into my belt and tugged my shirt over to hide it. Then I strolled towards the building, casual. When I was almost at the door, I fed Mia back her energy and felt her awaken, groggy and angry.

I walked past the front door, on to the next building. It was a small Indian restaurant. I paused outside, pretending to study the menu posted on the window. Anchoring myself, I stretched into the *sianfath* and sought inside the office building. There. Three of Dante's people held their positions outside the building, covering three exits. Two more lay dead in what must be a room off the foyer, their essences already sliding into the *sianfath*. There was nothing I could do to save them.

But in a hall behind the foyer was a hazy tableau of chaos.

The silver-green auras of five sidhe glowed, all alive. But none moving or fighting the dozen or so orange-hued humans surrounding them. I couldn't tell if the humans held weapons and they shifted and moved so much it was impossible to tell if they were threats or bystanders. Draining even part of their life-force was a risk. What if one had a weak heart, or I couldn't return the energy fast enough and killed an innocent? And there were so many, even weakening them would give me too much power. I'd either have to return the energy quickly or release it and destroy something. That idea appealed, but the last thing we needed was police showing up at a disaster site.

So how to get to the five sidhe out...wait, those were Dante, Calain and three of Dante's people. Where was Logan?

I retreated and found the thin green thread connecting us – the indication we were a couple and had shared intimacies. It led upward, through the building I stood beside. There, somewhere over my head, Logan stood poised, waiting. Waiting for what?

I stepped pretended to be absorbed in typing a text on my phone. I wandered a few steps towards the receiving office and snuck a quick look at the alley separating the two buildings. Wide enough for two small cars to pass. A long jump, even for a sidhe. I didn't dare look up, lest I give Logan's position away to anyone watching.

Logan? What the hell are you doing up there?

Stay out of this, Rowan. I'm going in to get them.

You can't. There are a dozen humans in there, probably armed. And Dante and the others are unconscious.

I know. But Dante's last three men are still waiting outside. Someone has to go in.

Let me—

No! Dammit Rowan, stay out. Unless you're going to use the skath-sheel Dante's right: you're not used to working in teams. Stay clear. I can't be worrying about you, too.

Screw you, Logan. I've saved your ass at least three times. Don't give me that "doesn't play well with others" crap.

He cut off our mental connection, slamming his thought-window with a finality that hurt. My chest ached with an unvoiced scream of rage. How dare he?

I stood for a moment, rooted to the concrete pavement, anger and hurt narrowing my thoughts into single-minded focus. Fine.

I turned back to the car.

EIGHT

Maeve. Are you and Erin alright?

<Yes, Logan. What's Rowan doing? She's just standing outside the building looking furious.>

Not important right now. I have to get into the building and get to Dante and the others. Can you shut down their phones and internet telekinetically? I don't want them calling for help.

<Of course. Done. Be careful.>

I stopped, appalled at my own childishness. Swearing, I swung around and headed for the frosted glass door. I pasted on an expression of eager anticipation and straight-armed the door open. It crashed against the wall, the sound reverberating in the open, marble-lined foyer.

'Oops.' I giggled. 'Sorry.'

Behind a black and white marble counter, a generously-curved twenty-something girl with scraped-back dark hair blinked at me. She cleared her throat and her eyes darted twice to the side room, where I knew two sidhe lay dead on the floor.

'Can I help you?' She spoke in Italian.

I replied in American-accented English. 'I'm trying to find the FedEx shop. Is it around here somewhere? I've got a letter to post to the States in a hurry.' I strolled towards her, patting the pockets of my jacket. 'Now where the heck did I put that? I just had it.'

I palmed a throwing knife and pulled out an open packet of M&Ms I'd bought at the Autogrill, laying it on the counter as I continued to mutter and search. Mia's pistol pressed into my back. I didn't want to use it if I didn't have to.

'There's no FedEx store in town, ma'am,' she said in English. 'The nearest one is in Prato. I'm sorry. We can't help you. We ship parcels for our business customers.'

'Oh.' I let my shoulders droop. 'Really? Can you show me where it is on the map?' I pointed to a map of Florence on the desk, distracting her.

She leaned forward. I grabbed her throat. Her neck felt soft. She choked and gargled, her face turning red, her nails scrabbling on my arm. But my half-sidhe strength outweighed her human abilities.

'You're going to stay quiet and I'll release you, yes?' I whispered.

She garked. I took that as assent and relaxed my grip a fraction. She sucked a shaky breath.

'Now,' I said, 'you're going to show me how I can get to where my friends are being held. And how to get there without going through that door behind your desk.' I nodded at the security door behind her. On the other side, I could sense the dim life-auras of the six unconscious sidhe.

Wait. Six? There were six now. And one was moving. Logan? No, our connection still led up to the roof. He was in this building, but at least three floors up. Who was the sixth sidhe? I couldn't tell without stepping into the *sianfath* and that would leave me physically vulnerable.

The security door opened.

'Pray, child, release the human,' a light, cool voice drawled. Framed by the doorway, the sidhe revealed seemed inhumanly tall and thin, for his head brushed the frame. His skin was a rich, dark gold – the colour of autumn leaves. The white-blonde of his hair and black of his eyes jarred against his skin and had to be fake. The shock of kin-recognition was strong, which meant he was probably full-blood sidhe and wearing contact lenses. If he'd just cast a glamour I would have seen through it.

I grabbed the woman under the arms and dragged her around the end of the counter. Anger had a way of making me even stronger, and I was pretty pissed off right now. She shrieked. I hauled her close and wrapped an arm around her throat. A small squeeze and a few seconds later she'd be unconscious. A couple more and she'd be dead.

'Who are you?' I said. 'Let my friends go and I'll let her go.'

The sidhe inclined his head, his eyelids half-closed as he assessed me. 'Alexander Dyson. And you?'

I froze, gaping. This was the Mors Ferrum's leader? This skinny prat in a pinstriped suit and shiny black shoes? He had a tie bar. And three pens in his jacket pocket. Seriously?

'Not going to tell me who you are?' he asked. 'I don't blame you. It's been so long since I used my real name I believe I've almost forgotten it. Eons ago, humans believed there was powerful magic in knowing a true name. I've often wondered how it worked.' He shrugged. 'But I digress.' His gaze hardened. 'Let the girl go and we'll talk.'

'Let my friends go.'

'You mistake my order for a negotiation,' Dyson drawled. 'I wouldn't normally waste my time on this. I don't care what happens to that young woman. Kill her, if you will. And I care little for half-breeds such as yourself. But there's something about you...' A feather-thought brushed against my shields. His eyes widened.

I tightened my grip on the woman. She gasped and clutched at my arm.

Dyson pulled a gun from beneath his jacket and shot my hostage. A dart slapped into her thigh and she jerked in my arms. A few seconds later the tranquiliser took effect and she sagged, her weight dragging at me until I was forced to let her slide to the cold marble. She collapsed in a graceless sprawl, her skirt rucked up and arms bent beneath her body.

Dyson loaded another dart into the pistol. I used his moment of distraction and flicked my throwing knife, aiming for the femoral artery. We were a long way from forests. A deep enough cut might kill him. He would bleed out in a few minutes if he couldn't heal himself quickly.

Without even looking up, he shifted to one side. The knife missed and clanged on the marble floor, skittering across the tile until it came to rest against the wall.

Hands grabbed my arms from behind, pinning them to my sides. Someone clutched a handful of my hair and wrenched my head backwards until all I saw was the white-painted ceiling. A whiff of sickly cologne almost made me gag.

The time to resist was right at the start of a kidnapping. My heart hammered blood into my ears. I crouched, crooking my arms, buying myself space. I shoved backwards and hauled my three captors with me as they clung to my arms. They were human; weaker than I, but there were three of them. Big, strong, armed with pistols still holstered on their hips.

'Restrain her, lackwit!' Dyson snapped.

The hands clamped tighter, cutting off circulation. Adrenalin made my legs tremble. I swallowed rising fear and kicked back. Something crunched beneath my heel. The man behind me screamed and released my hair. I twisted, folding one arm behind my back and the other before my body, bringing one of my captors into full view. He let go with one hand and reached for his pistol. I turned beneath his arm, dragging the two men together. They cracked heads and released me. I lashed a kick at a thigh nerve bundle. The man nearest collapsed, clutching at his leg.

A metallic click by my ear. My heart skipped a beat. I ducked. The boom of detonation shattered silence and pounded on my eardrums. Surging up, I caught the gun and shoved it skyward. *Crack.* Ceiling paster showered down, dusting my attacker's dark hair white. I folded his wrist. Something snapped and he screamed. The gun clattered to the marble floor. My elbow smashed his cheekbone. He sprawled on the ground, sliding a across the polished stone, coming to rest at Dyson's feet.

Dyson laughed softly into the silence. The dart gun's muzzle pointed at me. I'd wasted the chance to draw my own weapon.

'You'll have to do better,' Dyson murmured. 'Show me something impressive and I might let you live.'

There was nowhere to run or hide. If the dart contained the same sedative I'd been hit with before, I'd have about two minutes before falling unconscious. It wasn't long, but enough time to access the *sianfath* and purge the sedative from my system. The best option might be to let him dart me, then feign sleep while I worked out what to do next. But what if I was wrong and the sedative worked faster? I did *not* want to be in his power.

His finger tightened on the trigger.

'Why are you doing this?' I said, hurriedly. 'You're a sidhe. Why are you running an organisation that hunts your own kind?'

He lowered the gun. 'You know who I am? Fascinating. Now I am agog to know your name.'

I set my jaw and glared at him. 'Why are you killing your own people?' I inched one hand around behind my back, feeling for the butt of the gun in my waistband.

'Keep your hands where I can see them.' Dyson gestured with the dartgun. He sucked a quick breath, eyeing me curiously. 'You have no idea what I'm trying to achieve by running the Mors Ferrum, have you?

'What's that supposed to mean?'

'It means,' he said, amusement flickering across his narrow face, 'you and your misguided friends have spent over a hundred years hindering my attempts to save our race.'

'What?' I lowered my arms from their defensive position and gaped at him.

'You might want to ask young Dante exactly what he and his people are trying to achieve.' Dyson's lips twitched in a cool smile. 'Because, at the moment, all he's doing is obstructing my efforts. I'm using the Mors Ferrum to do the legwork of finding sidhe so I can save us from our own blundering idiocy.'

'What?' I repeated. 'The Mors is killing sidhe, not saving them.'

Dyson chuckled. 'Yes, before I took over, that's true. Now, although they don't know it, they're helping me find a way to save our species.'

I shut my mouth. No. There was no way... But I only had the word of Maeve and the others on what the Mors did. Michael had already admitted much of his experimentation on sidhe had been without the Mors knowledge. Was it possible he was completely rogue? That the Mors Ferrum were no longer a threat, and Dyson really was trying to help?

There was only one way to be sure.

'Why don't you come with me and see for yourself, my dear?' Dyson said. 'I could use more help.'

I made a non-committal noise, more focussed on anchoring myself and stretching a filament of my consciousness through the *sianfath*. I reached into the silvery-green aura surrounding Dyson. His thought-shield took the form of an elaborate fifteenth century

French chateau, complete with blue, conical roofs on stone roundel towers.

He glanced at the closed security door behind the counter.

I slid a tendril of thought into the cracks around the barricaded oak door of his chateau.

'Ah. We have company.' He tucked the gun back into his jacket. 'We shall have to take this up another time.'

'What…' I couldn't devote much to a witty comeback. I pushed through his shield, into an unlit entry hall; hollow and open, but strangely silent.

His smile became enigmatic. 'I have what I came for. I've lived too long to risk my plans for mere ego.' He swept a shallow bow. 'Your servant, madam.' Spinning on his heel, he strode to the front door.

'Wait!'

He turned back. Muffled thumps from behind the security door were followed by a shout of pain and a gunshot. I wavered. Logan's voice yelled an order to lay down arms. Another shot reverberated.

'What did you mean?' I frowned. 'How are you trying to save the sidhe?'

Dyson paused, one hand on the glass door. 'Suffice to say: if you stay out of my way, the world will be a far better place for our kind in the end.'

A small part of my mind pushed deeper into his, seeking truths in the oppressive, echoing history encompassed by his shields and holding his long memories.

'Now that *is* interesting,' he muttered. He took a half-step towards me, but stopped as something thumped against the security door.

Dyson scowled and made a chopping gesture.

Thread connecting us snapped. Pain sliced through my chest and I staggered, clutching at the marble counter as my knees sagged.

Dyson shoved the door open and closed it behind him, locking it with a card-key. Through the smoked glass, he smiled. He reached into a pocket of his jacket and pulled out a small padded envelope. He waved it at me and saluted.

A second sidhe emerged from a waiting car and they exchanged words. The newcomer glanced through the glass door at me and I gaped. Logan? No, on closer study, the man was older, with flecks of grey at his temples. It could only be Finn, Logan's father.

I looked fearfully at the back room. When I turned to the front door again, both sidhe were gone.

The security door burst open, smacking against the wall behind the counter.

Logan and three of Dante's people ran through, weapons out. Logan caught sight of me and hurried to my side, sliding an arm around my waist. Dante's team focussed their weapons on the three men still scattered at my feet.

'You ok? Did they hurt you?' Logan kissed me. 'You scared me.'

'Not those ones.' I leaned against him, still weakened and aching with an inexplicable sense of loss. 'But there was another. And he has the package.'

'He? Would you recognise him again?'

'It was Dyson.'

'Dammit!' Logan stared at the busy street.

'Logan?' I gripped his wrist, afraid he'd run after them. 'Your father was with him.'

NINE

<Dante? Are you safe?>

    Of course, Madre. They merely took us by surprise and darted us. You're correct about the sedative. It's extraordinarily effective. We shall have to be more careful.

    <Have you spoken yet to Rowan about disobeying you?>

    No.

    <She pulled out of the unity. Her headstrong action could have endangered you all.>

    Could have. Didn't. Because of her we almost succeeded in regaining the parcel. We also found out what Dyson looks like, and that he's here in Firenze. Along with Finn.

    <Finn? What did Logan say?>

    Nothing. He hasn't told me. I overheard his conversation with Rowan.

    <We need to be certain he won't—>

    You will do nothing. I will handle this my own way and thank you for not interfering. You've managed both these young people badly.

    <...>

    Madre, do you know what Calain hides?

    <Many things, I'm sure. As we all do.>

'Take the bodies back to Rome and return with reinforcements – Callia and Luigi, if they are free.' Dante finished instructing two of his team then closed and locked the safe house's iron-studded wooden front door. The great, wrought-metal gate outside clanged shut. One of the cars drove away, the engine's growl echoing between the high brick walls that lined the narrow Via di Montughi.

I followed Dante through a wide, white-plastered hallway to the back of the rambling villa. On the outside, the buildings were a jumble of red-tiled roofs and yellow-plastered stone walls, all set in a vast garden that served as a balm to my exhausted body and mind. The site seemed to have grown organically over hundreds of years; several mis-matched, two-storey buildings patched together and creating an internal maze of rooms and corridors.

The hall's grey marble floor gave way to pink and grey when we entered an airy lounge room of vaulted ceilings and gilded plaster.

Dante and I walked into an argument and I was tempted to keep walking. Wide French doors led out onto the garden and promised peace.

'You sonofa...' Logan shoved Michael up against a white-plastered wall, one forearm across his throat. 'You used Erin's phone and warned them we were coming.'

Michael's face reddened and he sank his nails into Logan's forearm. 'What the hell did you expect me to do, just go along quietly and let you win?'

'They killed two of our people,' Logan snarled.

Michael's lip curled. 'Two less sidhe is hardly going to make me regret my actions.'

Logan pulled a throwing knife from his belt and shortened his arm for a thrust.

'Logan!' Dante's voice whipped through the thick silence.

'Shit.' Logan shoved away. He ran stiff fingers through his dark, dishevelled hair. 'I was in their minds when they died...' His voice cracked and he sank onto a brown leather couch, holding his head. 'I felt them. Their agony...'

'Let it go, Logan,' Dante murmured, squeezing Logan's shoulder. 'You've been through this before. You know it does no good to dwell on their deaths. They're with the *sianfath* and probably more content than we are. And we both know this is not what's truly bothering you.'

Logan made a hasty gesture, as though rejecting Dante's words.

I sank into a studded leather chair and watched Logan. There was little I could do to help him. Showing empathy would shatter what little self-control he had and expose him further to Michael's ridicule. In Brisbane he'd almost killed everyone he loved and it fuelled a barely-concealed hatred for Michael. He wore the guilt of his actions like a cloak of lead. Now his Dark-aligned father was here, too, adding to his anger and confusion.

Michael rubbed at his bruised neck, smirking in a way that made me want to finish Logan's work. I glared at him as he dropped into the deep leather chair opposite me and put his feet up on the smoked-glass coffee table.

Erin, Maeve, Mia and the rest of Dante's people were not there, having scattered to find rooms in the ten-bedroom mansion. Wise, given the tension in this room.

Calain stood by the room's southern wall. Ignoring Michael and Logan, he stared through the glass doors, into a garden rich in autumn golds and reds. His brows were drawn close, his eyes hard and cold.

'What did Dyson say to you, Rowan?' Dante sat next to Logan and crossed his legs, his gaze resting shrewdly on me. His fingers drubbed restlessly on the golden timber of his cane.

'Is it wise to talk in front of him?' I jerked my chin at Michael.

Dante gave a wintry smile. 'Believe me, he'll never get a chance to betray us again. And I think it might benefit him to hear the truth.'

I fiddled with one of the sunken leather buttons dimpling the chair's arm. 'I think we'd all like to hear the truth, but I'm not sure what it is any more.'

'Explain?' Dante's attention sharpened on me.

Logan straightened. Only Calain didn't turn around. He kept staring out the window, arms folded.

'Dyson's definitely sidhe,' I said. 'As was the man he left with, Logan's father.'

Logan swore softly, his face pale and set.

'Dyson said…' I sucked a deep breath. 'He said for the last hundred years he's been using the Mors to find sidhe so he can save our race, not so he can kill us off.'

'What?' Michael clutched at the arms of his chair and half rose, sinking back again when Logan pointed the knife in his direction. 'You're lying.'

'Continue, Rowan,' Dante said.

'Not much else to say,' I replied. 'He said he was trying to locate the sidhe to help them survive and you were getting in his way – I assume he meant with your rescues of captured sidhe.'

Dante exchanged a quick glance with Logan. By the distant looks, they were communicating telepathically and leaving me out of the conversation. I checked on Calain but he remained silent and aloof.

'You have to be lying,' Michael said, his voice low and tense. 'There's no way the Mors Council would let him get away with helping you bastards.'

Dante glanced back and forth between me and Michael. He leaned back against the couch and held the cane behind his head. The elegant dark grey jacket he wore slid open, revealing a tailored white shirt and a gun holster under his arm.

'No, she's not lying,' he said. 'But for once I agree with you: Dyson can't be helping the sidhe. I've released hundreds...no, thousands, from Mors facilities in the last hundred years since Dyson came to power.' Darkness shadowed his eyes, and Logan's. 'Brainwashed, traumatised, scarred for life. No one does that to their own people in the name of saving them.' He pressed his lips together.

'Show me,' I said, folding my arms. 'Let me see those memories. I only have your word for all this and I don't know you. Even Logan only worked with you once, when you released Tomas Fairchild.'

'Rowan!' Logan's shock and Dante's quick intake of breath was enough to convince me I'd made some social blunder.

'You don't do that, Rowan,' Calain's deep voice rumbled. 'A memory share is reserved for the most intimate loved ones. People with whom you've shared the deepest *lorntinn* closeness. It involves letting someone into your most protected spaces, leaving you vulnerable.'

My cheeks warmed. Resentment boiled.

'You cannot ask it of me, Rowan,' Dante said, his voice hard, 'when you disobey a direct order.'

'I'm not part of your team.'

'That,' Dante drawled, 'is obvious. Nor will you be unless you curb your impatience and intemperance. I'm here to help you, but you trust no one – not even yourself.' His eyes softened. 'And because of that, whatever you do is doomed to failure; and you damn all of us.'

I ground my teeth. My throat ached with held-back tears and words but denial was pointless. He spoke only the truth, after all.

'Dante, back off,' Logan warned. 'A month ago she didn't know any of us. And after the way Maeve's treated her, you can't blame her for not believing you.'

'She'll not fail us,' Calain put in. His tone was matter-of-fact, but his gaze, as it rested on me, was troubled.

'You people are idiots,' Michael snapped. 'You have these powers but you have no idea how to exploit them to get what you want. You don't deserve them.' He sneered at me. 'You want his memories, just take them. If you can murder a hundred people, you can do that.'

I flinched and hunched a shoulder.

Michael sniffed. 'The Mors have spent the last ten years taking sidhe with the "dark" gene. We learned how to switch it on, and added them to the ones who responded to brainwashing.' He smirked then jerked a thumb at Dante. 'And even though you've released thousands, we still have an army that can equal you. More, because we control them and you can't function in a team of six.'

Logan turned a cold stare on him. 'Speaking of using powers. Now's a good time to get past that deep block in your mind and see what you're hiding.' He smiled thinly. 'And I guarantee it will be painful.'

Michael's eyes widened. 'Now, wait a minute.'

'An excellent suggestion,' Dante ordered, rising from his chair. 'Hold him, Logan.'

Logan shoved Michael deep into his seat and held him there, digging into the pressure points along the collarbone. Dante clamped onto Michael's wrist, holding hard when Michael tried to wrench free. Dante's eyes unfocussed as he probed the shield buried deep in Michael's mind. His brow furrowed.

Michael's body tensed. His eyes rolled back and his mouth gaped in a silent scream. Then the scream became real and echoed hoarsely in the vaulted room. Dante's neck corded and his lips drew back in a snarl.

'Merda!' Dante released Michael and stepped back, pale and shaking. 'I couldn't get through. That's never happened. Non capisco.'

Michael slumped in the chair, unconscious.

'I understand.' Calain eased his large body onto a three-legged timber stool, resting his elbows on his knees, head bowed. 'It's Dyson.'

'What?' Logan relaxed his grip on Michael's neck. Michael's head lolled to one side.

'Dyson set the shield.' Calain pointed at Michael. 'I've seen his work before. You won't get through it. I doubt even Ruadhán could.'

I scowled, irritated by the slight on my abilities. Part of me wanted to try, just to prove him wrong. More of me didn't. I was too angry and upset to think straight and I'd promised Paul I wouldn't kill his father.

'Where have you seen—' Dante began.

Calain interrupted with a peremptory wave. 'It doesn't matter. Dyson is over a thousand years old. He's learned from the best. Whatever Michael knows, we can't access it. We have more important things to think about.'

'If he's so old,' I said, frowning, 'why does he speak normally? You and Maeve both use old-fashioned words all the time. He doesn't.'

'He always was a good actor. And if he's running the Mors, he can hardly betray his true age by speaking in Middle English or Anglo Saxon,' he said wryly.

'How do you know so much about Dyson,' I asked. He was holding something back. I just knew it.

Calain hardened. 'I'm six hundred years old, child. I've seen a lot.'

'Don't patronise me. That's not an answer,' I shot back.

He hesitated, grimacing. 'I told you I fought him at the end of the nineteenth century. Burned down his laboratory and released hundreds of sidhe held captive there. Many of them had the same type of wall buried deep in their minds. Whatever else he may be, Dyson is persuasive. They all believed he was a great leader, doing great things. Even those he'd tortured.'

Dante scowled, rubbing his hands on his biceps. 'Now you mention it, I have also seen this shield before. But always in sidhe, so I never tried to get through it. I assumed it was their own, deepest level of shielding. I wonder—'

'This is all beside the point,' I broke in. The three men directed interrogative stares in my way. I lifted my chin. 'We're forgetting why we came to Florence: that damned parcel containing our DNA and information on all our powers. Dyson has it now. He waved it at me as he left the building with Logan's father. Why are two sidhe running the Mors and why do they want our DNA information?'

A tense silence fell over all of us. Logan groaned and dropped his head into his hands and Dante scrubbed at his scalp, dishevelling his dark hair. Calain leaned back in his chair.

'Mayhap Maeve and Erin should assist us in thinking this through,' Calain suggested. 'Maeve may know of some method by which to breach Michael's wall, and Erin is skilled in technology. She may be able to assist in finding the Mors's headquarters.'

'Mia, too,' Dante added. 'She's a genius with computers. But we have tried before, you know. To find their base, I mean.' He grimaced. 'Especially in the last three months. They're skilled in hiding it.'

'Do you know if they're holding any of your people there?' Logan scratched at the dark stubble on his chin and gazed off into the distance.

'Not for certain,' Dante answered, 'but it's a distinct possibility. Why?'

'If you have anything personal from one of them, Erin is a psychometric.' Logan shrugged. 'She could use the item to track them.'

For a moment Dante's eyes blazed with excitement. Then his face fell. 'No. I have nothing suitable here.'

'And even a *dilynna* doesn't work?' Calain put in.

'That means "follow" in the *Henath* language,' I said. 'Some sort of tracking thing?'

'Yes,' Dante replied. 'It's a thought you attach to another mind. Like a…fishing line stretched between you. It only works up to a limited distance – maybe a few hundred kilometres at best – before it fades. But no, it doesn't work. Every time we've put a *dilynna* on a Mors member, it's been severed before they've returned to their HQ.'

'Severed?' I shivered, staring at the cold grey marble floor tile under my feet, seeing again Dyson's mocking smile.

'What troubles you, daughter?' Calain rumbled.

'I tried…' I gritted my teeth. 'I tried to see into Dyson's mind by using the *skath sheel* to walk through his shields. But he cut the connection.' I glanced at Dante from beneath my lashes. 'Just as you did, but whatever he did *hurt*. Really hurt. It felt like a piece of me had been cut away.'

'God's blood!' Calain paled and wiped at his mouth.

Dante leaned forward, watching our father. 'What do you know of this?'

Calain grimaced. 'My mother, Aeona, called it the *torryl.*'

'The cut,' I translated from H*enath* for Dante's sake. I almost added that Aeona hadn't mentioned it in her book, but stopped myself. The book was my last link to my grandmother, full of her wisdom and advice about sidhe abilities. I didn't want to give it over to Calain or Dante.

Calain nodded. 'It was a technique developed by Tordal Ivaldison – the dark sidhe who forced Aeona to use her gifts on his behalf. She had the ability to kill him, so he and his son developed the *torryl* to counteract her *skath-sheel*. It cuts the connection, but also cuts away part of the *enath*. Every time you encounter it, you lose part of your essence, Ruadhán. And his control over you grows. If he cuts too much of you away, you'll become *demenath* - soulless. Undead, if you like.'

I swallowed. 'But there must be a way to counteract it. I mean, Aeona survived.'

'No. She ran,' Calain said. 'I was a babe of not yet two in the summer of 1405. Henry IV's army was on Abberley Hill. Owain Glyndŵr, as Prince of Wales, held Woodbury Hill, with the village of Great Witley between them. Tordal held me hostage, forcing Aeona to help the English king.

His gaze slid from mine. 'But Aeona said she had a vision the night before the battle. It revealed I was in danger. She took me and ran. She had been Tordal's weapon for almost a hundred years.' Calain's expression was bleak. 'She'd felt the *torryl* just twice in all that time, but it was enough to frighten her for a century – until she decided my life was worth the risk of defying Tordal.' He paused.

'And?' I prompted.

'There is no counter for the *torryl*.'

CHAPTER TEN

Have care, Padre. She's frightened enough as it is.

-Thankyou, Dante. Pray do not lecture me on dealing with my daughter until you are a parent yourself.-

This, from you? You've as little parenting experience as I. Perhaps less, since you've worked alone for half a millennia while I've been guiding youngsters her age for over a century.

-...My apologies. I spoke unwisely. You're correct on both counts. I fear Ruadhán is as unused to working with others as I.-

And now you've surprised me. Something I thought impossible.

'No counter for the *torryl?* None?' I gripped the seat arms and sucked a long breath, trying to slow my heart. But the memory of the pain Dyson had inflicted stirred fear that threatened to choke me.

Calain shook his head, his mouth thin and eyes dark with old pain.

I rose, stalked to the French doors facing the garden and yanked them open. The handle of one smacked into the plastered interior wall. The door-glass shattered, cascading onto the marble floor. I swore, hesitated then walked from room, ignoring Logan's call.

Footsteps crunched on the glass behind me. I broke into a run, desperate to get away from all of them, from everything. The villa garden was large, but not big enough to hide me, or to soothe my billowing fears. I needed to get away from all these men and their agendas. I needed to talk to someone who cared about me; the only woman who would understand; who might have an answer: Aeona. But I couldn't reach her, not here.

Logan called my name again. I kicked into high gear and sprinted around the corner of the villa, skidding on the gravel driveway. I let myself out through the walking gate and emerged into the narrow road. Lined with high brick and stone walls, there was room for only one car going one direction. I turned right and ran.

Winter hadn't yet stripped the trees and life still pulsed through the gardens hiding behind the walls. But it was slow and sluggish. I needed somewhere bigger and more robust to draw on. To my left, behind the wall, a swathe of the *sianfath* called. Ahead, a gap in the walls revealed an open gate and a gravel parking space.

I ran in and paused, breathing hard. To the right stood a grand, sprawling villa with crenulations on the third floor roof, dust-yellow paint and massive arched windows. Perched on the ridge, it overlooked a vast sweep of gardens. In the end wall, a small glass door said 'Exit' and 'Café'. The building must be some sort of publicly-accessible venue. My fears of intruding on private land evaporated and the gardens called me. To the left stood a smaller building, perhaps a dower house or similar. Ignoring both buildings, I ran straight ahead, towards the gardens.

My feet took me along broad paths of pale gravel, beneath trees glorious in their autumn clothing of gold and red. I came to a small lake surrounded by towering pencil pines and walled by moss-covered grey stones. The water was still and greenish, reflecting the storm-grey clouds overhead. On one side, a square pavilion overlooked the lake. Steps led down to the water from a dark door flanked by Egyptian statues and set into a dust-yellow wall. A white obelisk towered over the building on one side.

Dark, quiet and surrounded by forest. Just what I needed.

I made my way into the building's cool-dark and sank onto a cold concrete bench. Shivering against the autumn chill, I zipped up my jacket and settled my heart. I did a quick Google check on my phone to make sure I knew when I needed to be. Reaching Aeona at the right moment would be difficult, but at least I now knew when that moment should be. Calain had just told me. Had he done it on purpose?

I closed my eyes, extended myself into the *sianfath's* rich depths, and opened the door to my deepest core. A long hall extended before me, with doors to each side; my mental compartmentalisation of my own self, and of Calain's long life. At the end I found a thick wooden door, decorated with chunky black iron studs and leaf-shaped hinges. Taking a deep breath and focussing fiercely on the place and year I needed, I opened it and stepped inside, into Aeona Silverblade's memories.

I fell through the shadows of history for eternity, unable to make sense of the myriad of images flowing past, bombarded by moments of joy and spikes of pure agony. Then it all stopped and I stared at my hands, outstretched towards a guttering fire. Delicate, but with dirt ingrained beneath broken nails. Long sleeves of a thick, dark green material covered my arms, buttoned to the wrists. No. Not my arms; not my hands.

'Who art thou?' My mouth moved, but Aeona's voice emerged, quavering.

I tethered a tendril of myself to her body and stepped out, into the *sianfath*. Turning back, I saw her; dark grey eyes wide and mouth open. Fine reddish brows twitched into a frown as she studied me.

I still wore modern clothing and had no idea how to change it to something more suitable to the era. Aeona wore a simple, green woollen long chemise with a grey, sleeveless kirtle over the top. Her long, dark hair was tied back with a matching grey scarf.

'I don't have much time, Aeona,' I said, checking to see we were alone. She sat on a low stool, in a small room with wattle and daub walls and dirty rushes on the floor. Smoke from the central hearth wafted up to a thatched roof. On a rough timber table next to her, the remains of a chicken bone and a horn cup half full of some brown liquid bore testament to a recent meal.

'Why thou art a woman!' She glanced at my jeans-clad legs and blushed. 'From wither? What land lets their womenfolk array thy form so immodest? And thy hair!' She reached for me but her fingers passed through my short, auburn curls and she gasped. 'Art thou a shade? Nay. Art sidhe; and one with much strength, I sense.' She tilted her head. 'So not wither, but from whence, mayhap? Art thou sliding betwixt times?'

Oh, she was quick alright. I opened my mouth to tell her everything, but stopped. All the sci-fi stories I'd ever read about time paradoxes and affecting the future hijacked my thinking. If I wasn't careful, I could set her on the wrong course of action and I might never be born.

'I'm from the future,' I said, 'but I can't tell you much more or I'll screw up the time line.'

'Screw up?' She blinked at me. 'Thy words make little sense and thy manner of speech is most strange.'

'Sorry. Just hear me out.' I sucked a deep breath, organising my thoughts. 'If I've picked the right time, you're now somewhere in Wales with Henry IV's army, about to attack Owain's.'

Aeona nodded, gaping. A gust of wind rattled the walls and whistled beneath a gap under the slatted timber door. She shivered and wrapped a woollen cloak about her thin shoulders. Her narrow face was drawn, cheeks hollow. Dark circles shadowed her eyes, but there was a spark of mulish anger deep in her that made me wonder.

'My lord Tordal doth press me to use my gifts 'gainst Owain's army on the morrow.' She gestured at the door. 'They art encamped o'er the vale and a victory here could turn the rebellion in our liege's favour.' Rain pattered on the thick thatch. A steady drip of water splatted in one corner of the room and the chill deepened. She shivered again, clutching the woollen cloak close. 'But I'm sore wearied, my heart divided. And my poor bairn...' She bit her lip and covered her mouth with thin, blue-veined hands. Her shoulders shook.

I stood by, helpless to do more than watch. 'I'm sorry, Aeona. I know it's been tough for you, but I'm here to help – you and your son.'

'My son?' She sniffed, wiping away the tears with a corner of her cloak. 'But—'

The sound of nearby footsteps made me jump. Aeona paused and listened with both mind and ears, then shook her head.

'Tis but the watchman making rounds.' Her jaw worked and tears welled again. 'Tordal and Kieran hast tripled the watch outside my door 'ere sith a month agone when Owain's men came upon me unawares as I did nurse my babe.' Her fists clenched and opened. 'An they are right and justly wroth. Owain deserveth no less than my full wreche upon his foul pate,' she muttered, glaring at the door.

Horror struck me. I only half-understood her words, but it was clear something horrible had happened. Was I too late? Had I arrived at the wrong time? Was Calain hurt? How could that even be possible? My brain ached with the paradoxical possibilities. No, I couldn't be here if I'd arrived too late.

Footsteps sloshed past again. Thunder rumbled overhead.

'Aeona, listen. Calain is in danger,' I said. 'You must get him away from here today.'

'Calain? Nay, I cannot lose him.' She shot to her feet, paling. She took two steps towards the door before stopping. Her shoulders slumped.

'I cannot flee. Tordal holds him and his father hostage for my co-operation. But certes he wilt track me through the *sianfath* ere I use my powers. And use the *torryl* to cut away my very soul an I disobey. I dursn't risk it.'

'If you don't,' I said, 'Calain will die here, tomorrow.' I had no idea what would happen if she didn't leave. Wikipedia said the two armies engaged in a few skirmishes over the next eight days before the Welsh crept away under cover of night. But if Aeona stayed, in her current mood she might slaughter the whole Welsh army. Who knew what that would do to her, to Calain, and to my own existence.

'Tell me the whole,' Aeona demanded, straightening. 'How do I know thy words be truth; that thou art not some seeming sent by Owain? That blackguard deserveth naught but death. Mayhap thou art in his employ, seeking to prevent mine due wreche for his villainy.' She lifted her chin, regarding me haughtily.

I sighed, not seeing any way around it. 'I'm your granddaughter. Calain's daughter. But if you don't leave today, I won't be born. Do you know of your sister's book?'

Aeona sank onto the stool as though her knees had given out. Her eyes softened and she reached for me, only to let her arm fall when she couldn't touch me. 'My little one wilt have a daughter? Oh, thou hast given me fresh hope. Thy name?'

'Ruadhán,' I said.

She stared. 'Thy name doth bear the full weight of our whole race. But what book dost thou speakest of? Dost mean Mairi hath penned a book?'

'It contains her visions of the future.'

'She wrote them down!' Aeona frowned. 'Unwise, mayhap. What hast to do with me?'

'One of her visions involves Calain – and how he will, many years from now, help to save the sidhe from extinction by humans. So you see…' I spread my palms. 'You must get him away from this and give him the chance to father me, and to save our people.'

'Many years from now? And does Mairi still live in your time then?'

Hesitated. Would that knowledge change her choices? Unlikely. I shook my head.

'Then how…' Aeona made a cutting gesture, rose from her seat and paced the small room. 'Nay, it matters not. But there is so much I ken not. How art thou e'en here? I can only slip back the length of mine own memories.' Her shoulders slumped. 'And I've not been able to speak to mine own self. Would I couldst warn myself 'gainst so many things that caused great woe.'

'Aeona!' I recalled her attention. My energy levels were dropping fast. I tried to draw more power, but the sense of connection to the *sianfath* was attenuated, possibly by time; who knew. Whatever the reason, power drained from me like water from a leaking bucket.

She started. 'Thou art appalled, granddaughter, thy cheek most pale. Art well?'

'I don't have much time,' I said. 'There are three things you must do. Promise me?'

She nodded, then froze, staring at the door. 'Hasten, then, for I do feel Tordal approaching. He must not know of thy existence.'

I ticked off points on my fingers. 'You need to get Calain and his father away from here. They must go to Ireland, to a little village called Lothien.'

'But I—'

I cut her off. 'You'll join them later. First you must go home, to Scotland. Talk to your family. Ask their help. I need you to find a way to counteract the *torryl*. It threatens my life now, too.'

'But e'en if I find a way, thou'rt of the future. How canst I counsel thee?'

She was right. I rubbed at my forehead as thinking became more difficult. The world around me blurred and, just for a moment, I thought Logan called my name. No! Too soon. I had to finish this. I gathered what little energy I had left and focussed it on holding myself in this time and place, on my tether to Aeona.

'Mairi's book. Inside the back cover,' I said. 'Slip a note in there and I'll find it. Please. It's vital you find a way of stopping the *torryl*.' There was no point in putting the note into Aeona's book, for the cover was of leather and not lined. I'd never checked the back of Mairi's book, so it could be lined.

'Mairi's book of visions...aye...'twill be the very thing,' Aeona replied. 'Very well. I shall attempt. What is thy third instaunce?'

I hesitated. This was the one she wasn't going to like. 'You have to pass all your memories to Calain. They are what allows me to slip here and warn you. It's complicated. But you must lock them away because he's too young to handle them right now.'

Aeona gasped and clutched at her cloak. 'But why? That could destroy his mind! Why removest him from one danger, to thrust him full well into another?'

The door rattled and a fist pounded on it. A harsh, masculine voice called out.

'My lady. The master awaits without.'

'Anon!' she called. 'Abide and grant me but a moment's respite.' She lowered her voice to a whisper. 'Speak child, and with haste, for the time of decision rushes towards me and I mislike what I hear.'

'It gets worse,' I said. 'You need to leave Calain with the Williamson family in Lothien. Tordal won't let you go easily. You must ensure Calain survives and your life will be difficult. So you must leave him behind.'

'Leave my son?'

'If you want him to survive, yes,' I said bluntly.

She wrung her hands. 'And Kieran? What of him? Will we stay as husband and wife or will he remain with Calain?'

'Kieran!' I gaped at her. 'Kieran Ivaldison is your husband? But he's Dark sidhe!' Calain had mentioned Tordal and his son, Kieran, but had never mentioned Kieran was his father. Or had he? No. Why had Calain not spoken of it openly? What was he hiding?

'Of course he's mine husband!' Aeona drew herself up. 'I'd not bear children out of wedlock. Kieran hast governed my heart and sanity this last century. He's not of Tordal's mind. He hast protected me, as much as he might, from his father. Kieran's dearest wish is for the *sidhe* and humanity to live in peace. I must know what becomes of him.'

How could I tell her? When I'd slipped back in Brisbane and met her with Calain and Fionn, she'd mentioned Kieran had succumbed to the darkness. That he'd left her and died in a battle in France. What could I say that wouldn't break her heart?

'I...'

The door rattled again.

'Anon!' Aeona snapped.

'There's no time,' I said. 'I'm too far from my own time to sustain this any longer. Please, Aeona. Trust me. I know you've no cause. All I can say is: your son is a good man because of your actions in leaving this place, today. And he's our best hope of saving our people.'

She stared doubtfully at me. The guard outside thumped on the door again. Dust and bits of straw drifted from the ceiling.

'My lady,' he shouted. 'My lord is without and demands thine attendance.'

'Very well,' she replied, loud enough for him to hear, though her eyes were on me. 'Very well,' she repeated, more softly. 'But thou must promise in turn, granddaughter, thou wilt do *everything* in thy power to help my son achieve that end. For if I'm to spend my life fleeing Tordal's wrath, I must know thou wilt keep thy part of the bargain and make my sacrifices meaningful.' She hardened. 'Whatever it takes, no matter how distasteful. Agreed?'

'My lady.' A new voice, deeper and with arrogant, impatient overtones called through the door. 'Open now lest I lose patience with thee. Thy child calls.'

A child wailed outside, crying 'Mamma! Mamma!' in heartbreaking sobs.

'Calain!' Aeona took a step towards the door then sent a pleading look at me.

'Agreed,' I said, my heart sinking.

She fumbled with the wooden bar holding the door closed.

I released the anchor holding me to her and let myself slide back through the *sianfath* to my own time. Exhaustion dragged at me. The link to my body shimmered, tenuous and faint through the silver-green haze. The effort of hauling myself back into my own world seemed too great and the urge to release myself to the comforting oneness of the *sianfath* was nearly overwhelming. The taste of ozone and the prickling sensation of the *sianfath's* power were warm, familiar friends.

'Rowan!' Logan's voice. This time clear, though faint. 'Rowan, damn you. Don't you quit on me.' His voice broke. Was he crying? I'd never seen him cry. Could he possibly care that much for me?

His calls acted as a beacon and I followed the whisper-thin green thread linking us back to my body. Slipping in, I drew a shuddering breath into lungs weighted by sorrow, and lifted eyelids heavy with centuries of sleep.

Logan leaned over me. My head rested in the crook of his arm. We seemed to be on the gravel floor of the Egyptian temple. There were spiderwebs on the ceiling. The inconsequential thought made me smile, glad to be home to think it.

'Oh my God, Rowan.' Logan snatched me close and kissed my forehead. Tears dripped onto my cold skin.

'Logan,' I croaked. I tried to hold him, but my arms lacked the strength. I was in my body, but so drained I hadn't even the power to speak.

'Shit.' He stared at me. 'Hold on. I'll feed you my reserve.' He touched my chest and a strange sort of warm-honey sensation spread from his palm, deep into my flesh and bones. My extremities tingled, tiny needles prickled beneath my skin, and it became easier to draw each breath. So that was what a power transfer felt like.

Logan sucked a shuddering breath and grabbed at the bench for support, but kept his hand in place. I gripped his wrist feebly.

'Stop now,' I whispered. 'I can do it myself. Don't drain yourself.' I connected to the living world of the garden and drew in enough energy to restore myself. Weariness remained, dragging bone-deep.

I struggled upright and Logan joined me on the concrete bench. We sat, side by side, fingers intertwined. I returned his power and he straightened with a groan.

'Are you alright?' He brushed my hair back, anxious. 'What happened?'

'I forgot about the regulator organ thing I'm missing,' I said. 'Before, the pain in my head from fighting Calain's corrupted memory stopped me from overextending. With that gone, I just…ran out of juice.'

'God, Rowan,' Logan's voice cracked again. 'You almost died. If I hadn't found you…'

I leaned on his shoulder and breathed in the warm, comforting scent of his skin. 'I'm sorry.'

He caught me close. 'Please don't do that again. I can't lose you, too.'

I didn't know what to tell him, because the way things were heading, I couldn't see any way to avoid it. I'd just promised Aeona I'd do whatever it took to end this. And I had a bad feeling that promise could cost my life.

TEN

<What happened?>

I don't know, Maeve. She won't tell me. I just know we almost lost her.

<Foolish child. Why won't she heed me when I tell her to take care on how she expends her energy?>

Because you've given her little reason to.

<Logan!>

Stop it, Maeve. We both know you don't give a damn about her as a person. I'm not sure you care about anyone. Did you know my father is here? With Dyson?

<...>

Damn you, Maeve. You knew he might be here and you didn't say anything?

<I couldn't be sure. I only knew Dante's people had seen him several times in their incursions to Italian Mors facilities.>

And it never occurred to you I might be interested?

<I didn't want you going off half-cocked and hunting him down. We need you.>

What about what I need, Maeve?

'Tom?' I paced the gardens outside Dante's safe-house, turning in circles to watch for eavesdroppers. Logan had half-carried me back up the hill and into the house, where we'd walked into yet another argument. I didn't wait around to be abused and criticised by Erin and Maeve. I left them discussing what our next moves ought to be and slipped out into the garden to draw strength back and call Tomas Fairchild, still in Brisbane, Australia.

'Rowan?' He yawned. 'What time is it there? I was about to have an early night. You alright? I was starting to get worried. Saw the news of the plane crash and I've just had a couple of texts from Erin since. Everyone ok?'

'We're all fine,' I said. 'It's 12:20 in the afternoon. Listen, I need your help.'

'Anything,' he replied.

'Remember how we put all your old books into storage when we cleared out your house in Fig Tree Pocket?'

'Yes.' His tone held bitterness. 'I've had to rent a crap little apartment because my father's will is so fracking complicated it could take months to free up enough money to buy another house. So they're all still in storage. Why?'

'I need you to get hold of your copy of Mairi Silverblade's Visions book. Once you've got it, you need to slit open the inside back cover. There should be a note inside for me.'

'What? How?' He sucked a sharp breath. 'You slipped again, didn't you? You went back in time. Damn. I envy you.'

'Yes, but don't envy me, Tom. Not by a long shot.' Feet crunched on gravel nearby and I spun. Calain approached, watching me. I backed away, then spoke more softly into the phone. 'Just check for me, will you? It's vital. Call or text me as soon as you get it. I have to know what it says.'

'Sure, Rowan,' he said, sounding bewildered, 'I'll go get it first thing in the morning. But what's this—'

'Sorry Tom, gotta go.' I thumbed the End button and tucked the phone into my pocket.

Calain took that as a signal to approach and resumed walking. He thrust both hands into the pockets of his dark jeans.

'Logan tells me you overstretched yourself in the *sianfath*,' he said, his tone too neutral.

I shrugged. 'More like ran out of energy. But I suppose it's pretty much the same thing, isn't it? I guess I would have disappeared into the *sianfath* if Logan hadn't called me back. Sorry.'

Calain frowned. 'Nay. Erin had the right of it. You aren't sorry, not really.'

I glared at him and he held up an open palm.

'Apologies. I didn't mean to sound critical. Tis just...I'd not realised the mark my abandonment had left on you. You're afraid and untrusting of everyone. Even those who would help. So you feel you must do things yourself, unaided.'

I folded my arms. 'Stop pretending you understand me. You don't. Why didn't you tell me Kieran Ivaldison was your father? Tordal your grandfather?'

'Because it matters not who passed the dark gene on to me.' Calain sighed and scrubbed his fingertips over his scalp. Then he smiled wryly. 'We don't get to choose our parents, unfortunately, else we'd both choose another, I think.'

My arms loosened and I returned him a half-smile.

'Will you sit with me a while?' he said. 'We've had little time to speak since you returned my memories. I would like to know you better.' He indicated a grey concrete garden seat and round table, greenish with lichen, set beneath a silver-leafed olive tree. I sat, saying nothing.

'I am sorry, Ruadhán,' Calain said, touching my wrist. I jerked away out of habit and mumbled an apology when he sighed.

'No, the fault is mine,' he said. 'Anna told me your precognition is linked to a touch. I should have remembered.'

We sat in silence a while, staring at anything but each other. I shivered as the sun hid behind lowering clouds and long, blue shadows crept across the winter-brown lawn.

'I spent five hundred years preparing for your arrival,' Calain said, methodically tearing an olive-tree leaf into tiny fragments. 'Yet when you were born, and I held you in my arms, I was terrified. For all that time you'd been an ideal, a far-off possibility. Then, suddenly, you were real and I had no idea what to do.'

'Is that why you left? Because it was all too much?'

He flinched but it was too late to retract the sharp words.

'No.' He sighed. 'I suspect every new father feels something similar. Mine was merely weighted with a longer period of anticipation. I left because...because I was endangering you and your mother.' His attention slid to the trees and he shifted his position, angling subtly away. 'We were living in Germany at the time and I had a close call with Mors agents. I...had to draw them away before they discovered your existence. The life we led wasn't fair to you or Anna.'

'And not having a father was better?' I retorted. 'I spent years thinking you'd given up on us. That I'd done something wrong to make you leave.' I gritted my teeth against the sting of tears. 'When the migraines started I was terrified I'd inherited your mental health problems. I though I'd end up so depressed I'd think suicide was the best option. How could you do that to me?'

His hand shifted, then stilled, frozen in the act of reaching for mine again.

'I'm so sorry, Ruadhán. I left a letter...?'

'Yes,' I said, 'but Anna only showed it to me a couple of weeks ago.' Anger subsided. He was right. I probably would have let the hurt go earlier if I'd seen the letter when I was younger. 'I think she was worried about frightening me with it – you did talk about people chasing me.'

Calain grimaced. 'Another apology is in order, then. I'd hoped it would help you understand, not make you more fearful.' He sighed. 'It seems I've made many missteps in my role as husband and father, short though that journey was.' His mouth twisted into wry smile. 'My only excuse is that I was five hundred years out of practice. And so afraid of losing you both.' Pain sleeted through his storm-grey eyes.

I hesitated, then clasped his hand, shielding against precognitions. 'I've seen your memories of Fionn. And I met her, remember? I do understand…sort of.' A small knot of hurt unwound, deep within my body. He gave back a troubled half-smile.

I released him and rested my chin on my palm, one elbow on the concrete table. 'I just don't know what to do next. These people…I don't know who to trust. Logan, yes. But Dante, Erin and Maeve all have their own agendas. And I can't help feeling like I'm just a tool in your grand plan as well.' I looked directly at him. 'I don't know what you want from me. Any of you.'

Calain rubbed at the back of his neck. 'Have you not read Mairi's vision?'

'Sure. In the embrace of the *sianfath* and the *lorntinn,* the *ocair* may be the deliverance of those that dispossess the *Ruadhán Daoine sidhe.* But what's it got to do with me?'

He cleared his throat, shuffling his feet on the dirt beneath the bench. 'I'm the *ocair*, of course, though I still have no idea what that means – the key to what? I have no special gifts other than my ability to sense sidhe from afar, and tell Dark from Light.'

'That must be handy.' I grinned. 'Saves the badguys having to wear black.'

He returned a blank look. I let the smile go. Clearly not a big movie fan.

'It has been useful on occasion,' he said. 'But many Dark are unawakened to their nature.' He smiled wryly. 'Which lead to some most awkward situations early on in my life.'

I laughed. 'Now that I want to hear about.'

'The point is,' he continued, 'for many years I had no idea how I was supposed to embrace the *sianfath* or *lorntinn*.' Calain gazed at me and my heart stuttered at the depth of fear in him. 'Now I believe they are you, and Dante. It's not me who will deliver our people to safety. It's all three of us, together.'

I froze, shocked into stasis by the implications. Calain continued to watch me, like a soldier awaiting the explosion of a bomb.

'But how...' I faltered to a stop, not even sure what to ask. 'I mean, I can see Dante's group-connection ability could make him the *lorntinn*. But how can one person be the *sianfath?* It's...everything, isn't it? And even if I was, what am I supposed to do?'

'There, you have me. I know not.' His mouth twisted. 'Something that is the deliverance of those that dispossess us?'

I flung my arms wide. 'And explain to me why the hell we'd want do that, anyway? I mean, if we assume they are either humans or Dark sidhe, why would we help either of them? They both want us dead.'

'Again,' he said, 'I know not. Only that my task – our task – is somehow vital to the survival of our species.'

I rose from the seat and took a few paces away, turning back to glare at him. 'I thought you had this all worked out. Are you telling me Dante was right? That for five hundred years, you've been...what, faffing around hoping I'd come along and make sense of it all? Well, you're out of luck. I have no freaking idea what we're doing here.' I folded my arms, clenching my jaw to stop the flood of angry words threatening to pour from the deep well of my frustration.

'Ruadhán,' Calain said gently, 'we're in this together. None of us knows what's happening, or what's expected. But we'll work it out. Just—'

'No.' I backed away. 'Whatever you want from me, I can't do it. Logan and Dante are right: I've proved, over and over again, I can't work in a team. Can't be trusted or relied on. Now you're telling me the future of our people depends on my ability to do exactly that? Seriously?'

'Fret not, Ruadhán.' Calain's deep voice stayed level, his gaze holding empathy and understanding. ''Tis but speculation. We don't know for certain what is required. You could well be right: the *sianfath* in Mairi's vision might refer to the very stuff connecting our world, not you, specifically.'

A small knot of tension unravelled deep in my chest, but its core remained, wrapped around disbelief of his words and fear of his expectations. But for now... I wanted to believe him. I chose to believe him. The solution to this mess couldn't be on my shoulders.

I sighed and unfolded my arms. 'Have they decided what we're doing next? How we're going to get hold of the DNA information Dyson took?'

Calain stood and crooked an elbow like he was escorting me to a ball. 'That's what I came to fetch you for. We need your help.'

'With what? There are too many cooks in there at the moment. I'm sure they all have a dozen ideas...each.'

His mouth twisted into irony. 'You speak truth, daughter. We have ideas aplenty. What we don't have is focus.'

I groaned. 'You need a lightning rod. Someone for them to gang up on so they can make a decision.'

Calain laughed ruefully. 'Anna told me you were sharp-witted. You're right. They are divided. You do have a knack for…polarising this group.'

'That was not a compliment.' I glared at him. He merely smiled.

'Fine,' I said, sighing. 'What are the options?' I tucked my hand into the crook of his elbow and we strolled towards the villa.

'Dante and Logan are intent on infiltrating the Mors Headquarters and stealing the information back.'

I looked sharply at him. 'Is that possible? I thought Dante didn't know where they're based. And Michael said Dyson would disseminate the information straight away, so how is getting it back any use?'

Calain shrugged. 'Dante's people from all over the world have been updating him. Nothing has been leaked so far, that he can tell. We may have time. Erin and Mia haven't yet found the headquarters, so the option may be moot, anyway.'

Was it possible Dyson hadn't sent out our details because he wasn't against the sidhe? If that were true, why did he need the parcel?

'So, what are the other plans?' I asked.

He hesitated, grimacing. 'Maeve and Erin prefer a more radical idea.'

'And that is?'

He paused and stared off through the gardens, out across the city of Florence just visible through the olive trees surrounding the house. 'They wish to attempt two things. The first is switching off the dark gene in those sidhe bearing it.'

'The dark sidhe gene…maybe,' I said. 'If we had time and knew how to identify everyone with the gene, which we don't.'

Calain rubbed at the back of his head. 'It might be possible to identify them, actually.' He shrugged. 'As I said, I have the ability to tell those with the dark gene from those without. And sidhe from humans, at a distance, unseen. But my range is limited.'

'How limited?'

'Mayhap a kilometre or so, no more,' he admitted. 'So 'tis difficult to see how it could be of assistance in this venture.'

'Still,' I said, 'useful to know. It may come in handy. What was the other thing Maeve and Erin wanted to try?'

He hesitated as we neared the house. 'Unlocking the gene in humans to allow them to sense the *sianfath*. They believe doing so will align all humans with us, and against the Mors, making it more difficult for the Mors to gain a foothold or strike against us.'

'Change the humans?' I tugged free of his arm, unable to even process the magnitude of such a scheme. 'I thought you'd vetoed that already, when Maeve brought it up in Brisbane. Are we talking changing just a few key people, or the whole of humankind?'

Calain gave a one-shouldered shrug. 'I believe Maeve and Erin would prefer the majority of humans, all at once. I can see the sense in it, but it might not be possible.'

'It wouldn't. Not unless…' I sucked a sharp breath. 'Unless they think I could provide the energy…' I waited for him to jump in with a denial, but he didn't. He merely returned my horror with level empathy.

'I couldn't.' I backed away. 'It's not even possible. Is it?'

'Perhaps not all at once.' He frowned. 'As you say, I considered it when we were in Michael's warehouse in Australia. My concern is the effect using the *skath-sheel* had on Aeona, but Maeve seems to think you could handle it if the process were staged and monitored carefully. She and a few others would do the telekinetic work. You would provide the power.'

'No.' I backed further away. 'No way. The only way I could source enough power would be to kill thousands of people. You can't want me to do that.'

Calan closed the gap between us and squeezed my shoulder. 'No, but the truth is we have so few options we must consider all of them with unemotional thoroughness. We haven't the luxury of refusing out of pique or discomfort.' He frowned. 'Your ability to draw vast power is key to anything we do, daughter. It is time you took on the responsibility for which you were born.'

'No. You're meant to be the key.' I shoved his hand off. 'I didn't ask to be born and I didn't ask for any of this, either. What if I can't?' I grasped at that straw. 'What if it's not even possible to express that gene in humans? We don't even know how. And what if—'

'Enough!' Calain gripped my arms. 'There are too many what ifs to contemplate and I like them as little as you. But I also have more faith in your abilities than you do. Drawing power from people is not the only way. Aeona, at the end of her life, could draw on the Earth itself. But you're right about one thing. We don't know if changing humans is possible.' He stared thoughtfully at the villa. 'Mayhap we can test that, at least.'

ELEVEN

Are you certain this will work, Madre?
    <As certain as I can be. It's never been tried.>
    We'll be losing a valuable asset if it fails
    <Not so valuable any more. Disposable now.>
    Rowan may not agree with you.
    <Irrelevant.>

Reluctance dragged at my feet as I entered the villa. Logan, Dante, Maeve and Erin faced me with expressions ranging from concern to interest to scorn. Mia, who worked on a laptop at a desk in one corner, ignored me. Erin leaned over and whispered something into Mia's ear and the sidhe woman gave a bark of laughter as her fingers flew over the keyboard.

My cheeks grew warm and I gritted my teeth. So ridiculously high school. I ignored her and sat on one of the spindly-legged, harp-backed salon chairs placed against the wall.

'So?' Maeve addressed Calain but looked at me.

He swept a hand in my direction. 'I've told her the options, but it falls to you to convince her of the rightness of your path, Maeve, for you know I like it not. The risk is great.'

'Of course it is,' Maeve said, crouching before me, 'but can you imagine how the world would be changed if we did this? If the humans could understand what we do and how their actions affect everything?' Her expression radiated only earnest morality. But I'd seen that before. She was an excellent liar.

'And what would the cost be?' I said, tucking my fingers under my legs. 'To them. To me? There's always a price, Maeve. People could die. Even if I find an alternate source of power, the gene-manipulation could have horrible side effects.'

Erin snorted. 'So what? A few thousand, even a few hundred thousand – or a million humans die. What of it? There are too many for the planet now, anyway. Culling them is a mercy to the *sianfath*. If the natural world is going to survive – if *we're* going to survive – we need to reverse population growth. I wouldn't weep over a few million deaths if it saved the whole freaking planet.'

'Really,' I said, pursing my lips, 'and yet you were pretty cut up about Ian.'

Erin glared, paling. 'He was *sidhe* and worth a thousand humans.' She curled a lip. 'Certainly worth more than your pathetic, half-breed life.'

'Is that what bothers you about me?' I asked, holding hard to artificial calm. 'That I'm not a full-blood sidhe? Well, yep, my mother is human so I'm not excited by the idea of culling them just because you have an unfounded superiority complex.'

'Unfounded!' She half-rose. Mia gripped her wrist and drew her back down, laying an arm around her shoulders. Erin leaned into her and glared at me. Mia kissed Erin's forehead and murmured something. Erin flushed.

Across the room, Logan folded his arms and frowned at me. I sighed. Something about Erin just got under my skin, but I wasn't proud of who I was around her. Maybe I should just shut my mouth and stay away from her.

Dante broke the awkward silence with a tap of his cane on the marble floor. 'Ladies, we must cease hostilities and focus our efforts on what's important. We must either retrieve that information from Dyson, or find some other way to incapacitate the Mors Ferrum before they distribute your data and a full scale war against the sidhe breaks out. Either way, finding their base is crucial. However, since Mia and Erin are having no luck so far in finding the Mors Headquarters—'

'I've still got about two hours' worth of analysis to do on the latest data, sir,' Mia put in. 'But I do think, with Erin's help, we can narrow it to within a few city blocks. Then we can send teams to watch the area.'

'Grazie, Mia,' Dante said, bowing in her direction. 'Unfortunately, two hours, plus whatever time it takes to find, and launch an assault on the building, may be too late. We must act now. Once Dyson gives the DNA information and details on our powers to all his people, our days are numbered.'

'If Dyson is sidhe, and my father is working with him...' Logan scowled. 'Why hasn't he just told the Mors what powers are possible before now? He must know what scope exists amongst the women. He must have met other female sidhe. His parents, at least. Do we know anything about his past? Calain?'

Calain, who sat at a small, circular desk of rich red timber, bowed his head. 'Very little. I have crossed paths with him several times, but tried to keep out of his way. He had no real ability to do any damage up until he took over the Mors. Since he has obviously hidden his species from the Mors, perhaps he couldn't give away too much knowledge without revealing his own secret.'

Logan and I exchanged doubtful looks.

Dante studied his father with distant interest. Then he tossed his cane high and caught it, pointing the leaf-shaped knob in Calain's direction. 'Beside the point, for we have no way of knowing his motivations. The fact is, we cannot immediately mount an assault on his offices.' He pressed his lips together and his fingers whitened on the cane. 'We have no other option but to at least attempt to convert humans to our side. Unless someone has a better suggestion?'

No one spoke. I couldn't think of anything, either.

'So,' I said, my throat constricted, 'what do I do? How can we test the gene conversion idea?'

'We use Michael,' Maeve said, her tone matter-of-fact.

I stared at her. 'Are you serious? We can't. I promised Paul he wouldn't be harmed and we have no idea what this will do.'

'What you promised is irrelevant,' Maeve said.

'Not to me. I—'

'Have you forgotten already what he did to you, to Logan, to all of us?'

'No.' I ground my teeth, biting back the retort that she was hardly any better. 'But I also remember he was trying to cure his son of an incurable disease.'

Maeve waved dismissively. 'He's our best chance. Making him aware of the *sianfath* will serve the dual purpose of making him an ally, and testing our theory.'

Dante nodded, pressing his cane to his lips as he gazed at his mother. Logan said nothing. He leaned against the wall, with his arms folded and his eyes fixed on his feet.

'Oh my God.' I shot to my feet and paced the floor, my boot heels echoing on the marble. 'I can't believe how...clinical you are. All of you! Logan are you still so angry at Michael that you'll make me do this?'

Logan hurried over and gripped my shoulders, holding me still. 'Stop, Rowan. You know I wouldn't agree to anything that might hurt you—'

I shook free. 'It's not me I'm worried about. Can't any of you see that?' I swept a horrified look around the room. All of them, even my own father, stared back at me in various stages of bewilderment or, in Erin's case, scorn. I uttered a slightly hysterical laugh and sank back into my chair. 'No, of course you can't. You're just the flip side of the Mors and you can't even see it. Fine.' I sucked a quick breath, throwing my shoulders back. 'Whatever. Do I have to look Michael in the eyes as I kill him?'

'Don't be dramatic,' Maeve said. 'It won't kill him.'

'Oh?' I sent her a mocking look. 'Exactly how sure are you?'

'I'm sure,' Erin said, lifting her chin. 'A PhD in genetics worth of sure, if you must know. Unfolding the gene and reactivating it will just put him in touch with the *sianfath*, nothing else. Not much harder than what you and Jen did to Logan and that didn't bother you.'

'I didn't exactly have a lot of other options,' I said.

'And you don't now, either.' She rolled her eyes. 'The trickiest bit will be doing it delicately enough to keep the DNA intact. As long as you're careful with the power you feed to Maeve, it will be fine.'

'Come,' Maeve said, rising. 'You're being ridiculous, both of you. All of humanity will be better for being part of the *sianfath*. Who knows, perhaps they can even merge with us in the *lorntinn* and truly understand what it means to be part of a community.'

I glanced away.

'Calain. Dante?' Maeve nodded. 'Michael is asleep in one of the guest quarters. I believe it would be wise if you joined us. The rest of you stay here. We need to concentrate and you would distract us.'

'But what about me?' Erin said, rising.

'You've already shown me what to do,' Maeve said, with just hint of condescension in her cool tone. 'I, too, have a PhD in genetics, remember? I believe I understand well enough. You and Mia are best off focussing on finding the Mors.'

Erin glowered.

Logan caught my wrist and drew me into a quick hug. 'Be careful,' he murmured, sweeping a thumb over my cheek.

I nodded, unable to speak, and ran from the room.

I found the others waiting in Michael's bedroom, gathered around his still form like vultures. I shuddered and joined them, staring at Michael's lax face and helpless body. He lay, fully dressed, atop a blue and grey geometric patterned quilt. His head lolled to one side, his mouth open and hands relaxed by his body. He looked innocuous and ordinary; not at all frightening. Pity sparked in me and I clenched my fists. There could be no space for such thinking or it would derail my focus. As Erin said, this would be delicate work and I needed to concentrate.

'Calain,' Maeve said, 'I'd like you to monitor us. Without the regulator organ, Rowan has trouble controlling the amount of power she releases and we need to know if she's too close to being drained.'

I opened my mouth to protest and shut it again as Maeve sent me a weary look. She was right, but it irritated me to admit it.

'And Dante,' she addressed her son, 'I'd like you to manage our connections in the *lorntinn*. Rowan needs to learn to trust you and she has a habit of shutting people out of her shields when she feels threatened or afraid. We can't have that happening in the middle of this procedure or it could be fatal for Michael, and possibly for me, also.' She flicked me a measuring look beneath her lashes. I held my tongue.

'Unlike what you and Jen did to Logan,' she continued, 'I'll be both uncurling *and* activating. Jen was only de-activating a single gene, which is much simpler. So you must keep the flow of power smooth.'

I nodded and swallowed. Everything about this made me uneasy, but for no reason I could pin down. The feeling wasn't even strong enough to call a genuine precognitive event, so I couldn't back out on that basis. On impulse, I touched Michael's wrist and checked forward, into his future: blackness; emptiness.

'And?' Dante asked.

I shook my head. 'Nothing. Hopefully that means it goes well.'

'Perhaps we should sit,' Maeve said. 'This could take a while.'

Calain and Dante brought in chairs and we scraped them across the polished marble floor, arranging ourselves with awkward fussiness around Michael's body.

'Very well.' Maeve straightened her back and touched Michael's arm. 'Rowan, draw as much as you can from the gardens around the house. It should be more than adequate for this procedure on one person. When you're ready, signal Dante and allow him to connect us all. Then feed the power to me, slowly. Calain, you direct her and help her keep the flow steady.'

I suppressed a flutter of fear and closed my eyes. I extended filaments outside the house, avoiding the silver-green forms of the sidhe inside the structure, and the two who patrolled the grounds. Once beyond the walls, I sought the richness of life embodied in the olive orchard and the gardens. Their energies were turgid with the approach of winter so I drew a little from each tree so as not to kill any. Holding the prickling silver-green energy within myself, I reached out to Dante and slipped through his shield.

Now.

Very well. But you must relax your guard, sister, or this will not work. Let me in.

Reluctantly, I opened my thought-castle. Most of it. The deepest rooms – those holding the core of who I was, and those holding Aeona's and Calain's memories – I kept sealed.

Dante said nothing, but I felt his disapproval as he flooded into my thoughts. Calain's mind joined us, then Maeve's; all three merging in a shifting, confusing mess of brilliant, indistinguishable one-ness. I allowed myself to be drawn in, uncomfortable, bewildered by the joy with which the others seemed to embrace the open-ness of their connection. It was like watching through a half-open door as a family sat down to Christmas dinner: alluring, compelling, but intimidating as well. They were my family, but I was still outside; not quite with them.

Ready Maeve? I interrupted their silent bonding.

<Begin.>

-*'Ware, daughter,*- Calain's thought intruded. -*Art still wearied by thy previous venture. Watch thine energy levels.*-

A part of me found it amusing that his thoughts reverted to archaic forms of speech, even as I focussed on trickling energy through to Maeve.

She stiffened as the first pulse of power reached her, but she absorbed and twined it through the *sianfath*, into Michael's body. I watched in fascination as she slipped the silver-green stuff deep into him, into the core of his body, into his bones, and began the transformation from the inside, out. On the bed, Michael stiffened, twisting beneath the quilt.

You're hurting him!

<No, he's not aware of pain. It's just his muscles contracting as I alter the DNA. Dante, show her.>

Dante gathered all of us into a single unit and sharpened our focus, diving deeper into Michael so we all saw what Maeve did, on a microscopic level. Mesmerised, I almost forgot to keep the flow of energy steady and Calain had to remind me.

Countless time passed. The room grew cold as the sun dropped lower and shadows lengthened in the garden outside.

I checked my internal energy levels and drew a little more, just to be safe. The bright flow pulsed through the *sianfath* and into Maeve. Calain's steady presence was an anchor to which we held firm as the *sianfath*'s energies buffeted us. Dante acted as the glue holding us together. I checked the doors, deep in myself, and found them still sealed. But Dante's presence pervaded every niche of my mind and I felt him watching every move.

Stop it, Dante. This is private.

Nothing can be private if we're bonded properly in the lorntinn, sister.

Too bad.

No, you don't understand. You must release your—

Enough, Dante.

Something warm touched my wrist. Dante's shape solidified inside my mind as he used his abilities to invade my inner sanctum. Together we stood inside the bowels of my castle, surrounded by stone and iron. I wore jeans and a tshirt and stood with my back to the thick doors guarding my inner self and my father's memories. Dante wore a long-tailed dark jacket, with a simple black cravat and a diamond pin. His hair was shorter, brushed sleekly back. He pointed his cane at the door.

You have to let me in, Rowan. If we're to work as a team we have to trust each other. I'm not here to judge you. He reached towards the sealed door protecting my deepest core, the source of my powers, my fears, my worst memories. Letting him in would give access to all that...and access to my powers.

What if *that* was what he really wanted? What if that's what this obsession with the *lorntinn* was all about – control over my abilities? And that must be why Maeve had asked him to join us – because he could get through my shields when she no longer could.

Something primal in me reacted.

'No!' With a surge of power, I shoved him clear of my thought-shield, wrenched my wrist from his grasp and slammed the front door on my mind, rejecting him.

I opened my eyes and glared at him in the real world.

He frowned back. 'Rowan, you must—'

Maeve gasped and clutched at her head. Michael's mouth opened in a gargling scream. His body convulsed.

Dante reached for me again. 'Rowan! Let me back in. Maeve's work isn't finished and you've cut her off. She's bound to him, too deep to get out on her own. She hasn't the power. We have to help or they'll both die.'

I looked to Calain, but he was watching Maeve, fear stark in his eyes. Maeve slumped across the bed, feebly scratching at Michael's arm. Michael's back arched, his mouth pulled wide in a grimace. He collapsed, limp, his head slack and eyes closed again.

I pulled away from Dante. 'I can do it without help.'

I stretched into the *sianfath* and drew more power. I anchored a tether to my body and stepped through Maeve's shields. I found her in the sunroom of her elegant Georgian mansion. She was curled in a corner, her hands to her temples as they were in the real world. I gripped her wrists and fed power into her until she uncurled and blinked at me in dismay.

Finish it.

<I...I can't. It's too late. I opened his DNA but you took the power away too soon and I couldn't...>

So what do I do?

<Nothing. His heart has stopped. It's too late.>

TWELVE

What's happened? Is Rowan ok?
  <Stay out, Logan. She's just upset.>
  I can help. She'll listen to me.
  <I said stay out. We have this under control>

'No!' I plunged from her mind, into Michael's body. If I could feed him the power directly, as I had Logan, weeks before in Cairns, I could shock his heart and get it stared again.

Vaguely, I heard an argument taking place in the room around me as I drew in enough power. Michael's body still held a few, feeble glimmers of the human-orange energy. I reshaped my power to match his signature, dropped to my knees beside the bed, and laid my hands on his chest. A sharp burst of energy stabbed through my palms, into his flesh. His body convulsed, arms and legs jerking. Nothing. No heartbeat.

'Rowan!' Maeve gripped my arm. I shook her off, refocussing on Michael. I'd promised Paul. No matter what Michael had done, I'd made a promise and I couldn't let Michael die because I'd been selfish and stupid…and afraid.

'Rowan, let us help.' Calain added his plea to Maeve's but I ignored both of them. It wasn't their problem to fix, it was mine. I'd done this; I needed to undo it.

I shocked Michael. Again his body convulsed and flopped unpleasantly on the bed. A small, brilliant orange kernel of non-light slipped free of his form and drifted into the *sianfath*. Michael's *enath*. If I let that go, it was all over. In desperation, I snagged it, tucked it into my thought-shield and drew more power from the gardens. Several trees died, their leaves falling in a shower of death to the dry ground.

Again, I flung power into his body. Nothing.

'Don't you dare!' With a yell of frustration, I slapped at the grey marble floor and released a surge of energy. The stone exploded in a shower of dust and stone-shrapnel. A piece stung my cheek and brought me to my senses. I couldn't afford to waste so much.

I drew more, heedless of the trees withering under my touch. I straightened and laid my hands once more on Michael's chest. This time I focussed the energy, concentrating on his heart muscles, feeling the nerves. I sent a precise shot of energy into the nerves responsible for contracting the heart. His body juddered. He sucked a soft, quick breath. And another.

A faint heartbeat fluttered beneath my palms and I let out a sob of relief. The bed swayed and shifted as I watched. No. That was me. I clutched at the mattress, but my thighs gave out and I sank onto my heels. The mattress's edge seemed like an excellent place to rest my forehead.

'She did it.' That was Calain's surprise, somewhere down a long tunnel.

'Yes,' Maeve replied, 'but she's given too much again. Help her, she can barely stay upright.'

Someone dragged me away from the bed and I protested, but couldn't break free of their grip. Maeve was right: I'd underestimated how tired I was after the slip through time, drained myself too close to the bone again in restarting Michael's heart. I still held his *enath*, deep in my mind, but I hadn't the power to return it to his body yet. But he lived and that was enough for now. I could return his essence later, when his body recovered.

Right now, I needed to sleep. I sank into oblivion.

When I woke my limbs were heavy, like my body wasn't yet ready, even if my mind was. I was tempted to roll over and drift away again, but a nagging memory drove sleep from my thoughts. Michael. Was he still alive? I sat up and took stock.

I lay in an enormous, four-poster bed straight out of a costume drama – thick, dark wood pillars carved with fruit and cherubs held up a green velvet canopy. My watch said it was three pm. Two hours had passed. I flung off the heavy, gold satin duvet and dragged on my boots. Someone had taken my throwing knife belt off and laid it on the carved bedside table. I hesitated, then strapped it on and tugged my shirt over it, more comfortable with it on than off. Mia's gun was gone. My leather jacket lay over a chair. Although the house was warm, I gave in to a vague sense of rightness and shrugged into it.

Next I checked inside my thought-castle and sagged in relief. Michael's *enath* remained inside, drifting, emanating vague feelings of misery and loss. A faint, orange thread still connected the spark to his body and that gave me hope. I needed to eat and regain a little strength, then I'd return it.

It took a few false starts, down dark corridors echoing with history and wealth, before I found my way back to the lounge room. I paused outside, listening at the door. A room full of telepaths would know I was there, if they wanted to.

'I've told you all along,' Erin snapped, 'she's a loose cannon. You can't have someone like her on the team. She's a danger to us all.'

'We know the risks,' Maeve replied. 'The fact is, Rowan has a unique gift. One we need to destroy the Mors Ferrum once and for all.'

'But she's told you,' Erin said, her voice rising, 'she's not willing to drain them and she's not capable of the self-control needed to change all the human DNA, either. So what use is she?'

'You underestimate her, Erin.' Logan said quietly. 'Why do you dislike her so much? What's she done to you?'

'You can ask me that?' Erin's voice was shrill. 'You? After what the two of you did to my family?'

There was a brief silence and the pain in Logan was almost tangible, even through the timber door. When he replied, his voice was strained.

'You were against her from the minute you met, Erin. You're just using Ian's death as an excuse. Why?'

Another silence followed. Someone coughed and a chair scraped on stone.

'It doesn't matter,' Erin said, sounding more in control, but still on the edge. 'The point is, we can't rely on her.'

'I will admit,' Calain said, sounding tired, 'I fear for her. I'm afraid her upbringing has made her over-cautious of us, and is causing...difficulties.'

'Difficulties?' Maeve weighed in, scornful. 'Do you call leaving Michael Eisen catatonic because she was too proud to accept help, just a difficulty? Be honest, Calain, your daughter is more of a liability than an asset. She's headstrong, un-co-operative, untrusting and untrustworthy. If Mia and Erin find the Mors headquarters, how on Earth are we supposed to fulfill Mairi Silverblade's prophecy using someone like that?'

'Unfair, Maeve,' Logan put in. 'Rowan's only those things because she's afraid.'

'Afraid?' Erin scoffed. 'I've never seen anyone less afraid. She swans right in and does whatever she wants without thinking for a second how it affects anyone else.'

'You're wrong, Erin,' Logan returned. 'She thinks so much it freaks her out.'

'What does?' Dante put in. 'What is it that freaks her out, as you say? For I confess I'm struggling to find a reason to work with her, even with her extraordinary gifts. A team is as strong as its weakest member. Right now, she is our weakest member. We will fail if we rely on her.'

'And,' Erin jumped in, 'she'll start the job and quit because it's hurting a few humans. She's afraid to do what's necessary.'

'No. She's afraid of herself,' Logan said. 'Afraid she'll accidentally kill us. She's keeping us at a distance because she knows how much it hurts to lose someone she loves and she's not willing to risk it.'

'We've all lost people, Logan,' Erin grated.

'And we all had other sidhe, and our ability to merge with others in the unity, to help us through it,' he responded. 'I'm disappointed and worried about her lack of faith in us, too. But remember, Rowan's new to all of this; to us. She's been thrown into this at the deepest end you can imagine. Maeve hasn't given her any reason to trust. Neither have you, Erin. Let her come to terms with everything before you push her to save the whole damned world.'

'We have no time for that,' Dante snapped. 'If we find the headquarters, we have to move. As yet, Dyson has still not released our information. We don't know why, but we have to use this chance to take the whole organisation apart while we can. If we wait, it will be too late. We must get into that building, soon.'

I leaned against the timber panel next to the door and swallowed down pain and ego.

'Why are you so all-fired keen on getting to the Mors headquarters, Dante?' Logan asked, his voice close to the door.

'Leave him, Logan,' Maeve murmured. 'He has his reasons.'

From further afield, Calain spoke up. 'If we can't entrust Rowan with the task of changing human DNA, what can we do to fulfil the prophecy?' He sounded worried.

I was letting him down. Five hundred years of planning and waiting was unravelling because I wasn't able to be what they needed. I'd failed Ian and Erin. I'd failed Paul and Michael. Now I'd failed my entire species and possibly doomed all of us. But how could I be expected to trust people I'd met only a day, a week or even three weeks before? I'd spent my life running and hiding, trusting no-one. They expected me to throw that aside and welcome them all just because we shared DNA?

Was I wrong to be afraid of giving Dante access to my gifts?

And what if they were all wrong? What if this conflict – all this anger at the Mors Ferrum – was misplaced? What if Dyson *was* working for the same ends we were? If we could end things peacefully, wouldn't it be easier? Surely I was right to avoid killing people, wasn't I?

I leaned against the dark panelled wall, staring up at the white ceiling with it's thick, dark-oak exposed beams.

The truth was: I was alone. Even my mother – who had protected me, uprooted her life time and time again for me, encouraged and guarded me – never understood what it was to be so different, so afraid of hurting people. Before, I'd feared my speed and strength and the damage that might do. Now, the damage I could inflict was unthinkable. And behind me was a room full of people who wanted me to be a weapon in their insane war against mankind; against their own people, even.

There had to be a better way. Just giving myself up to Dante's *lorntinn* and opening my inner self to these people couldn't be my only option. Not if doing so meant giving control of my abilities to Dante and Maeve.

But what if it was the right thing to do?

No. I'd brought Michael back without relying on them. His *enath* still tingled, deep in my head, an itch I couldn't scratch. If I could do that, when Dante thought I needed a whole support team, maybe I could find a way to resolve this without any of them. Then I wouldn't be putting anyone but myself in danger, either. Yes, there had to be other options. Some other way of bringing humans and sidhe together.

First, I needed to return Michael's *enath*, so I could tell if the DNA uncurling worked and humans would survive. Given he was one-sixth sidhe, though, correcting his gene expression didn't mean it would work on all humans. And even if it could, where would I get the power to do it for the whole world? Worry gnawed at me but I pushed it aside. I'd work that out later. Right now, I needed to fulfil my promise to Paul and bring his father back. Figuring out how to help the rest of humanity could sit on my extensive To Do list for the moment.

I pushed off the wall and strode along the corridor towards Michael's room.

Halfway there I paused, uneasy for no reason I could determine.

Pressure built in the back of my skull.

'Shit.' I spun and sprinted back down the hall. 'Logan. Calain! We've got incoming!'

I skidded around a corner and shoved the door open. It smacked into the wooden panelling startling the occupants. They studied me with varying expressions of irritation and concern.

'We've got incoming,' I repeated. 'Get your people ready, Dante.'

He shot to his feet, fingers whitening around his cane. His gaze became abstracted then he refocussed on me.

'The perimeter is still secure. Are you sure?'

'She's never wrong, Dante,' Logan said. 'Ever.'

I sent him a grateful look.

He frowned. 'Do you know who, or how soon, Rowan?'

'No. It's a strong feeling, though, so they must be close.'

Dante's jaw clenched and his brows drew together. 'Very well. Calain, take Michael to the safe-room in the basement. Erin, you too. Maeve, you and Logan are with me. Logan, you'll need a weapon.'

'I have my throwing knives,' Logan replied, touching the belt beneath his shirt.

'Why don't we all go to the safe-room,' Erin said, glancing at Mia, who stood at the window peering into darkness.

'Because the house isn't fire-proof,' Dante said grimly.

Erin paled and gasped, wrapping her arms around her stomach. 'But how would anyone know we're here? I mean, Michael's been under guard or out to it all day. The Mors Ferrum don't know about this house, do they?'

Dante shook his head.

She stared at me, her eyes narrowing in suspicion.

'Don't glare at me,' I snapped. 'I didn't tell them.'

'You *were* talking with Dyson in Florence,' she retorted.

'We didn't exactly exchange phone numbers. I tried to drain him and he cut me loose, remember?'

'Wait,' Calain's deep voice cut through our hostility. He considered me thoughtfully and rubbed the back of his neck. 'It is possible they have tracked us here through you, Rowan.'

'See! I said—'

'Enough, Erin,' Maeve snapped. 'We don't need your ill-mannered childishness right now. We need information and solutions. Either help or get into the safe-room, but leave Rowan alone.' She addressed Calain, ignoring Erin's growl of anger. 'Calain?'

'If Dyson has the ability to use the *torryl* against you,' Calain said, 'then mayhap he also has the skill to track you through the *sianfath*. Tordal was able to do so with Aeona. He followed her for over a century, tracking her down every time she used the *skath-sheel*.'

Logan straightened. 'Are you saying Dyson is Tordal Ivaldison?'

'No,' Calain said, flatly. 'Not possible. Tordal is dead. I know for certain.'

'How?' Dante said sharply.

'I beheaded him, myself,' Calain replied. 'But mayhap he taught Dyson before he died.'

The pressure in my head increased and I winced. 'So, what do we do? They're almost here.'

THIRTEEN

<Does she know?>

-No. And I'll thank thee to hold thy tongue, Maeve. I'll tell her in mine own time.-

<Don't leave it too late.>

'We need to lead them away from here,' Dante said, tapping his cane against his lips. 'We can't carry Michael's body around and Erin's vulnerable. Mia, get them into the safe room. We'll draw fire and lead them away.'

'No,' I said. 'If I leave and use my ability somewhere else, they'll come after me. They're not after you.'

In the silence that followed, I wanted someone, anyone, to disagree. They didn't.

The sense of foreboding increased until I feared the onslaught of a migraine I thought long-gone. I sucked a breath through my teeth and rubbed at the back of my head.

'There's no time to go far and the lane outside the house is narrow. They'll block us in.' I glanced out the window at the burnished afternoon light. 'I can get away through that garden over the other side of the lane. Steal a car and circle back, later. Or meet you somewhere else.'

'I'll come with you,' Logan said, stepping forward.

'And I,' Calain added. 'If you use the *skath-sheel* to draw him, you'll need protection while you're vulnerable.'

'No,' Dante said, stepping forward, 'not you, Calain. You said Dyson has been chasing you for a hundred years. And you are the *ocair*, even if we don't yet know what that means. We can't put the two of you into his power should something go wrong. We need to split the three of us up. Calain, you stay here with Erin, Michael and two of my people. I'll take Maeve and three of my people and go out through these gardens. Logan, you, Rowan and the rest go that way.' He pointed in the direction I'd intended to go. 'Stay in the *lorntinn* with me as long as you can. We'll rendezvous at the secondary house in two hours.'

Calain's mouth pursed and he scowled. I touched his arm.

'It's alright. Go. I'd rather you were away from me, anyway.' I kissed his cheek. 'I promised Anna you'd be safe and I think the worst place is near me, right now. I'll be ok, I promise.'

He hesitated, grave. 'It goes much against my will to leave you thus, daughter. Promise me you'll do whatever is necessary to come through alive.' His eyes hardened. 'And if you have the chance, kill Dyson. Don't waste time talking to him. Just kill him.'

I said nothing.

'One more thing,' Calain said. He kissed my forehead and stared intently into my eyes, much as he had fourteen years before when he'd left Anna and me. 'Do not let Dyson capture you. Do whatever you must. Do you understand? He must not...use you against us. As I said: he's persuasive and if he takes more of your *enath* he'll begin to control you.'

I nodded. 'Let's go, Logan. We're out of time.' I sprinted out the front door, not waiting to see if Logan followed.

As I burst through the entrance, three shadows detached from the wall nearby and fell into step with me. Dante's people: Angelo and two others I didn't know by name. Logan appeared at my side and the five of us ran out the front gate.

In the narrow road outside, the high brick fences either side seemed to close in as the pressure built in my mind. Ahead, tyres crunched on the asphalt.

'That's them,' I said. 'Just around the next corner. We need to get off this road.'

'Here.' Angelo pointed out the same entrance I'd used earlier and we changed direction.

My feet slipped on the driveway's loose gravel and I almost fell. Logan caught my elbow and dragged me upright. Behind us, the purr of a car engine ceased and doors slammed.

'Shit.' Logan glanced over his shoulder. 'They've seen us. Angelo, we need somewhere to make a stand. The garden's too open.'

'This way,' Angelo said, nodding at the café door in the end of the huge house.

'We can't take this somewhere the public might get hurt,' Logan said.

'It's a museum,' Angelo replied, running to the door. 'There's no-one in there at the moment except a couple of staff. They're about to close up.'

'A museum?' I panted. 'How is that helpful?'

'It's the Stibbert.' Angelo's mouth quirked. 'It's a weapons museum. The curator is a sidhe. Friends with Dante. That's why Dante bought the villa across the road – to have access to a source of weapons if needed.'

'Oh.' I followed him willingly through the glass door, with Logan and the other two sidhe close behind.

'Farima,' Angelo said, locking the door behind us, 'you watch this entrance. If they break in, don't take them on your own. Hide and follow them. Pick them off from behind if you can. You've been here?'

The slender sidhe woman pulled out a nine-mil, checking the clip. 'Yessir.'

'Hey!' A stocky, dark-haired man stood behind the café counter, staring at us in wide-eyed concern. 'Who are you? You can't come barging in here.' He gulped and raised his hands at the sight of Farima's weapon. 'Don't shoot me!'

We had no time to waste on civilians. I slipped into the *sianfath* and drained enough of his energy to put him to sleep. He crumpled behind the counter, knocking a tray onto the floor with an ear-splitting crash.

'Rowan?' Logan glanced at me in question. 'Is that wise?'

I waved him aside. 'We're supposed to be drawing Dyson away from the house, aren't we? That's what I'm doing.' I concentrated, extending further into the house. There, at the opposite end, three more humans. I pulled their power, biting down on the taste of ozone and resisting the urge to take it all and use it against our approaching enemy.

'There are three more,' I said. 'In an office at the opposite end of the house. They're asleep, too. Now what?'

Angelo looked out the glass door. 'They're coming in. Farima, hide. We're going further into the house. Follow me.'

He trod with the usual sidhe stealth through a swinging timber door in one end of the small café. We passed along a narrow hall and through another door, into a hallway that made me gasp. Dramatically lit behind huge panes of glass, stood a dozen exquisite sets of Japanese Samurai armour.

I touched the glass, readying the power nested in me to break it and take one of the stunning katana on display.

'Not this display,' Angelo warned. 'It's alarmed. We don't need the police here. Upstairs.' He jerked his chin towards an exit. 'Most of the smaller cabinets aren't wired and there're plenty of weapons just hanging on the walls.'

With one last, longing look at the ornate samurai helmets and armour, I ran after him and Logan.

We raced up a narrow set of stairs and stopped short at the next floor. I blinked, unable to even grasp the grandeur of the space. Enormous rooms with high ceilings – and more gilding, marble, and ornate plasterwork than should ever be in a sane person's house – extended in every direction. But I barely had time to assimilate the Persian rugs underfoot, or the gilded eighteenth century French chairs flanking a twenty-foot high carved timber fireplace, when glass tinkled in the distance.

'They're in downstairs. Rollo.' Angelo gestured to the last of Dante's team with us, a lean, older sidhe with a long ponytail and a burn-scar on one cheek. 'You go that way. Find more weapons. Hide and do the same as Farima – pick them off from behind after they pass you. Meet us in the great hall. We'll make our stand there.'

'Yessir.' He snapped a salute and slipped away into a darkened hall, his footfalls silent on the marble.

'Right,' Angelo said, sucking a deep breath, 'you two stick close. The lighting is crap in here, so try not to trip over anything and make noise.' He flickered an ironic smile. 'And believe me, there's a lot to trip over.'

We ran through more lavishly-overfurnished rooms: bedrooms with velvet and silk drapery, a sitting room with a flower-painted harpsichord, a room lined with racks and racks of antique flint-lock pistols and rifles. In one room, a display of crossbows hanging on the wall caught my attention and I reached for one.

'No point,' Angelo called. 'Strings are too old and there's no bolts. Don't stop. We'll get to the good stuff, I promise.'

He sprinted through another dark room and skidded to a halt in front of a display of basket-hilted longswords. They were chained together with thin steel chain that snapped like pasta when he yanked it. He selected a sword and twirled it before holding it out to Logan. Logan waved it aside.

'I don't have the training for that style of grip. Get me a shortsword.'

'I'll need a katana,' I put in.

Angelo pointed. 'Middle-eastern room. This way. No katanas, but there're some similar middle eastern swords. In the Great Hall. You pick up what you need on the way through, Logan.'

We passed through more rooms, too fast to appreciate the sheer volume and beauty of the weaponry on display, and slid to a halt in what could only be the Great Hall. Two rows of knights in armour, mounted on life-sized armoured horses, rode in stately fashion down the length of the hall. Their colours flew, steel gleamed and I half-expected the horses to neigh and toss their heads in protest of our hasty entrance. The scent of rusting steel and dust hung in the air and our footsteps clattered up to the vaulted ceiling, lost in darkness overhead.

On either side, cases of rapiers and swords lined the walls. Angelo gestured Logan to one case and waved me on to the other end of the room. Timber splintered as Logan wrenched a display case open and selected his choice of sword. Angelo led me into a smaller room that made my heart stop in envy. The intricate decorative workmanship of the shields, helmets and armour on the Persian knights begged hours of close study. A dozen lavishly-dressed, armoured warriors stood silent in the centre of the small room.

I pointed to a glass case of curved blades.

Angelo shoved the case away from the wall and yanked open the back. He drew out a long blade in a delicately-painted scabbard and passed it over. I hefted it, feeling the weight.

His eyes glazed and he nodded to someone I couldn't hear.

'Hurry up and choose. Farima says they're searching each room. It'll take them awhile, but they'll get here soon enough.'

'Why don't we just leave through the other entrance?'

He cast me an impatient look. 'Do you really think they've left it unguarded? Besides, we're here to draw them away. Running won't help protect the others, will it?'

I flushed. He disappeared back into the main hall. I tucked the blade through my belt, rummaged through the cabinet and pulled out two smaller knives, stowing them in my boots. A chainmail coif and coat tempted me, but they would be heavy and I wasn't used to fighting in armour. Best to rely on my speed and strength. One more weapon caught my attention and I picked it out. A katar punch-blade with a black handle gilded with tiny flowers. It nestled nicely in my fist. I tucked it into the small of my back and returned to the great hall.

Logan grinned, twirling two short swords. 'I could get to like this place.'

Angelo gripped his shoulder. 'Now's not the time for playing around. Find a spot and get ready to ambush them. Dante wants this Dyson character alive.'

'But Calain said—'

'My orders are to take him alive,' Angelo said coolly.

'Why?' Logan asked.

'Because we need to know the truth.' Angelo held up a palm as I opened my mouth to object. 'They're coming. Take up positions.' He pointed at me. 'If we have to fall back, stick close to her, Logan. Rowan, use your damned power. I don't want to lose anyone today.'

'If Dyson's here, I can't, remember? He'll just cut me loose.' I said. 'Unless you want me to turn undead on you?'

He swore. Three gunshots echoed somewhere in the vast maze of a house. Glass shattered and someone screamed, high and shrill. Angelo and Logan grinned.

Excluded from their communications, I looked askance at Logan.

'Farima. She's fine,' he supplied.

'How many are there?'

'Hard to tell,' Angelo replied. 'Farima thinks maybe a dozen. She got two and escaped through a secret passage. They won't find her and might waste time hunting. Down side is they'll now be a lot more cautious.'

'Is this the best place to make a stand?' I asked, checking the balconies on the next level up. Angelo followed my gaze.

'No access to those.' He pointed at the door we'd entered through. 'Most will come through there and we can bottleneck them for a while, but I've only got two clips. You?'

I grimaced. 'Someone took Mia's gun off me. I have six throwing knives. Rest is hand-to-hand.'

'Same here,' Logan said. 'But there are spears on that wall. Could be useful.'

Angelo nodded. 'Grab some. You and I will take the entrance. Rowan, you guard our backs in case they send someone in through the Middle-eastern room. We're one storey up so you should hear them coming.'

Angelo and Logan padded away to the other end of the hall and flanked the narrow door. I slipped in behind a standing suit of armour, beside a huge wood-canopied pew, and watched my entrance. My palms slicked with sweat and I wiped them on my jeans. Off in the distance, something large fell and crashed. I trembled and my mouth dried up. Blood thudded in my ears as I strained to hear footsteps coming up the stairs.

A short burst of static sounded in the Middle-eastern room, followed by a deep voice cursing and the click of a radio being switched off. I drew all six of my throwing knives out and laid them in my left palm. I could throw both hands, but my right was more accurate.

The Middle-eastern room's door was visible, but someone would need to stand squarely in the centre for me to be sure of hitting them at this distance. I stood a good twelve feet from the door. I hefted the first knife, measuring the distance. I should have paced it out before hiding.

Too late, now.

FOURTEEN

-Protect my daughter, Logan.-

I'll do my best, sir, but I think you're underestimating her. You all are.

-Whatever happens, don't let her fall into Dyson's hands.-

What the hell do you mean by that?

-Just prevent it, by whatever means are necessary.-

Logan, I have at least one incoming this direction. I sent the thought to him. He acknowledged but said nothing else, his concentration elsewhere.

A soft footfall scuffed on the marble in the next room and I stilled, watching the door. I was tempted to send out a tendril of myself and just drain whoever snuck through the house. But I couldn't risk Dyson's cutting me to the core.

A head poked around the corner and retreated. I stayed still. If they thought no-one watched this entrance, perhaps I could lure them into the open before throwing any knives. I had six and couldn't afford to waste any. A rack of spears behind me held my back-up plan, but they were clumsy weapons for close attack.

My body throbbed with the power I'd drawn from the museum staff. Not a lot, but enough for a distraction.

A cry of pain rang through the hall and I tensed. But Logan's mental presence, now tinged with triumph, hovered at the edges of my thoughts, so I relaxed. Someone swore and there followed a whispered exchange of heated words from the hall's opposite end.

Echoes distorted the content but I could guess the Mors people were reluctant to advance.

A lean figure darkened the doorway before me, peering towards the other end of the hall, oblivious to my presence. He wore a vest and gripped a nine-mil with two hands, professionally. I waited, breath held. He gestured to someone behind and stepped silently into the room. A second man emerged – thickset, bulging with muscles and also wearing body armour. Two I could manage. Three would be too many. One would get a warning out.

I threw two knives in quick succession; faster than either man could react. The first knife lodged in the lean man's throat. His eyes bulged, mouth opening and closing on screams that never sounded through his severed trachea. Blood pulsed down his neck and he collapsed to the floor. His gun fired as it fell, loud in the hall. The bullet ricocheted off a marble pillar. Glass over a display of swords smashed, cascading to the floor.

My second knife was less successful. Either by luck or speed, the muscular man moved at just the wrong moment and the knife lodged in the wall behind him. He wrenched it from the plaster and hurled it back at me, aiming his gun at the same time. I grinned. I'd played this game many times with Anna. I threw my third knife and leapt from behind the thin wooden pew. He pulled the trigger. The timber exploded into shards. I snatched the returning dagger from the air and curled into a roll that took me behind a mounted knight. The katar blade in the back of my belt dug into my kidney.

The thickset man swayed and slumped to the ground, my knife protruding from his chest. I breathed out a sigh of relief. I'd bet on his vest being ballistics armour, rather than stab-armour and had guessed right. The knife had passed right through without stopping, taking him in the heart.

Rowan?

Not now, Logan. Busy. Two down. You ok?

Yes.

Something metal crashed to the ground at his end of the hall and two shots rang out from the opposite side. Presumably Angelo. I slipped back to the pew and concealed myself again, watching.

The pressure in my head had eased as the attack began. Now it redoubled, almost blinding me.

Logan, get ready. I think they're about to mount an all-out assault. They've just been testing us.

Shit. His presence faded and Angelo swore as he received the message.

I debated clambering into the suit of armour standing next to me. But there was no point. A bullet would go straight through. Instead, I plucked three spears from the wall and leaned them up against the pew.

Shouts erupted from both ends of the hall. Five figures burst through my door. I flicked my four remaining throwing knives, not waiting to see which ones connected. Two bodies piled to the floor. The other three men scrambled over and surged forward. More filled the space behind them. Gunfire echoed in the hall. I snatched up a spear and drove it into a body. He staggered back, clutching at the shaft protruding from his stomach. I pressed forward, shoving him into his companions.

Two stumbled, tripping over their injured companions on the floor. They fell in a thrashing tangle of yelling rage. I yanked the curved Turkish sword from my belt and one of the daggers from my boot. All the guns these idiots carried had fallen out of my reach.

A report cracked. A suit of armour toppled and scattered across the floor and the crash of metal reverberated off the walls. Another gunshot blasted and more glass shattered. One of the Mors men regathered his feet and pointed his pistol at me. He was too close. I kicked into high speed and covered the few steps in a fraction of time.

I slashed with the sword, cutting at the gun. He pulled the trigger.

The report slapped against my eardrum. Somewhere behind me, metal clattered. The gun flew free and skittered across the floor. He snarled and grabbed my wrist, trying to wrench the sword from my grip.

I moved with him and drove a dagger through his vest, into his liver. He blinked at me, his mouth falling open. Releasing me, he sank to his knees and grabbed at the dagger. I wrenched it free.

A metallic click by my ear.

'Don't mo—'

I ducked and swung. The sword blade sliced through cloth and flesh and wedged into bone. I sent a shaft of energy along the blade. His flesh blackened and crinkled. He screamed. I kicked at my attacker's stomach and yanked the blade free. He clutched at the gaping red and black wound in his arm. My stomach twisted.

Rowan? It was Logan's voice. *We've cleared this exit. Get over here and we can get out.*

Coming. I ducked behind the armoured knights ahorseback and sprinted to Logan. He stood in the doorway, watching both directions anxiously. Bodies lay piled in bloody heaps all around. Angelo leaned against a wall nearby, blood staining his right side. Logan pointed Angelo's gun back over my shoulder. He squeezed the trigger and glass shattered at the opposite end of the hall. Return fire blew chips out of the wall and showered me in plaster dust.

I ducked through the door and Angelo followed. We hurried a few steps down a narrow hall. I checked behind. And stopped.

'Logan?'

No answer.

'Leave him,' Angelo growled. He reached for my arm but I twisted away.

'You get out if you want,' I snapped. 'I'm not leaving him.'

Angelo glared. 'I can't let you bet taken by the Mors. Dante was clear on that.'

'Was that a threat?'

He sagged against the wall. 'I'm in no position to make threats, Rowan. Just get out, please? I'll cover you.'

'Nope. Not leaving either of you.'

Another shot echoed through the massive hall and Logan slipped through the door. He put his back to the wall and cradled the pistol against his chest. His face was ashen, his eyes bleak as he stared at me.

'He's here,' he said, voice flat.

'Dyson?' I swallowed.

'My father.' Logan's mouth hardened, eyes flinty with hatred. His fingers flexed around the gun.

I reached for his wrist but he moved before I could stop him. 'Don't—'

He was gone, back into the hall, gun raised.

A gunshot. And another. Glass. Metal. Screams. The smell of blood and cordite.

I swore and leapt through the door, sword in one hand, knife in the other.

Another shot rang out close by. I threw myself to one side and something punched me in the left arm. I landed on my right side and skidded across the marble, sliding into a sheltered position behind another suit of armour. Only then did pain register. My left arm dangled uselessly. Both sword and knife had been jarred loose and lay on the floor, out of reach. Blood poured down my chest and dripped onto the marble floor, the scarlet pool spreading with the rapid fluttering of my heart. Dizziness darkened my vision as pain tore through my arm.

The meagre power left in me wasn't enough to heal it, but the flow of blood slowed.

I bit back a sob and scrambled to my feet, my back against the wall.

Boots clattered across marble and four figures towered over me. Each pointed a gun at my head. My weapons – boot knife, katar blade in my belt and karambit in my shirt – were out of quick reach.

Rowan!

Desperation and fear blasted Logan's cry into my thoughts. He fought hand to hand against a man his own height and equally as quick. Finn. They traded blows, blindingly-fast, lethal. Logan reeled back, blood pouring from a gash on his forehead. A cabinet smashed, showering him with glass. Finn pulled a gun from his belt and aimed it at Logan.

'No!' I anchored myself and stepped into the *sianfath*, stabbing tendrils into the four men before me, and Finn. I drew life from them, stopped the bleeding in my arm—

And screamed. Something sliced through my connections and ripped away part of my soul, tearing me apart from the inside. I sagged to the floor, panting, whimpering, tasting blood from where I'd bitten my lip through.

Silence descended on the room, followed by the crunch of glass as footsteps approached.

'I did warn you, my dear girl,' Dyson's smooth tones reminded me. He stood before me, lean, dressed in a tailored grey suit, a light haloing his pale hair. 'Surely Calain's told you by now the outcome of doing that more than three or four times?'

'What do you want?' I said, low and harsh, glaring up at him. I wasn't about to try standing. My legs wouldn't support me. The power I'd taken from Dyson's men had drained from me with his cut, as though each tether had reversed and poured their life back into them. The four men appeared unaffected, standing by Dyson, their guns trained on me. Finn arrived hauling Logan, whose head lolled alarmingly. Blood streaked Logan's face. His eyes were unfocussed. My arm throbbed and warmth slipped down my wrist.

Dyson pointed to my arm. 'Draw what you need from the gardens to heal yourself. I won't stop you.'

I did so, filling myself to capacity with energy. Hopefully I could hold it and not have the power tear me apart from the inside. At least that would give me one, last-ditch weapon if they took everything else from me.

I pushed up the wall again, leaving bloody handprints on the gilded wallpaper.

Logan?

I'm...alright. I'm sorry. I lost it. I should have left, not gone after him. I put you in danger.

I tried...

I know.

'Now,' Dyson said, gesturing. Finn brought Logan closer, a pistol to his temple.

'We have a dilemma,' Dyson finished.

'Oh?' I replied, trying to sound casual. I slipped a hand behind, into my waistband, and found the katar's comforting grip. 'I don't see how. You seem to hold all the cards.'

Dyson smiled, his thin mouth stretching wide. 'But you would appear to hold all the *power*.' He pointed at my chest and I blinked in astonishment. He could *see* the energy I had stored? No other sidhe but me could see the *sianfath*. How...?

'My men are under orders to kill this one and the other, should you release that energy in my direction – or, indeed, at any of us,' he said. 'So, I'd like to offer you a solution.'

'I'm listening,' I said, flexing my left hand, testing its strength. The bullet wound was healed, but I was still weak from loss of blood. Only water and food would fix that.

Dyson clasped his hands behind his back and paced two steps in either direction before me. Just far enough out of reach that I couldn't get to him with the katar blade even if I'd been in perfect health. Behind him, Logan watched me, stoic anger in his expression as his captor pressed the gun into his head.

Dyson nodded at Logan. 'I'll let your friends go – and I'll call off the people I have hunting the others in your party.'

'In return for?' I studied him narrowly.

'You,' he replied, cocking his head. 'You remind me of someone I knew many years ago. I think we can help each other.'

Could he have met Aeona? It was possible if, as Calain suggested, Dyson had learned the *torryl* from Tordal.

'What do you want from me?' I asked.

He shrugged. 'I told you what I'm trying to achieve. I think your…abilities could be useful.'

Calain's warning rang in my ears – don't let him capture you. Epic fail.

'So, if I come peacefully with you, you'll let Logan and Angelo go free, alive and healthy?' I said.

'Rowan. No,' Logan hissed. His father cocked the pistol.

'Please,' Dyson said. 'There's no need for such brutality, Finn. Let him go. He won't go anywhere. Not while she's still here.' His thin smile slipped into the knowing and I shivered. He could undoubtedly see the thread connecting Logan and I as evidence of our intimacy.

Logan glared at his father and hurried over to me. I released the katar blade and returned his hug. His arms wrapped around me and he froze for a second when he touched the blade.

'Don't,' I whispered. 'Let me handle this.'

He drew back, his jaw clenched and his eyes narrowed in indecision.

Don't go with him, Rowan.

I don't think I have much of a choice. Trust me, Logan.

'Yes,' Dyson's smile became truly amused. 'Do trust her, Logan.'

We both gaped at him and exchanged horrified looks. He'd heard our private exchange. How as that even possible? I paused, thinking fast. All the things I'd intended to tell Logan, I couldn't.

'Rowan—'

I fended him off, palms flat towards him. 'Don't, Logan. Just don't. And don't try to come after me.' I sucked a deep breath and threw my shoulders back. 'I'm not risking any of you again. In fact...' I dragged Calain's signet ring, now slippery and sticky with blood, from my left hand. 'Here. Give this to Erin. I know she admired it.'

I curled his hand around it as Logan blinked at me in astonishment. 'Tell her I love her, too, but I don't want her following me and I know the ring has a tracking device in it.'

Logan's fist tightened around the gold and emerald jewel. He swallowed.

I addressed Dyson. 'I'm keeping my promise. Keep yours. We stay here until Logan and Angelo are safely gone from here and away from your men. Then I'll go with you.'

Dyson nodded to his men. They separated, half the guns shifting from me to Logan. With several backward looks, Logan helped a groggy Angelo to his feet and the pair of them disappeared through the house. The silvery-green thread connecting me to Logan stretched reassuringly through the *sianfath.*

Several silent minutes passed until I felt them get into a car and speed away down the narrow lane. Then I returned my awareness to the Stibbert great hall and confronted Dyson, raising my chin.

'You kept your word, so I will, too. Where are we going?'

Dyson's mouth twitched into an empathetic half-smile. 'I do apologise my dear, but this could hurt a trifle.' He made a slicing gesture.

The connection to Logan fell away and loss punched me in the stomach. I dropped to my knees, winded and in agony, too breathless with pain to even cry out. Weakness flooded my limbs and I had no choice but to let Dyson's men carry me bodily through the Middle-Eastern room and downstairs to the front entrance.

They bundled me into a car and yanked a black bag over my head. They didn't need the bag. I curled around the hole in my heart, unable to speak or think through the hurt, or see through the tears.

FIFTEEN

He cut your connection to her?

Yes. But I don't think he'll kill her. He said she could be useful.

Merda!

Dante...it's my fault. I saw Finn. I had a clear shot but he moved and I stayed to try again. She came back for me.

Logan, once I would have lectured you on letting emotion overcome logic. I can no longer do so. You made a mistake. Don't make the same one again. Rowan is more important than revenge on your father.

...

Meet us at the new safe house. We must plan our next move.

Dante, why did Calain say I should do anything it took to stop her falling into Dyson's hands? Is he hiding something, or is he just afraid Dyson will use her against us?

I don't know. But I think it's time we found out, my friend.

Dyson's men manhandled me out of the car an unknowable time later. It felt like no more than twenty minutes, but I was so groggy it could have been longer. Extending into the *sianfath* would just invite trouble, so I relied on my physical senses to try and get some idea of where I might be. The ground underfoot felt uneven but solid, not dirt, perhaps some sort of rounded paving stones. A car crawled past. The growl of its engine bounced back so there must be walls or buildings close by. Footsteps hurried by and voices spoke in English, Mandarin and German. A woman yelled something in Italian about following a flag and being almost at the Palazzo. We were somewhere with a lot of tourists. Perhaps the centre of Florence, somewhere near the Palazzo Vecchio?

All of which was useless information, because I had no way of getting it to Logan or Calain. My only hope was now Erin and she was the least likely person to come to my rescue.

I stumbled over a step and the men either side of me tightened their grip on my arms. A door closed, solid and heavy, behind me. The lock snicked into place. Someone tugged the bag off and released my arms. I blinked and flicked hair out of my eyes.

'This way, my dear.' Dyson strolled ahead of me along a narrow, white-walled corridor. Hemmed in by four large guards I couldn't do much but follow. The hall opened into a vaulted space with an elegant white stone staircase, exposed timber ceiling, and colourful frescoes of what looked like shields high on the white walls. Off to one side, a small timber door was set into a thick stone wall. The door might lead outside, but the chunky iron lock would be difficult to pick with the slim metal lockpicks hidden inside the lining of my bra. The picks were designed for modern locks. This door lock looked to be about four hundred years old at least. Ironic.

A woman in a labcoat emerged from a low door in the opposite wall. She hurried over, only to stop when she caught sight of me. Dyson waved her aside. She reversed her course without speaking and vanished back through the door, down a set of narrow, brightly-lit steps.

I followed Dyson upstairs, climbing the white marble staircase, reassured by the boot knife's scrape against my ankle, the warmth of the curved karambit under my breast, and the katar punchblade beneath my shirt. Why hadn't his men frisked me?

At the top of the stairs Dyson opened a thick timber door and waved me inside, motioning the guards to stay out. I crossed the threshold and paused. I'd expected something dark and ancient. Instead I found myself in a modern room not unlike a university library. One wall was lined with books. Several shiny black desks that looked like they'd come flatpacked from Ikea were lined up in a neat row before the shelves. Each desk had a pair of elegant, art-nouveau type lamps with square cream shades. At the far end of the room the afternoon light from two arched windows was filtered by white gauzy curtains.

The door shut behind me and Dyson strolled past. He didn't stop, but headed for a narrow door inset into the far corner.

'What is this place?' I asked. My footsteps fell silently on the prosaic, square-tiled floor.

'The Dante Society library,' Dyson said over his shoulder.

I blinked at him. 'What?'

Dyson's thin lips pulled into a wry smile. 'No, not Dante, the Conte di Lucca. Dante Alighieri, writer of Dante's Inferno.' He waved a lazy hand. 'A group of enthusiasts who seem to see Dante as a visionary of sorts. They have meetings.' He shrugged. 'They make a good distraction from what really operates out of this building – the Mors Ferrum. In here.' He unlocked the door and bent to go through the opening.

I ducked through the entrance and followed him up a narrow, spiralling stone staircase. The steps were worn and shallow, indented in the middle by the passage of thousands of feet over hundreds of years. The timber walls were dark, my path lit by a few, yellow bare bulbs, dim overhead.

We emerged into a wide, open room lit by five arched windows, two in the eastern wall and three in the western. Thick timber beams held the timber-lined ceiling up and the walls were of plastered stone. But there any semblance of the original medieval structure stopped. Placed in an orderly fashion around the room, were fifteen grey desks. Each sported a minimum of four state of the art computer screens and hardware. At each desk sat a worker, with a headset and microphone hooked over one ear, attention fixed on the screens and fingers ticking over keyboards and touchpads. every screen showed a bewildering array of flickering images I had no hope of interpreting from a distance. The workers wore casual clothing: jeans and tshirts. Jackets were draped over chairs as the room was warm. Soft jazz music played from invisible speakers, mingling with the low murmur of voices speaking in a variety of languages as the workers communicated with people unknown.

Dyson jerked his head towards a single, enclosed space in one corner of the room. A small box of an office. As I passed the workers I heard snippets of conversations.

'…take him out. Protect the asset.'

'…activate only on our signal.'

'…No. Get confirmation of the gene before you move in…'

'…are they endangering humans? Fine. Let them go. Just tag for now. We'll pick them up later.'

'…not yet ready to activate all the assets. Hold for our signal.'

'…authorised to proceed with the therapy.'

'…standby for activation.'

My presence didn't seem to bother anyone. I rated no more than an assessing glance as I passed each desk. One woman, with extraordinary green eyes and blue-black hair, stared through me, her expression devoid of interest. But it was impossible to ignore that every worker was fit and in the twenty to forty age-group, aware of my existence, poised to act if needed…and many were armed with a nine mil on their hip.

This was not a place I would get out of. And not a place Logan and Dante would get into, either. That spiral staircase was a killbox.

Dyson paused with his hand on the office door. 'Finn, will you ensure our guest has fresh clothing and check none of our people have been tagged with the *dilynna*. I suspect that boy of yours is resourceful'

Finn's mouth twisted into a wry smile. He bowed. 'Yes, my lord. Pity we didn't take him as well. He'd have been a good addition.'

I gritted my teeth and glared at him. 'You'll answer to Logan one of these days.'

Finn's smile widened. He turned away without replying.

Dyson chuckled. He indicated the bustling office. 'What do you think of our little operation?'

'It's smaller than I expected.' The spiteful words were out before I could censor them and I flushed.

But Dyson only smiled and opened the door. 'Never mind, my dear. We're growing every day now, though perhaps not in the way you might think.'

I stepped into his office and blinked again. It was, Tardis-like, much bigger on the inside. The plasterboard box visible in the other room was just an anteroom into a much larger space. This was the antithesis of the office outside. The dark timber ceiling was lower and the three arched windows along one wall closer-spaced. The walls were of rendered brick and hung with exquisite silk tapestries depicting stylised battles from all eras, and places: Persian, Indian, Chinese, European. All beautiful workmanship, though the silk was faded.

A plush Burmese cat strolled across the slate floor, swiped against my leg and yeowled at Dyson before curling up on a brilliant red Turkish rug in front of a heater. Dyson scratched the animal behind the ears.

Scattered around the rug were four heavy armchairs with deep-buttoned upholstery of brown leather. A low timber coffee table of dark oak, stained with dozens of water and wine-marks, was the focal point for the seats. The room looked…warm, inviting. Masculine but comfortable.

A strong sense of the *sianfath* also imbued the room with a power that revived my flagging strength. But the only plants were two potted rubber trees near the windows. I extended a little of myself, seeking the source of power. There. On the roof overhead. A massive, density of plant life. Probably a hot house, given how cold winters were here.

Dyson headed for a rough-hewn timber sideboard, lined with shelves. Every shelf was crammed with a bizarre and eclectic mix of knickknacks: watches, jewellery, hats, even a shoe and a toothbrush. From a cabinet between the shelves, he selected an unlabelled bottle of liquor and poured a nip of golden liquid into two plain glasses. I waited, awkward, inspecting a tapestry. He returned and passed me a drink.

'Thanks.' I sniffed the alcohol and screwed up my nose. I didn't like to drink, normally. My whole life had been about keeping tight control of my speed and strength so I wouldn't hurt anyone. Drinking was exactly the wrong thing to do.

Dyson raised his drink to his lips and sipped, watching me from beneath lowered lids. A half-smile quirked his thin lips.

I threw the drink back in one gulp and gasped as it burnt my oesophagus and settled uncomfortably in my stomach. The fumes went up my nose and I coughed, eyes watering.

Dyson chuckled. 'Waste of hundred-year-old scotch, my dear.'

I sniffed. 'What are those?' I pointed to the shelves full of oddities.

He shrugged. 'Memorabilia. Of people I'd like to find again one day. People I wasn't able to…keep in my life for one reason or another. Do you like my tapestries?'

Accepting the abrupt change of subject, I nodded.

'This is me.' He pointed to a figure on horseback in the middle of the nearest artwork. The image depicted a battle between an Ottoman army and some other I didn't recognise. 'I was fighting alongside Harald Sigurdsson during his years in exile from Norway, when he was commanding the Vangarian Guard for the Byzantine Empire. That's Harald.' He indicated another armoured figure.

'Oh,' I said. 'When?' The alcohol warmed my stomach and spread relaxation into my shoulders and thighs.

Dyson tilted his head to one side and tapped his lips. 'After so many years one forgets the details, but sometime around 1040, I believe. Harald was a fine leader. Would have made a much better King of England than Edward or William the Bastard. But…' He shrugged. 'It wasn't to be. Entertaining while he lasted, though.'

I put my glass on a sideboard. 'Is that how you see humans? As entertainment?'

His lips quirked again. 'How aggressive you are, child. Think about what I just said.' He strolled to a chair and sank into it, crossing his lean legs at the ankles. 'I've been alive for over a thousand years. I don't get emotionally attached to humans anymore. They live such short lives.' He stared into his glass before downing the golden liquid in one swallow.

He set the glass aside and indicated a seat opposite. 'Please, sit. We have much to discuss.'

I hesitated, but there weren't any other options. So I sat on the edge of the creaking leather, my feet firmly on the floor so I could rise quickly.

'What do you want from me?' I said. My tone was more belligerent than I intended and I fidgeted when he looked wearily at me.

'I'm tired, my dear,' he said, leaning back in the chair. He pressed a thumb to his temple. 'The Ruadhán sidhe believe carrying the Dark gene is some sort of horrible disease; that it automatically makes you an evil dictator trying to take over the world.' He barked a laugh. 'I don't know if you've ever thought about it but running an entire world would be both wearisome and unrewarding. So many people complaining. So much paperwork. So much death just to maintain power.'

I started, for I'd said something similar as a sarcastic joke to Logan just a few days before.

Dyson rubbed the palm of his free hand down his thigh, as though scrubbing it clean. 'The truth is: the Dark gene doesn't lead to mental instability or megalomania, as Maeve and her ilk would have you believe.' He gave a weary sigh. 'It just means you aren't blind to reality anymore.'

'Reality's subjective. Which one are you talking about?'

'Humans are incapable of looking after this world,' he replied.

'That sounds a lot like rationalisation to me,' I shot back. 'What about Hitler, Khan and the others? They were Dark.'

Dyson shrugged impatiently. 'I'm not saying the dark gene's never paired with idiocy. But there are many who've never so much as killed a kitten, let alone laid waste to entire countries.'

'So, you're just trying to save humans from themselves? A moment ago you said you didn't care about them anymore. Why would you want to save them?'

'Don't be a fool, girl,' he snapped. 'I don't care about humans, but we're stuck with them. They're short-lived, short-sighted, self-destructive and probably a lost cause. I care about my people. Your people. The sidhe – both Dark and Light. If the Council had listened to people like Tordal Ivaldison fifteen hundred years ago, we wouldn't be facing the environmental disasters we are today.'

'Tordal!' I clenched the chair arms. 'So you did know him?'

Dyson raised surprised brows at me. 'Of course. I fought by his side for close to two hundred years.'

There was so much I wanted to ask, but I didn't want to look like a burbling idiot, so I took a deep breath and tried to settle my mind on one question at a time.

'What did he advise fifteen hundred years ago.' I frowned. 'And who are the Council?'

'Were. They're a defunct body of elder Ruadhán sidhe who used to feel the need to govern us all. As though a scattered population of wildlings could ever be brought under the control of a single group.' Dyson sucked a quick breath and leaned forward. He blinked and rubbed at one eye. With a noise of frustration, he pulled a small plastic container out of a pocket and proceeded to remove his dark contact lenses. When they were out, he sighed in relief.

I gaped in momentary amazement. I'd seen all shades of grey and blue amongst the sidhe I'd met so far, but none like Dyson's eyes. They had the characteristic dark rim, but the irises were so pale as to be almost white. The effect was startling and memorable and I could see why he wore contacts.

'As to what Tordal proposed...' he grimaced. 'I wasn't in agreement at the time, but now I can see how it might have been our saving grace, had the Council agreed.'

'And?'

'And,' he said, 'Tordal wished to eliminate all humans, once and for all. The Council denied him. He then spent several centuries trying various methods of achieving his aim. Warfare. Plague. That sort of thing. But the world was not as closely tied as it is now, so the ability to kill en masse was limited and, alas…' Dyson smiled wryly. 'He always underestimated the speed with which humans breed.'

'And yet you fought by his side, even though you say you didn't agree with him.'

Dyson shrugged. 'What can I say? I was young and searching for meaning. I'd spent two hundred years as a mercenary, fighting alongside good men like Harald, only to see them wither or sicken or be slaughtered. I was tired of losing people I cared about, so I stopped caring about humans and focussed on sidhe. Tordal's words appealed to me. He talked about protecting sidhe; about making the world ours again. I agreed with his philosophy but, in the end, not with his methods.'

'Really?' I folded my arms. 'So, after a couple of centuries killing for him, what was so dire it changed your mind?'

Dyson smiled. 'You still don't believe me? Very well. I'll show you, then.'

'Show me? How?'

He held out his hand, palm up. 'Search my memory. Go back to the date I tell you and you'll see exactly what made me leave. And why I'm using the Mors as I am – for our advantage.'

'Your memory?' I stared at him in disbelief. 'But I was told that's—'

'A gesture of ultimate trust amongst sidhe?' His smile softened. 'Yes, so it is. So, I extend the hand of trust.

Still, I hesitated. Could Maeve and Calain have been wrong about him? I had no real reason to trust Maeve and Dyson had given me none to distrust him.

The cat stretched and yawned on the rug. It strolled over to Dyson and leapt into his lap in one fluid movement and curled into a ball, tail twitching. Dyson stroked the animal.

'Come, child,' Dyson said, his tone touched with impatience. 'I know you can slip in time.'

I gasped. 'How...?'

He chuckled. 'Because I remember you coming to me in the summer of 1405. So you must be able to.'

1405 was the time I'd slipped back into in Aeona's memories. It couldn't be a co-incidence.

'You knew Aeona,' I stated. 'You were there. During that battle against Owain Glyndwr's forces.'

'I was. But you need to see it from my perspective. Then you'll understand why I left Tordal. And why I'm trying to protect our people. Come.' He extended a hand to me. 'I'll guide you to the right time. When you get there, just watch and listen. I'll know you're there. You'll need to reassure me you're not an enemy. But once you've done that, you'll see why I chose as I did.'

SIXTEEN

-I charged the with her care, Logan. To prevent her capture. Instead anger at thy father overcame thy judgement-

I know, sir. Believe me, I know, but even if—

-God's blood! Don't you see, you fool? He'll use her against us. As h...Tordal did with Aeona. I knew I should have gone with her-

Would you really have me kill her to prevent this? When you've waited five hundred years for her birth?

-If needs be...yes. I know what it did to Aeona. What she did under duress for Tordal. I would not wish for my daughter.-

Is that the only reason?

-...-

I tethered myself and slipped into Dyson's French chateaux. This time he opened the door for me and led me to a room in the back of one wing. There, he paused before a small, heavy timber door.

#Through here. The same day you came to Aeona, in the summer of 1405, but early in the morning. Find me in the same house. I was speaking with Aeona, trying to convince her to leave.#

What?

#You'll understand when you see her. To convince me of your good will, you'll need to say this: "I'm here to help you achieve the goal you decided on this very morning." Do you understand?#

Yes, but what was that goal?

#To ensure the sidhe's survival, of course.# He opened the door. *#Don't stay long as I cannot allow you to draw power from people*

in this area lest you overstretch and kill by accident. For I know you don't wish that, either.#

I said nothing, confused by his concern. I pulled in a little power from garden above, and from the several dozen people just outside the building, and squirreled it inside myself. Then I stepped through the door.

Once again, vague impressions of people, fear, time and death swirled past as I tried to concentrate on the date and place. The sense of motion stopped and I solidified into a place and time. I blinked and swayed, struggling with disorientation. My mind fought with Dyson's for control of his body. I withdrew, giving up control, recalling his words.

I'm not here to hurt you. I've slipped through your memories, with your permission, from the future.

There was a long pause, filled with tumultuous emotions: anger, fear, worry. His eyes opened and I saw, through them, the same room I'd been in with Aeona.

#Who art thou? From whence dost thou come?#

The future. You sent me here, yourself. How else would I be able to get here, but through your memories?

#Why should I trust such a canny shade? What's thy purpose?#

You told me to say: I'm here to help you achieve the goal you decided on this very morning.

There was another pause and his focus turned inward, onto me. I couldn't see through his eyes, only sense the overpowering strength of his mind battering against mine.

#'Twould appear thou dost speak truth. How canst thou help?#

He said you're trying to convince Aeona Silverblade to leave. You need to start that. I'll finish it for you, later. For now, I'll just watch.

I pulled back again and waited, husbanding my strength.

The slatted timber door opened and icy rain gusted into the tiny cottage. A cloaked female figure entered and slammed the panel shut with a cry of anger. She leaned against the timber and beat the wood with a fist, sobbing.

'Aeona, weep not. We'll prevail.'

She gasped and spun, thrusting her hood back. Astonishment warred with disbelief and hope. Tears gathered, spilled and tracked through the grime on her cheeks.

'Oh, *Kieran!* I thought thee gone forever.' She flung herself into my arms and I retreated in confused haste as she kissed the body I occupied.

Kieran? This man was Kieran Ivaldison? Alexander Dyson was Kieran Ivaldison. My grandfather? The leader of the Mors Ferrum. How could that be?

And why had Calain said nothing? He obviously knew. Every moment of his reticence and hesitation was now perfectly understandable. He knew who Dyson was yet hadn't said. Why? What did it gain him to withhold such vital information?

I paused. But when I'd visited Aeona and Calain in the fifteen hundreds she'd spoken of Kieran as long dead on a French battlefield. Had she been misinformed, or had she lied to Calain? But again, why?

Did anyone in my life tell the truth?

I regathered and pushed back into Dyson...Kieran's awareness. He drew Aeona closer to the small fire and chafed at her cold hands as I watched from behind his eyes.

'Husband.' Aeona touched his mouth and he kissed her fingers. 'Where hast thou been? That day, a month gone, when Owain's men came upon me...'

'I'm sorry, my love,' Kieran replied. 'When I found what they'd done, I was so enraged I could scarce think beyond revenge.' He hung his head. 'I didst leave thee when I should have stayed by thy side. But mine heart held such darkness I feared...'

Aeona sucked a quick breath. 'Art not...?'

'Nay,' Kieran replied. 'Tordal's teachings hold. But none of those who sought to harm thee survive, nor their commander, nor theirs. Suffice to say Owain's army is the lesser and mine heart lighter for my actions, though their blood will e'er stain me, I fear.'

'But thou wast gone a month.' Aeona looked into the fire.

Kieran leaned forward. 'I left only so long as to regather my wits, for they'd nigh abandoned me in my wreche. I feared to come near thee lest...'

'Nay,' Aeona replied, sighing. 'Thy choice was wise, husband, for in thy wreche and grief thou art stronger than thou knowst. Tho my heart was sore with fear for thee, I do forgive and am o'erjoyed thou art safe back now.' Her jaw hardened. 'The humans, tho... Them I canst not forgive. They deserve all thou didst and all I shall do on the morrow. Tordal does ask of me the ultimate and I find the darkness in mine own heart such that I no longer wish to gainsay him.''

'Nay, love.' Kieran scowled. 'What dost Tordal require of thee?'

Her eyes were dark with bitter anger and hurt. 'That I should suck the life from Owain and half his army on the morrow. Lay waste to them and theirs and use the power to level the other half. And I find the thought...draws me.'

'Ah, my sweet love, do not!' Kieran caught Aeona in his arms and held her as she sobbed into his shoulder. 'There are better ways. 'Twill be aright, anon, I promise thee. But thou must not allow Tordal to bend thy will to his. Thou hast stood a century 'gainst his blandishments and threats. Stay thy hand, yet.'

Aeona thrust herself away and mopped her cheeks with the corner of her cloak. 'Because I thought the humans worthy of my sacrifice, but now…' Fresh tears welled and her nails dug white pits into her palms.

'I know,' Kieran said. 'But think on Calain. He needs thee now. Such devastation thou'lt wreak on the morrow couldst kill thee. Thou canst not leave him to be raised by Tordal.'

'Calain…' Aeona bit her lip and glanced narrowly towards the door. 'Nay, 'twould be best for him and all our kind if I did slaughter all humankind for the beasts they are.'

Kieran stroked her hair, his thumb brushing her cheek. 'Thou art wearied and heartsick, my love, for that path is the very one thou hast fought gainst this last century. And the destruction of humankind will serve no purpose, for they art as much of the *sianfath* as we. There is a better way. Let us leave. We can unite the sidhe. Take our rightful place again as masters of the *sianfath*.'

'Nay, the humans deserveth not such kind masters.' Aeona straightened and tossed her auburn braid back over one shoulder. 'Mayhap Tordal has the right of it, husband, and I the wrong.' Her chin lifted. 'Speak no more to me of this. My mind is fixed. From this day I shall work towards the downfall of humans, no matter what the cost to me and mine. Now leave. I must rest afore the battle on the morrow and thy father keeps better house than I in this hovel.'

'Aeona!' Kieran rose to his feet, following as she stalked to the door. 'Thou canst not turn me out, into this foul day. We must speak more.'

'No!' Aeona wrenched the door open and rain spattered on the rushes at the threshold. 'Thou wouldst seek to change my mind and I'll have none of it. Go to thy son and thy father. Care for Calain.' Kieran reached for her, but she stepped back. Tears coursed down her cheeks once more and mingled with freezing rain. 'Go!'

Kieran stepped into the grey morning and flipped up his hood. She slammed the door.

I shared his confusion and anger, his despair and uncertainty. None of this made sense.

Kieran, I—

#Get out of my mind, wraith. I fear more now than I did before.#

Don't. I'll return to Aeona later and speak with her. She'll change her mind, I promise.

#I want to believe thee, but...#

Something tugged at me and my energy levels plummeted. I released my tether on Kieran's body and slipped back through time to my own.

I dragged my eyelids open and stared vaguely at the dark timber ceiling. I seemed to be lying on the floor, on a rug smelling of cigars and dust. Something hard pressed uncomfortably against my back.

A thin, shadowed face appeared and I flinched away.

Dyson...Kieran held out a hand and I allowed him to haul me upright. My knees buckled so he assisted me into one of the deep leather chairs. He pressed a drink into my hand but I pushed it away. My mouth was dry and my brain fuzzy. The last thing I needed was more alcohol.

'It's a sports drink, my dear,' he said mildly. 'I was monitoring your blood sugar and energy. You were low on both, so I pulled you back. You appear to lack the regulator organ for the power you draw. You should have mentioned it. When did you eat last?'

I took a swig of the drink, the lemony-tartness soothing my mouth and throat. I drank the entire thing before replying.

'I can't remember. This morning, maybe?'

'Unacceptable.' Dys...Kieran pressed a button on the wall. A disembodied voice responded. Kieran requested two orders of fettucine carbonara before returning to my side. He sank into the chair beside me and smiled.

'So, now you know,' he said.

'No.' I sat up straighter and accepted a second lemon drink. This time I drank more slowly, savouring the rush of energy and sugar as it hit my exhausted body.

I examined Kieran – my grandfather – and felt only confusion. He'd treated me with nothing but respect. So who did I believe? Calain or Kieran?

'I don't understand. Calain said Aeona left because she couldn't kill humans any longer, but she said…' I waved a helpless hand.

'I know,' Kieran sat back, the leather creaking beneath him as he crossed his legs. 'Your visit that evening to her – after you'd come to me – convinced her to leave in order to protect Calain. But I'm afraid it didn't dim her desire for vengeance against humans.'

'But *why*? Why did she hate them so much?' I held the cold drink to my aching head, trying to make sense of it all. 'People who knew her – my father included – said she was trying to save humans from the Dark sidhe.'

'Did they?' Kieran's pale eyes were intense. 'Think about it. Did those people say Aeona was saving humans, or did they say she was working against the Dark sidhe. For those are two different things. One can easily be working against the Dark and also be attempting to eliminate humankind.'

I groaned. 'I don't know any more. I don't know who to believe. Or who to trust. Why should I help you, anyway? How do I know you're any more truthful than everyone else?'

Kieran sucked a quick breath and leaned forward. 'Who is your father, my dear.'

I rounded on him, wide-eyed. 'You mean you don't know? Aeona didn't tell you after I saw her?'

'No. I suspect, but I'd like it confirmed.'

I put the bottle of lemon drink aside, rose and paced the room, debating. If I told him, I could be held against Calain as hostage. But

Kieran already knew I had people who cared for me: Logan. I was already a hostage, should he wish to play that game. But he hadn't, so why would that change? Unless he was hunting Calain, as my father said.

Kieran's thin smile showed. 'Let me put you out of your misery, my dear. I suspect Calain Gilmore is your father, and also the father of Dante, Conte di Lucca. Would I be correct?'

I stilled, then cursed myself because that reaction gave the truth away as much as agreement. But I said nothing and kept my back turned to prevent him reading my expression.

'Which means,' he continued, 'Dante most likely carries the Dark gene, as Calain does. But you don't, for I can sense the Dark in sidhe. Interesting.'

I whirled, fearful. 'But I've already switched it off permanently, in both of them. And Logan. So they're no use to the Mors.' It wasn't true. I'd helped Maeve alter Calain's DNA and Logan's, but we'd not had time to alter Dante's. There was still a danger his could be switched on if he were captured.

'Ah.' Kieran took a sip of his drink and regarded me over the brim of the glass. 'Now that *is* interesting. I did not realise Maeve had worked out how to do that. And you said you did it? You're telekinetic?'

'No. I meant…' I stumbled to a halt under his cool expectation. 'I'm not telekinetic. I just helped, with the energy draw.'

'You have Aeona's gift in full, then?' He didn't seem impressed so I nodded. 'Yes, I suspected that when I felt you invade my shield in the receiving office.' He sighed and stared off into middle distance. 'You look much like her. I miss her, still.'

He made no moves to hurt or impose his will on me, so I sat back down and stared at him. The cat brushed against my leg. I stroked it absently, avoiding Kieran's piercing intensity.

'Why did you leave her? Why was she so angry with humans?'

Kieran's expression became bleak. 'The answer is the same for both questions, in a way. I left because she was so angry. And she was angry because of what had happened the month before we left Tordal.' He threw back his drink and a knock sounded at the door. He rose and opened it.

The scent of food wafted into the room and my stomach rumbled. Finn and a human carried a small table and two chairs in and set the food up at the opposite end of the room, then departed without speaking. Finn sent me an amused smile so like Logan's characteristic half-twist of the lips that my heart ached. Then he closed and locked the door.

'Shall we eat?' Kieran seated himself and poured a glass of pale white wine. He held it out. I shook my head but joined him at the table.

The carbonara's creamy flavour and salty accents were exactly what I needed and I said nothing more until my plate was empty. I drank water. I couldn't afford my brain to be any more muddled than it already was. Kieran picked at his food, eating little and drinking less. He watched me, though, with apparent pleasure.

When my stomach was full and I sat, crumbling bits of garlic bread into dust on my plate, I slanted a look at him.

'So? Why did you leave and why was Aeona so angry?'

Kieran placed his wineglass on the white tablecloth.

'Because Tordal set too light a guard around her and Owain's men found her. Owain's spies told him Aeona was the source of Tordal's success on the field. She and her child – our child – were taken by his men. Aeona was told she must help Owain as she had Tordal. She refused, because that would have meant killing me.' Kieran's eyes glittering like diamond chips. 'So Owain's captain murdered the baby.'

I gasped. 'But that's impossible! Calain's alive.'

SEVENTEEN

Can Erin do it, Logan?

Yes...at least she says she can.

Alla buon'ora! I'll get the team assembled and call in reinforcements.

Why is this so important to you, Dante? Finding the headquarters, I mean?

We must retrieve Rowan.

That's not all, though, is it?

It's all that matters to you. Did Calain say anything more?

No. Maeve?

If she knows what he's hiding, she's not telling, either. I suspect she doesn't know.

Can we trust him? He was under Mors control for the last few years.

Now you sound like Rowan, my dear boy. You can trust me, at least.

Kieran directed a cold stare at me. 'Not Calain. Our daughter, Iseult.'

'Iseult? Your *daughter?*' I wrapped my arms around myself, barely able to take in his words. 'So Aeona...how did she get free of Owain?' I didn't want to hear the answer. I knew what it must be and the thought sickened me.

Kieran's lips stretched into a parody of a smile. 'She drained Owain's men and destroyed the building in which they held her.

Tordal and I were leading a force to find her when we met her coming back.' He swirled the liquid in his glass. 'I regret to this day I didn't stay with her after that. I may have been able to change her thinking, had I done so. But I fell into grief and took vengeance on as many of Owain's men as I could find, leaving Aeona to find her own path through anguish. She never really recovered.' He lifted his eyes to mine again. 'She buried the anger deep. It burned a slow, hateful fire in her that poisoned our love and our lives.'

'But she said you'd left because the Dark gene had corrupted you.'

He shook his head. 'No. As I said, the gene doesn't necessarily make each carrier into a megalomaniac. Tordal had long since taught me how to control the…impulses arising from the gene's influence. No.' He sighed. 'I left because I could no longer stand to see Aeona tearing herself apart with her obsession. I went back to find Calain, but he'd left the Williamson's home and I had no way of tracking him. So…' He shrugged. 'I travelled. As far around the world as I could go. But I could never escape the pain. Eventually I returned to England and Ireland to see if I could help my people.'

'And Aeona? What did she do while you were gone?'

'I don't know the details, of course, for she died while I was away.' He covered his eyes briefly. 'But I know she tried to use her gift against humans. There were reports of whole villages, dead of unexplained causes.'

'That makes no sense,' I protested. 'She could have just gone back with Tordal if she just wanted to kill humans en masse.'

'Indeed.' Kieran inclined his head. 'But she blamed Tordal for not guarding her and Iseult well enough. And she was afraid of him. Of his ability to use the *torryl* against her. She would never return to him. I believe she indoctrinated Calain against him. I heard Calain killed him sometime in the sixteen hundreds. Pity. Tordal was one of the most gifted strategists I've ever met.'

'OK, stop,' I said, throwing my napkin onto the table. 'Just stop. I can't even…I just can't. This is too much to take in and I don't know whether to even believe you. I've met Aeona and that's my *father* you're talking about.'

'Yes.' Kieran leaned back in his chair, twirling the stem of his wineglass. 'But how well do you know either of them, really?'

I shoved up from the table and stalked away, staring out the window into darkness. Night had fallen and the street outside was hard angles, deep shadows, artificial lights, and people mingling and laughing as they hurried off to unknown destinations.

'But if Aeona was afraid of Tordal, and he could trace her through the *sianfath* when she used her gift, why would she risk using it against humans,' I asked, turning back to glare at him.

Kieran rose gracefully and strolled over to me.

'An excellent point.' He tapped his lips. 'Perhaps she did find a way to counter the *torryl* after all, and never told me. She did spend several months with her sister before joining me in Lothien. And Mairi was a skilled technician. Always seeking new techniques and ideas for using sidhe abilities. Perhaps they found a way?' He smiled gently.

I could always go back and ask her; confirm his words. But bone-deep weariness ate at me from the inside. I sighed and scrubbed at my face.

'I'm tired. I can't think straight.'

Kieran bowed. 'Of course you are, my dear. I apologise. There's a room for you right through there.' He pointed at a narrow door set into a corner of the room. 'I'll have Finn bring you fresh clothing and whatever else you might need.'

'Not him,' I blurted.

'Ah, of course. You've heard about the tragedy of his wife's death.' Sadness aged him. 'Unfortunately, that's true. But the imbalance caused by his Dark gene had gone untreated, so he's hardly to blame. He is safe now, I assure you. And not a day goes by he doesn't regret his action, and the loss of his son.'

I said nothing. It all sounded so plausible. If he was lying, he was extremely good at it.

He indicated the corner door. 'Your room. I'm afraid it's not spacious, and there are no windows – but you understand.'

I folded my arms. 'I'm a prisoner? What happened to the hand of trust?'

He inclined his head. 'It goes both ways, my dear. Thus far you've done nothing to earn mine.'

That stung but I said nothing because it was undeniable.

He led the way to the door and paused in the act of turning the ornate iron handle.

'By the way, do you know the exact wording on Mairi Silverblade's prophecy?'

'Why?' I flicked him a quick, assessing look.

Kieran opened the door and revealed a narrow, wrought-iron spiral staircase leading up into darkness. He flipped a switch and a warm yellow glow lit the stairs from above.

'Because I've often wondered...' He stared off into middle distance. 'No, nevermind. It doesn't matter.'

'What?' Even though he was probably just manipulating me, I couldn't suppress my curiosity.

'Mairi died many years ago, I understand?'

I nodded. '1415. In Lothien. She removed the barriers you'd put into Calain's mind that held back Aeona's memories.' I shuddered at the memory of her burning. 'She was burnt at the stake.'

'Ah.' He sighed, shoulders slumping. 'I'm sorry to hear that. She was a kind person.'

'But what does her death have to do with anything?'

'Does her prophecy contain any specific dates?'

'Only Calain's birth year, why?'

He shrugged. 'I just thought I recalled Aeona saying Mairi's visions were only of things that happened during her lifetime, not beyond. But I was probably mistaken. After all, Calain was born when she lived. It was a long time ago. Sleep well.'

He turned away then back again. 'I forgot – your phone won't work in your room.' He indicated the walls. 'Something to do with signal strength.'

'Do you expect me to believe that?' I almost laughed.

'Not at all.' He chuckled. 'But we've done so well being polite. Goodnight…granddaughter.'

I stepped through the door then paused. 'It says: *And in the year of our Lord 1403 a key shall be born in the realm of the three crowns. In the embrace of the sianfath and the unity, that key may be the deliverance of those that dispossess the Ruadhán Daoine sidhe.*'

Kieran stilled, his expression abstracted. 'The deliverance… Interesting. Thankyou.' He flashed me a smile and closed the door behind me. The lock snicked.

I stood with my foot on the bottom stair for a long time, just staring at the door. Why had I told him? I didn't trust my own father but, after two hours, I trusted Kieran enough to tell him the prophecy that might bring his kind down? I must be insane.

Swearing under my breath, I climbed the tight staircase and emerged into a small attic-room. A sloping timber-lined roof and solid walls offered no chance of escape. The creaking timber floor meant anyone below would know where I walked, no matter how lightly I trod. Even the tiny ensuite bathroom had only a flue for ventilation. With no desk or chairs, my only option was to lie on the narrow, iron bed. It squeaked beneath me with each movement.

I pulled out my phone. No signal. I had no way to charge it and the battery was at only forty-five percent. I shut all the background apps and switched the phone off to conserve power in case I got a chance to call or text Logan.

A test of my range for standard telepathy yielded no results. Either I wasn't doing it right, or Kieran had some way to block me, or Logan and the others were beyond my telepathic range. That left only my ability to slide through the *sianfath* to find them. But I was reluctant to attempt it with Kieran close by. His first two cuts into my soul were agonisingly clear in my memory. It might be my imagination, but I felt incomplete now.

Was that why I'd told him Mairi's vision? Because Kieran now controlled me to some extent? I shivered and pulled the thick blankets up. There didn't seem to be any other explanation for doing something so dumb. What else could he compel me to do?

Or was I overthinking it? Kieran didn't seem the villain I'd been expecting.

So far, he hadn't lied to me – at least, not that I could tell. But Calain, Maeve, Dante, and even Logan all had lied. Why hadn't Calain told me who Dyson was? He'd said Dyson was persuasive; that sidhe he'd released believed Kieran to be a great leader. Was Calain worried Kieran would persuade me to join his cause? Buy why? Could it be that Kieran was in the right?

Was it possible I'd fallen into the wrong side of this war, right from the start? After all, I only had Maeve's word that the Mors and the Dark sidhe were even the enemy in this. If they weren't, what did Maeve and the others *want?*

They wanted to use me. But for what? Did Mairi Silverblade's vision hold some clue?

I considered it again, rethinking each word, checking the translation from *Henath* to be sure I had it right. Kieran's response had been underwhelming. 'Interesting', he'd described the word 'deliverance'. And he was right: either Maeve or Ian – I couldn't remember which – had said Mairi's visions were restricted to happenings in her lifetime.

So how could Mairi have predicted Calain's being the *ocair* in some great event six hundred years in the future? Was it possible Aeona and Mairi had concocted the whole vision? For whose benefit?

The question hung in my mind, unavoidable; the answer inevitable.

Mine.

If Aeona was fixated on destroying humanity, then the vision could only be aimed at me. My visit to her would have told her two things: she was no longer alive in my time; and I had her abilities. Which made me the perfect candidate to eliminate humans on her behalf.

But how? How could just working with Calain and Dante achieve that?

Unless... I sat up in bed, staring wide-eyed at the blank walls. Unless their plan to uncurl human DNA to allow re-connection with the *sianfath* was a lie. That would explain why Calain had sounded so surprised when Michael survived. Calain, Maeve and Dante – they'd all expected Michael to die.

Which put a dark slant on Dante's appearance in my mind at that crucial time. Why pick that moment – when Maeve was deep in the delicate telekinesis of uncurling the DNA – to insist I open myself to the *lorntinn?* Unless doing so would put me and my gifts wholly under Dante's control. Or perhaps he'd been trying to distract and goad me into making a mistake, allowing Maeve to test their experiment while making Michael's death look like an accident. Then, if they could convince me it was an accident – that humans would survive the process – they could set up the bigger run-through under the guise of uncurling human DNA en masse. And use me to kill millions of people.

I leaned forward and held my head. No. Surely that couldn't be right?

I fell back onto the bed, tears burning hot paths down my cheeks.

Who did I believe?

The blare of sirens, muffled by stone walls, woke me an unknowable time later. The bedlight was still on but there was no way of telling whether it was night or day. My body felt heavy and soft, as though not yet ready to face the day. I switched off the light, but my brain had woken up and wouldn't rest. The same endless, unanswerable questions revolved in my head until I felt like screaming.

I flicked the light on and checked the time on my phone. Five-forty am and twenty percent charge. Still no signal. No point in trying to sleep.

At the foot of my bed lay a towel and a pile of clothing that hadn't been there when I went to sleep. Someone had snuck into the room quietly enough not to wake me. I shivered and slipped down the narrow staircase. The door was locked from the outside. I shot home the inside bolt before returning to shower in the tiny ensuite.

I dressed in the jeans and utilitarian white tshirt provided then slipped on my leather jacket and considered my arsenal. My throwing-knives were lost in the Stibbert Museum. All I had was the boot knife, the katar, and my curved karambit. The katar, after a bit of modification to my throwing-knife belt, slipped into that. The belt went around my hips, under the baggy shirt. The karambit tucked back into the special sheath sewn into the front of my bra. A cursory pat-down should let it pass for underwire. Maybe.

Under the other bra-cup, the underwire was specially-modified to be lockpicks. Hopefully the lock on this door wasn't another clunky medieval one. Slipping the two slim pieces of steel free, I tiptoed across the creaking floor and down the staircase. I drew back the bolt and smiled. The lock was modern and not a deadbolt. Easy.

It was the work of minutes to torsion and rake the pins until they fell into place. Should have taken less time, but I was out of practice. The mechanism clicked free and the handle turned. I eased the door outward and peered into Kieran's cosy space. Cold, empty and lit only by the faint glow of dawn through the windows. The cat, curled up in one of the chairs, cracked an eyelid at me but didn't move.

I slipped into the room and spent a few minutes investigating every possible exit, but there were none. The windows were both un-openable and on the third storey of a sheer wall. The only other door was the one leading to the main office. If there was a secret exit, it was a good secret.

I paused before the door into the office and squared my shoulders. Nothing ventured, nothing gained. I tried the handle. It twisted beneath my palm and I stepped boldly into the office. There was no point sneaking.

The room was unchanged. Every desk occupied, every screen alight with quickly-changing images. A low murmuring of voices issued instructions to invisible agents out in the world. No-one paid me the slightest attention. I stepped again, watching them. Still nothing.

Were they all blind and deaf?

Or, perhaps, I wasn't a prisoner.

EIGHTEEN

<If we're going to do this, we shouldn't wait any longer, Dante.>

I don't have enough people for support, yet. This is important. I don't want to lose this chance.

<She may not be there, you know.>

I know, Madre. But I have to hope.

<It's been months, Dante. Focus on here and now.>

With my head high, I strode confidently to the exit, avoiding eye contact with the Mors agents seated at each desk. No one protested.

'Ah.' Kieran's voice halted me within a metre of the door to the stairs. 'There you are.'

I turned, grinding my teeth as I pasted a smile on.

He strolled across from one of the far desks, amusement lurking in his pale eyes. Dressed in an immaculate dark blue suit, red tie and white shirt, only the smoothness of his gait and the sharpness of his cheekbones gave away his non-human origins.

Finn glanced up from where he leant over one of the phone operators. He nodded politely to me, but his grey eyes held a disquieting glimmer of ironic enjoyment. Dressed in jeans and a grey shirt, he looked so much like Logan my heart skittered.

Kieran reached me and bowed with old-world courtesy. 'I trust you slept well?'

I shrugged. 'What do you want from me, Kieran?' I hadn't meant to be so blunt, but I was tired of being kept in the dark, literally and metaphorically.

He straightened and looked down his nose before softening into a rueful smile. 'Then again, there are times when you are nothing like Aeona and that always comes as a surprise. I still find the modern manners of women a little confronting.'

'Equality's a bitch, huh?' I retorted, stung.

'No, indeed,' he returned, 'but rudeness is. Come.' He placed one hand in the small of my back, then indicated the study from which I'd just come. 'Let's have breakfast.' He withdrew the katar blade from my knife-belt and inspected it.

'Hey!' I reached for it, but he kept it out of my grasp.

'What a singularly lovely blade,' he murmured. 'Original 17th Century, I believe. However, you won't need it here, I promise.' He returned it and showed his back, heading for the study.

I hesitated, Calain's instructions ringing in my ears. If I killed Kieran now I could end the war between the Mors and the sidhe – assuming I believed Maeve and Calain's version of history. But if Kieran was being truthful, then killing him could set the safety of the sidhe back a hundred years. In his absence, someone with a real anti-sidhe agenda would take his place as leader of the Mors Ferrum.

Kieran paused beside a desk and murmured something to the woman sitting behind the screens. She turned blank green eyes on him and nodded without speaking. She rose from the desk and glided past me, devoid of expression. It was the woman I'd seen yesterday. The dark rim around her eyes spoke of sidhe heritage, but I felt none of the usual shock of recognition indicative of sidhe blood.

'Come,' Kieran waved me onwards. 'Nes will bring us breakfast and we can discuss your contribution to our cause.'

I followed him into the room and sat at the same small table we'd shared for dinner. He made no mention of my door being open and I wasn't going to bring up the subject of lockpicks.

The door opened and the woman, Nes, entered, carrying a loaded tray. She slid it onto the table and stood to silent attention, staring straight ahead.

'That's all, Nes,' Kieran said. 'Thankyou. Return to your watch.'

She spun on her heel and exited, still without speaking.

I watched her leave. 'Is she mute or something?'

Kieran poured coffee from a silver jug into a tiny cup. 'No, why?'

'She just doesn't seem…normal.' I sipped the espresso and gasped at the strength. I normally drank cappuccino.

He set a silver plate cover aside and picked up cutlery before answering. 'She's sidhe.' He took a bite of scrambled egg, watching me from beneath lowered lids. 'And *demenath.*'

I gasped and coughed, choking on a mouthful of espresso. '*Demenath*, as in…?'

A forkful of mushrooms went the way of the egg before he answered this time. 'Yes, I have her soul in keeping.'

My appetite vanished and I pushed the plate aside. 'Why?'

Kieran followed suit, patting his lips with snowy linen. Thoughtful, he leaned back, placing the napkin precisely in his lap and smoothing the cloth across his knees.

'She's sidhe, but without the dark gene, and she's been trained to resist brainwashing. So, when we captured her it was either this or kill her.' He smiled faintly. 'And I'm here to save our people, not kill them.'

'Captured her?' I folded my arms.

'She was part of a team breaking into one of our facilities. They kidnapped thirty of ours. We caught two of theirs. Hardly a fair trade.' He sipped his coffee. 'But she's a telekinetic with a long reach, and I find them most useful. So we kept her here to watch over our field agents.'

There were so many questions I wanted to ask but they stuck in my throat. Could she still think for herself? Was there a way to return her soul? Most of all I wanted to ask: Is that Nesim Kaya, Dante's wife? But I couldn't. If she was, and I told Kieran, he would have more leverage over Dante and I wasn't prepared to sell out my brother.

I held my tongue and picked up the fork again, eating with intent, rather than pleasure.

When we finished breakfast, Kieran leaned back and watched me from beneath drooping eyelids. I sipped too-strong espresso and tried to appear relaxed.

'So,' I said, setting aside the tiny cup, 'what do you want from me?'

Kieran spread his hands. 'I want the war to end between the Dark and the Ruadhán sidhe. I want our people to be united. I want the humans to stop destroying the *sianfath*.'

'That sounds…reasonable. What's my part in that grandiose plan?'

'First tell me what Maeve, Calain and Dante intended to do to fulfil the prophecy?'

I rolled my eyes. 'You know I'm not going to tell you.'

'Because you're still loyal to them? No, I suspect it's because you don't actually know.' He laughed. 'None of them know, do they?' He rose and strolled slowly around the room, hands clasped behind his back. 'Calain has carried this knowledge with him for five hundred years and not yet worked out how to bring it to fruition? Perhaps I overestimated him.'

I stayed silent, watching.

'Well,' he said, lifting his chin, 'let me tell you what I believe should happen.'

I waited and he continued.

'I believe returning to humans the ability to sense the *sianfath* would solve most of our problems in one blow, don't you?' He pointed at the office door. 'And the package from Eisen tells me which gene we need to reactivate to allow that.'

I froze, trying my level best to keep my expression bland.

Kieran considered me. 'But your reaction tells me you have already considered this action. It would take immense power and I suspect you're the only one who could provide it. Ah...' He threw his head back and laughed. 'Of course. *That's* why Maeve and Dante have cultivated you so assiduously. If Calain is the *ocair,* then you're the *sianfath,* and that would make, who...Dante?...the *lorntinn.* He does seem to have a gift for creating teams who willingly sacrifice themselves for him.'

I studied my own fists, clenched in my lap. He guessed too accurately and read even my silences too well.

Kieran crouched before me, gripping the arms of my chair, caging me. I shied back.

'What can I do to convince you, my dear, I want what's best for our people? What will make you help me?'

'If you're being honest,' I said, 'then I need to know that changing human DNA won't kill or harm them.'

'Very well,' he said. 'How?'

'Let me call Dante. We tried it. On Michael Eisen.'

Kieran stilled, his brows lifting. 'Indeed. Ruthless of you, my dear. I'm all admiration.'

'Not my idea. Sorry to disappoint you.'

'Why do I sense it didn't go as planned?'

'Because it didn't. He's catatonic. I...hold his soul.' I lifted my chin. 'Let me return it so I can make sure he'll survive the procedure.'

Kieran frowned and rose, stroking his chin as he strode to the window. 'But Dante has his body, I assume. So what do you propose I do?'

I joined him. In the grey dawn, just a few early-rising tourists straggled through the empty streets below, clutching coats close against the morning chill, laughing, intent on devouring every tidbit of history from the ancient city's banquet.

'An exchange,' I said.

'You for Michael? Why would I do that?'

I shook my head. 'Nes for Michael.'

'Nes?' He blinked at me and I shrugged, glad I'd been able to surprise him.

'Show me how you return her soul, so I can learn the technique,' I said. 'Then give her back. I'm assuming she was one of Dante's people, so he'll agree. He values his team and dislikes Michael.'

'I see,' he eyed me shrewdly. 'And you gain the knowledge you seek and the assurance humankind will survive. A wise negotiation, my dear. Agreed. Come.' He headed for the office door. 'You may use one of our landlines to contact your brother and arrange the exchange.'

'Where at, though?'

'Not here,' he smiled. 'I'm not so trusting as to give away our headquarters location. The Piazza of the Palazzo Vecchio. Even at this hour it will be populated and safe enough for both parties. Tell them to bring their vehicle as close as is allowed and we'll meet them.' He strolled over to a city map of Florence, hanging on the wall, and pointed to a street. 'Here.'

'Logan.'

'Rowan! Where are you? Are you alright? Has he hurt you?'

'No. Shut up,' I said. 'Bring Michael to the piazza outside the Vecchio. Kieran's agreed to an exchange.'

'You?' The hope in his voice almost undid my calm.

'No. A sidhe of Dante's team.'

'No deal, then.' His tone hardened, implacable.

'Logan don't argue with me. Just do it. This is important.'

'Why?'

'I can't tell you. Just…trust me.'

There was a long, tense pause. I wanted to communicate privately with Logan, but there was no way. Kieran was able to hear my ordinary telepathy and cut through my *sianfath* connection. Ironic that, in a telepathic race, my only hope was through verbal communication.

'Alright,' Logan said. 'In forty-five minutes, exactly.'

'Just Dante and Michael. No-one else.'

'What? No. You can't expect—'

'Stop. It's the only way.'

He said nothing for a long moment, then cleared his throat. 'Rowan, is my…father…?'

'He's here. But you stay out of this, Logan. He's been cured. His Dark gene is under control.'

Logan swore.

I chose to ignore that and ploughed on. 'Did you give my ring to Erin?'

'Yes,' he said. 'She said thank you and she'll treasure it. She said…' his voice broke, 'it will always connect her to you – especially on the fifteenth of July.'

I hung up, trembling as I put the phone back in its cradle.

When I straightened, Kieran was considering me thoughtfully. 'Did I have things wrong, my dear? The link I severed was between you and the young man. But you gave your ring to another?'

I sucked a breath and sighed. 'We're close. Like sisters. But we've been arguing a lot and I needed her to know I loved her.' I lifted my chin. 'After all, I had no idea if I was going to live through the night.'

'And the fifteenth of July?' Kieran's mind brushed against my shields, testing the door to my public mind. I held firm.

'Her birthday,' I said. 'We'd planned a trip. She doesn't think I'll be coming back for it. That's what the message meant. She'll remember me.'

Kieran paused so long my heart pounded and I fought to keep a calm expression. Finally, he inclined his head and swept an arm at the exit. I resisted the urge to sigh in relief.

'Let us proceed, then,' he said. 'Nes. Attend me, please.'

The wall-clock read six-fifty. Which meant, if I'd understood Logan's message, I had just twenty-five minutes – until seven-fifteen – to decide who to ally myself with; who was telling me the truth.

The green-eyed sidhe rose from her desk and joined us, her blank expression eerie.

Kieran touched her wrist and motioned me closer. 'Watch as I return her soul. Finn?' The sidhe nodded and pulled out a dart gun. He trained it on Nesrin's back. Three other men stood close behind the sidhe woman.

'What the hell?' I glared at Kieran.

'A precaution. She'll be…disorientated when she's restored to her normal self. Her last memory will be of her forcible separation from her companions.'

I hesitated but couldn't see an alternative. I joined him in the *sianfath* and watched. He withdrew a shining silver-green globe from the depths of his thoughts and approached what I assumed was Nesrin's thought-shield. It had the appearance of an abandoned concrete bunker; a cube of crumbling concrete and rusted reo-bars, like something from World War Two. What sort of upbringing had she had to make that her safe-house? Kieran opened the bunker's front door and tossed the globe in like a grenade. There was a flash of greenish non-light within the structure. Fallen bricks and broken concrete reassembled themselves. The illusion of decrepitude vanished and the bunker took on a more solid appearance.

That's it?

#Well, it does take a little practice to get the door open, and their inmost shield must also be open to receive it. But you have the ability to walk through shields. You shouldn't have a problem.#

Is that how you can hear people's private conversations? You've learned how to open a door?

#Ah, I can't give away all my secrets, my dear. Shall we go?#

I retreated to the real world.

Something struck my forehead and pain flowered. I staggered back, half-blinded, and snatched the bootknife out. I wiped at my eye with the back of a wrist. Blood.

'Who are you? Where am I? What have you done to my team?' Nesrin struggled in the grip of three human men, her strength almost besting theirs. She glared at me and at Kieran.

'Dart her,' Kieran said. The sound of the shot reverberated in the enclosed space. Nesrin sagged, the curses blurring on her tongue.

Kieran touched my forehead. 'I do apologise, my dear. She was quicker than my man expected.'

'It's fine,' I said. 'OK if I heal myself?'

'My dear girl,' he said gently, 'you don't have to ask my permission. Just draw from outside my people.'

I checked the clock again. Seven a.m. Fifteen minutes. It was now or never. If I wanted to side with Kieran, all I needed to do was stay here in this fortified building and Dante's team would never be able to reach me. If I wanted to side with Logan, I needed to get Kieran outside, now.

NINETEEN

<What if she's leading us into a trap?>

-We won't know until it's sprung, Maeve.-

<Ooh – you're just as frustrating as ever, Calain Gilmore.>

-So I understand. Come. Dante's men are in position. Use thy telekinesis to aid them.-

I touched my forehead again and rubbed the blood between my fingertips, staring at it abstractedly. The steel blade in my right hand glinted, ominous. Who did I believe? Was Kieran the monster Calain and Maeve made out, or was that one more in a string of Maeve's lies? I glanced around the operations room, straining to hear the murmured conversations of Kieran's men as they oversaw the Mors Ferrum field agents. Once again I heard, over and over, the term 'standby for activation'. Activation of what? Who?

An uncomfortable, all-too-familiar pressure built in the back of my skull. I clenched my teeth to hold back a groan and clamped down on the urge to warn Kieran. My premonitions always seemed to mean danger to me. But would it come from Kieran, or from Dante and his team?

Dammit. There was no way of knowing, yet I had to decide.

In my pocket, my phone vibrated silently with the signal I'd received a text.

I straightened and found Kieran watching me, enigmatic. Holding out my bloodied fingers I nodded at the bathroom door in one corner.

'Mind if I clean up?'

Kieran inclined his head.

Silence followed me as I strode to the bathroom. My heart thudded. I waited for a yell, a shot, a warning. Nothing. I closed and locked the bathroom door, leaning on it as I yanked my phone free. Five percent battery and no signal again. I thumbed the message icon.

Message in back of book reads: "Riposte. Inner canst not hold against blood." That's all. Hope that helps. Lv Tom.

I stared at the message in disbelief. Riposte was a fencing term, but I had no idea exactly what it meant. What the hell? Inner what? How was that helpful against the *torryl*? Had Aeona found a way to counter it or not? Was she just using me as a tool, or was Kieran?

I checked the time. Seven ten. I was out of time. I had to decide now. The phone screen went black.

Soft footsteps sounded on the parquetry floor outside the bathroom. I rushed to the sink, lay the dagger aside, and washed my face. I drew a tiny amount from passers-by outside the building and healed the cut on my forehead.

After staring at my pale image for several seconds, I closed my eyes briefly and swore.

I grabbed the dagger, opened the door and returned to Kieran's side.

'Let's go get Michael. If we're going to do this, we'd best do it fast and discreetly. As you said: tourists.'

Kieran indicated the path between the desks to the exit. Two humans, Finn, and three sidhe fell in with us. Two more carried Nes. All wore sidearms and moved with the smooth, balanced stride of trained martial artists. As we exited the operations room, Kieran nodded to a woman who sat at a desk next to the door. She pushed a button on her keyboard and spoke into her microphone. More reinforcements? I had to assume Kieran would expect Dante to bring more than just Michael along to this exchange. So how many?

Logan would come with Dante, Calain, and possibly half a dozen or more of Dante's team. And Erin would probably be there, given she was the psychometric and would be using my ring to find me. What about Maeve? Would they bring her for her telekinetic powers, or would she refuse to take the risk?

Kieran's people clustered close as we descended the narrow spiral staircase, crossed through the library and down the broad, white marble steps to ground level. Even the humans moved with uncanny silence; only the occasional swish of cloth or scuff of a shoe on stone indicated their presence. The human closest to me had neglected to put on deodorant and the fear-stink of his sweat betrayed his unease.

I flexed my fingers around the boot-knife as we approached the door to the world outside. The pressure in my skull increased and I ground my teeth in an effort not to groan and wince.

'Once we're in the street,' Kieran said, his voice low and calm, 'I want three in front and three behind us at all times. It's unlikely they will keep the agreement and send Michael with one man.' He met my swift, frightened glance with irony. 'If we are attacked aim to kill but try to keep it discreet. Even this early there will be a police presence in the piazza. I can blind up to fifty humans to our activities, but no more.'

I hid my surprise as best I could but the twitch of his mouth said I'd given it away. Could he blind people literally, or did he just mean some sort of illusion; like the glamour all sidhe could cast to make themselves appear more human? I nodded, as though in agreement, and focussed my attention streetwards as the door opened.

Two sidhe stepped out, scanned the street and waved us to join them.

Outside, the cool morning air carried the faint scent of old alcohol and garbage. Morning sun fingered sly, pale beams between close-crowded medieval stone buildings and glistened off the new-washed, rounded cobbles underfoot. I shivered and flipped up the collar on my jacket as the pressure mounted in my head and my body trembled.

'You seem ill-at-ease, my dear,' Kieran murmured, studying the street. 'Do tell me why?'

'Yes.' The word forced itself from between my lips. 'Th...there's something...wrong.' I couldn't prevent the admission. I bit the inside of my cheek. Normally I could stop myself blurting out premonitions. Why was I speaking now?

Kieran slanted an amused glance at me. 'I suspected as much. Where are they?'

I sucked a hissing breath, half-blinded by the pressure and the effort of not spilling all my suspicions. 'Don't...know. Close.'

He sighed and signalled his people. They shuffled us into an alley that offered protection on two sides, at least. Beside me a darkened glass shop window reflected only my distress and the backs of the men and women guarding me.

Kieran leaned in, his lips close to my ear. 'How did they find us? Tell me.'

I bit my lip and tasted blood, but to no avail. The words spilled free. 'Erin Fairchild. Psychometric. The ring.'

'Ah!' He straightened. 'You really should have trusted me. I hate to have to kill more sidhe, but you're leaving me no choice.'

'Don't,' I grated. 'Don't hurt them. It's me you want, not them.'

'You're so wrong, my dear,' he whispered.

I thrust the dagger at his gut. His fingers wrapped like cold steel around my wrist and halted my blow with frightening ease. He twisted my wrist. Tendons and bones snapped in a sickening series of little pops. Pain lanced through my arm. I screamed and sank to my knees on the wet cobbles. The dagger clattered to the ground.

'Guard her,' he ordered. 'Dart her if she tries to escape.'

A silenced shot *phutted* nearby. Glass shattered behind me and I flinched, covering my head. Dark figures leapt from nowhere and attacked Kieran's men. I knelt in the midst of chaos, one hand useless, afraid to draw from the *sianfath* and heal it lest Kieran cut me to the core. All around, glass lay in glittering shards and crunched beneath booted feet.

A hoarse scream sounded and a black-clad body fell heavily on the ground in front of me. I snatched a silenced nine-mil from his lifeless grip and held it awkwardly in my left hand. Drawing a slow breath I tried to steady my heart. Pain throbbed through my broken wrist. The melee of flying fists and struggling bodies pressing close made it difficult to tell friend from foe. Kieran's white head appeared, then vanished before I could line him up.

Two men, struggling for possession of a gun, staggered and fell into me, knocking me off my knees and to the ground. The gun flew from my grip. I tucked into a half-roll and gasped as pain from my broken wrist whited out the world. Another silenced shot went off near my head. A body fell on mine, weighing me down. I shoved it aside and the dead man flopped onto his stomach, staring back at me in silent accusation. Blood darkened the cobbles. One of Dante's men.

Glass cut into my cheek. I had to heal myself. Had to take the risk. Kieran couldn't focus on me and all of this at the same time. A siren sounded in the distance. Nearby, a shout went up, followed by a scream and another shot.

'Sister!' A bloodied hand appeared in my vision.

'Dante!' I let him haul me upright. My right arm hung limp. Blood dripped into my eye from a fresh cut on my forehead.

Dante assessed me. 'Heal yourself. Draw from the Mors.'

'I can't,' I said, teeth gritted against pain and a lump of fear in my throat. 'Kieran...Dyson is here. He'll cut at me if I use the *sianfath.*'

He swore and drew me further into the alley, away from the worst fighting. 'Where is he?'

I peered over the combatants. 'I can't see him. Dante, his name isn't Dyson. He's Kieran Ivaldison – our grandfather and Calain's father.'

'What?' Dante directed astonishment to me. 'How...No.' He cut off his own words. 'There's no time. We must get you away.'

'I don't think it'll be that easy.'

Dante studied the street. Six of Kieran's men lay, crumpled and bloodied, in the street. Dante shrugged.

'My people have it under...' He stared off into middle distance and swore. 'You're right. There are more. A lot more.'

'We must find Kieran.'

'No,' Dante said, 'it's more important to get you out of here.'

I gripped his arm. 'You don't understand! He has Nes, your wife. She was my bargaining chip but he sensed the trap.' I scanned the bodies on the ground. 'She's not here. He must still have her.'

He hesitated, frowning. Logan and Calain appeared from around the corner, both bloodied but alive. Logan wrapped his arms around me, half-lifting me off the ground. I stifled a cry of pain and he released me.

'I thought I'd lost you,' he murmured.

I leaned into him, breathing in the warmth of his skin and basking in the reassuring touch of his mind. 'Where are we?'

'The Palazzo dell'Arte della Lana — the ancient wool guild building right in the middle of Firenze.'

I glanced up at the three storey medieval stone structure and shivered.

'Dante,' Logan said, 'let's get out of here before they return.'

Dante said nothing, his attention fixed on the building housing the Mors Ferrum.

'Dante?' Logan repeated.

I explained about Nes. 'And Finn's here somewhere, too.'

Logan blanched, the small muscles in his jaw working. 'He'll wait.' But he studied the Palazzo.

'If they've taken Nes back in there,' I said, 'we can't get her out. That place is like a fortress.'

Dante turned on me, intense. 'But you've been inside. You know the layout. This is closer than we've ever been. We *must* get in there.' He clutched at my arm and I winced.

Logan pushed Dante away from me. 'We can't. You taught me that. Nes knew the deal. We can't risk you, Calain, or Rowan.'

'There was a woman in a labcoat, too,' I offered. 'She went into a basement level. There must be more of ours in there; experiments. Maybe there's an underground entrance.'

Dante swallowed, haggard. 'Yes, the Mors often have those. But they're always barred and bolted and guarded from the inside.' He shook off Logan and strode down an alley to the back of the building. He stopped and pointed upwards.

'There.'

A narrow, arched flyover bridge connected the second story of the blocky Palazzo to the gothic Orsanmichele church behind.

I considered the bridge doubtfully. 'They wouldn't leave that unguarded. And you'd still have to get into the actual offices. It's impossible. There's a narrow, spiral staircase. A killbox. They can just stand at the top and pick you off. There's no other entrance.'

'Exactly.' Dante's mouth stretched into a mirthless grin. 'Which means if we blockade the front and back entrances, as well as the underground ones, then the only way they can get out is through that. And through the church. Then we'll have them.' His expression blanked as he communicated with the remainder of his team.

Calain appeared at the alley entrance and joined us.

'Are you mad, Dante? We have few enough left as it is. Your wife cannot be our priority.'

Dante rounded on his father and gripped his cane in both hands. Logan grabbed Dante's arm, his fingertips white.

Ominous pressure built in the back of my skull. I shoved between the men, snatching at Logan's wrist.

The sharp phutt of a silenced gun. Blood spraying across my face and Dante's. Logan's body, collapsing to the cobbles. Finn's twisted smile.

I cried out and pushed Logan. He stumbled sideways, clutching at Calain, who staggered under his weight.

Something punched my right shoulder. Blood spattered across Dante's chest. He gaped, reaching for me as I fell to my knees. A scarlet rivulet dribbled down the sleeve of my jacket and dripped onto the worn cobbles.

'Crap,' I muttered. The world sagged and twisted into surrealism. 'Dante, get Logan out of here. That shot was meant for him. Finn pulled the trigger.'

Dante crouched beside me. 'On Logan? Why?'

'Kieran knows I'd do anything to protect him,' I said, my voice fading with the world. 'He's trying to make me use the *skath-sheel* so he can cut my connection and make me *demenath*. Get out of here. All of you.'

'We're not leaving you.' Logan knelt beside me. He pressed a hand against my shoulder. 'Let's get her under cover.'

Calain and Dante slid their arms under me and lifted. I almost passed out with the pain. They carried me around the corner, hidden from the Mors building. The world blurred as they laid me on the cold cobbles and agony slashed through my body. Dante's eyes glazed again and he smiled grimly.

'We have all the exits under surveillance. We'll know if they try to escape.'

Logan lifted his palm from my shoulder and swore. 'It's bleeding too much. Draw from me and heal yourself.'

'I can't!' I moaned. 'Kieran will cut me the second I try. He's waiting for me to do that.'

'Dammit, Rowan!' Logan snapped. 'You can't keep rescuing me. Heal yourself. We'll take care of Kieran. You're going to bleed out.'

'Where's Erin?' I whispered. 'And Michael?'

'Two blocks away. In the car, with Maeve. Why?' Logan swept the quiet alley. Calain and Dante stood watch over me.

'Get them, and Calain and Dante away,' I said. 'He wants one of them for something. Get them all away. Then I'll heal myself.'

'There's no time,' Logan said. 'You're as white as a ghost.' He lowered himself to the ground and drew me close. 'Rowan...please! I can transfer some energy, but not fast enough to heal that.'

'Shit,' I said. He was right. Life drained from me every second I delayed. I had no choice.

I extended myself, sending thin tendrils creeping into the *sianfath* in the hopes Kieran wouldn't detect me. I wanted to drain his men, but couldn't tell who was who. Even within the Mors headquarters, green and orange life signatures intermingled in confusing chaos; impossible to distinguish and no way of knowing who was Kieran's victim, *demenath,* and who was on his side.

I left everyone inside the building alone. Draining even one would alert Kieran. Instead, I extended beyond Dante's team, into the piazza a few streets away. Even at this still-early hour, several dozen people swarmed outside the Vecchio, their pulsing, orange life a beacon and my saving.

Energy flowed into my body, healing and restoring. The bullet in my shoulder worked its way out and tinkled to the stones. Bones in my wrist knitted.

'Hurry,' Dante said. 'They're on the move. We must stop them. It's our best chance to break this organisation once and for all.'

I struggled to my feet, exhausted but physically in better shape. My clothes were sticky with blood and I'd lost my boot-knife somewhere.

'Give me a few more seconds,' I said, leaning on Logan's supporting arm.

Dante scowled. I opened my mouth to tell him to back off.

Kieran sliced through every thread of me. He cut close to the bone, hacking away my connection to the *sianfath*, leaving me breathless, limbless, blinded and writhing in agony as I tried to slam my innermost shields against him.

Then he tore out my soul.

TWENTY

Logan! Get her out of here.

What about you?

I must try to get Nes out. This may be my only chance.

You heard what Rowan said. Dyson wants one of us for something. You're the most likely candidate. I can't let you stay.

You have no choice. Get her away. That's an order.

I cowered, the merest fragment of me, behind the inner shield that hid my core and Calain and Aeona's memories. Kieran had taken most of me. He possessed my body. A shadow of thought was all that remained free. A beleaguered memory of self.

So I watched from within, helpless as Logan tried to coax me to run. My body remained motionless. Twenty Mors agents appeared and surrounded us. With guns trained on us, there was little Dante or Calain could do. More agents arrived, herding Erin, Maeve and four of Dante's people.

I railed against my self-imposed prison as we were marched back to the wool guild building. This time I was searched and my katar blade found and removed. Hope sparked when they missed the karambit, but I suppressed it. How much of my thoughts could Kieran hear?

How could I even be thinking? As my body followed Logan up the white marble stairs, I considered my situation. Somehow, I was able to think and reason, even if I couldn't control my body. Was it because I had locked myself into this room, with Calain, Aeona and my own deepest memories? Had keeping this deepest part of myself closed off – a thing most sidhe didn't do – somehow given me a way to keep part of my *enath* safe? If so, how could I use that?

Kieran had my body, but could I control my gifts?

We were marched up the spiral stairs, into the Mors headquarters. A large, central space had been cleared of desks. Kieran's men herded us into the middle. Logan held my hand but I couldn't move a muscle to respond to the reassuring squeeze.

The door opened again. Finn emerged, followed by Kieran – who carried Dante's leaf-headed cane – and by more of his men, then Mia, Erin and Maeve. Logan glared at his father and took a half-step in his direction. Calain restrained Logan with an arm across his chest. Finn laughed and saluted his son mockingly.

Two Mors agents carried Michael's body on a stretcher and laid him on top of a hastily-cleared desk. His chest rose and fell. A drip swung on a stand attached to the stretcher, the tube taped to the back of his wrist.

Erin clung to Maeve, both women pale and trembling. At some unspoken signal, the Mors separated Mia and the remaining four of Dante's team, leading them away. Mia glanced back twice. Dante shook his head.

'Wise words,' Kieran said, nodding to Dante. 'She will die if any of your people attempt escape. Keep your people under control and you may yet live, yourself.'

Dante's eyes widened. I groaned inside. I hadn't had a chance to tell him Kieran could hear private conversations. Logan must have forgotten to relay that piece of information; or Dante hadn't believed him.

Kieran turned Dante's cane, caressing the pale, golden timber and admiring the leaf-carved knob.

'Lovely craftsmanship. Rowan wood, isn't it? Ironic that rowan-wood was believed to deter the faery folk in the bad old days.' Kieran chuckled. 'Where did you get it?'

'From my father,' Dante grated.

'Your adoptive father, I presume.' Kieran pointed to Calain. 'Your real one wasn't around much, was he? Come, come. We all know who we are. Let's not pretend.' He nodded at me. 'Young Rowan here has been…helpful. Told me who you are, what you do…' He indicated Erin. 'And when you were about to spring your trap.'

All eyes shifted to me in horror. I stood, unmoving, drowning in anger and frustration, unable to defend myself. Logan released me. Then, after a moment, he re-entwined our fingers. I wanted, more than anything, to respond.

Slapping the cane's knob into his palm, Kieran paced around our huddled group. He stopped before Calain and examined him.

'I'm not fond of your new visage, son,' he said. 'But I understand how it came about. Well played, Maeve.' He inclined his head. She lifted her chin, but fear showed in the quiver of her lips.

'Now, follow me. All of you.' He led the way into his office. I followed, compelled, pulling Logan with me. The others trailed behind. Kieran's men carried Michael.

Once inside Kieran's sanctum, with the door locked, Kieran displaced the cat off a chair and sat. He waved a laconic hand at the couches and seats scattered around the room.

'Please, sit.'

Finn leaned against a wall, watching us from beneath half-closed eyelids, sardonic.

Calain drew himself up, his jaw working as he glared at his father. 'What's to stop us from killing you, right now?'

Kieran pointed at me. 'Her. She's my weapon, now.' His command arrived in my head and I was helpless to resist. I sent out tendrils of self into the *sianfath*, spearing them into the bodies of my friends, my lover, my family. And I drained all five to the point of unconsciousness. Their bodies hit the floor in a series of thuds that resounded in the silent room. Only I remained standing, throbbing with barely-contained sidhe power, aching to release it explosively into Kieran. Unable to do so.

He gave a new order and I returned the energy. Most of it. I cracked the door of my sanctuary open and drew a fraction into the darkness with me, holding it like a candle flame to guard against the monsters locked in with me. But the monster was me and no amount of light would protect the world, now.

Logan and the others staggered upright, groaning and clinging to each other. They left a wide gap between me and them. The Burmese cat strolled up the Erin and rubbed against her. Erin gathered the animal close, like a protective shield between her and me.

'What have you done to Rowan?' Logan said. 'She would never do that to us.'

Kieran pointed Dante's cane at Calain. 'Merely what you should have done. You had this girl in your control from childhood and you ran away. Let her grow up without any guidance. We could have saved our people a decade ago if you'd shown some backbone, boy. *She* is our key to success.'

Calain raised his chin. 'She's not a weapon. She's a young woman with the right to lead her life and make her own choices.'

'You *fool!*' Kieran rose in one fluid move. 'Don't you see what I can do, now?'

'What?' Calain stood toe to toe, the same height, but half again as broad in the shoulders and far more imposing. Yet, somehow, Kieran's gaunt intensity was more frightening.

Calain glared. 'What are you going to do? Tell us what your grand plans are. We're agog and breathless for your wisdom, father.'

'Sarcasm does not become you, son,' Kieran said.

'This was what you always wanted, wasn't it?' Calain's voice was low and hard. 'An admiring audience of loyal followers? That's why you left Mother, wasn't it? Because she was more powerful than you, but wouldn't use her gift to further your damned ambition.'

Kieran's mouth twisted. 'How little you know me. If I'd wanted to rule the world, I could have done it long before now.'

'So, what do you want?' Logan said. 'What's the point of kidnapping all the sidhe you have. Of the brainwashing. The release of the Dark gene. Of holding Rowan – and us – captive? What. Do. You. Want?'

'As I've said already, to Rowan,' Kieran replied, 'I want the sidhe to be safe. For the world to stop tearing itself apart. For our people to co-exist.'

'You're lying,' Dante said, thrusting forward. 'You want peace? Why then have your people tortured ours? Every single sidhe we've rescued from your laboratories has suffered horrifically. How do you justify that?'

Kieran looked down his thin nose. 'It was necessary for the greater good. When you live as long as I have, individual lives are less important than the species' survival. I've done what I had to.'

'And what, exactly, is the greater good?' Calain ground out. 'How are you intending to ensure our survival?'

Strolling over to the wooden side-cabinet, Kieran poured himself a scotch and stared meditatively at the eclectic collection of souvenirs on the shelves. He touched a small picture frame holding a folded square of grey cloth.

'I was hoping to use Rowan's gift to uncurl the DNA in humans and let them sense the *sianfath.*' He regarded Maeve and Calain shrewdly. 'But Rowan tells me you already attempted that, and this was the result.' He pointed at Michael Eisen's unconscious body, now laid out on the floor along one wall.

Maeve bit her lip, her cheeks flushing.

Locked inside my own shields, I thumped the door and groaned. I couldn't tell them. I should have said something before. Now there was no way of letting anyone know Michael still had a chance. That I held his *enath.*

'So,' Kieran continued, 'our only option is to switch off the Dark gene en masse, then convince all our kind to work together again. Think of how much more we could achieve if we were one people, instead of fighting amongst ourselves.'

In the shocked silence that followed, Logan and the others exchanged wordless looks ranging from disbelief to hope.

Kieran cleared his throat. 'You might as well speak aloud. I can hear your conversations. Your public-room shields are ineffective, I'm sorry.' He inclined his head. 'A little trick I learned from Aeona.'

Dante frowned. '*You* want to switch off the dark gene? How does that...?' His mouth pressed thin and bitter. 'I do not believe you. No one who has treated our people as you have, wants peace. Besides, the Mors have been switching the gene *on.*'

'No, no,' Kieran held up a thin hand. '*Michael Eisen* has been switching the gene on. That was his own private campaign, unknown to me. However the technology he discovered is exactly what we need.'

'What if he means it?' Erin grabbed at Dante's arm. 'What if he's just as sick of the fighting as we are? After all, he's a sidhe and he's in charge of the Mors Ferrum. He has the power to stop everything. Shouldn't we listen?'

'If you'd seen what I have,' Dante said coldly, 'you wouldn't think so.'

Kieran sighed. 'He has a point, my dear. I have had to use…somewhat drastic measures in my search for a solution. People…sidhe…have been hurt and I regret that. But sacrifices were necessary.' He studied at Calain and Maeve. 'You both know that. You've both made sacrifices, too. Your children, Maeve. Missing your daughter grow up, Calain; knowing her destiny.'

'Poor examples,' Calain growled. 'Both of those are the result of actions by the Mors Ferrum.'

Kieran glanced between Calain and Maeve. His lips twitched into a sympathetic smile. 'If you say so.' He waved his drink gently. 'The point is: my efforts, and Michael's, and yours have led to the revelation we need to alter our future. This is the culmination of Mairi's prophecy.' He indicated me. 'With Rowan's help, Calain, you have the ability to find Dark sidhe all over the world. With her power Maeve can alter their DNA, and Dante can weld them into the *lorntinn*.'

At Maeve's gasp, Kieran smiled again. 'Yes, Rowan told me the correct version of the prophecy, and that Dante and Calain are the other parts of it. She trusted me. Now you should, too. Together we can fix our species. Then we can put this world on a less destructive path.'

Logan pushed past Calain. 'If she trusted you, why is Rowan *demenath*? Why don't you free her to tell us herself?'

'A misunderstanding,' Kieran dismissed his objection. 'She believed I was going to hurt you. She felt turning on me was her only choice. I can understand how she feels.' He swept all of them with an amused look. 'After all, none of you have been open with her, have you? You've all been trying to use her for your own ends. So she trusts no-one.'

'And you aren't?' Logan shot back.

'Not at all, son,' he replied. 'I'm hoping she'll agree to help of her own accord. Once you have, she'll follow. I'm keeping her this way only until you agree. Then she'll be freed to help us.' He tilted his glass to me. 'If, of course, that's the best way to proceed.'

I listened intently. Could he be telling the truth? Surely not. He must know my first words would be to discredit him.

'That sounded remarkably like an ultimatum,' Calain said dryly.

'I do apologise,' Kieran returned. 'It was not so intended.'

'And what if she refuses to help?' Maeve said. 'As you say, she doesn't trust any of us.'

'A valid point.' Kieran tapped his lower lip and inspected each of my companions. 'But we know the importance of this. Are you prepared to leave the future of our race – of this world – to the whims of a stubborn child? As is, she will use her gift at my discretion.' He pointed at Dante and Calain. 'She's just the powerhouse. You two are the ship and the guide, respectively. Those roles require conscious decision-making.'

'You can't mean to treat Rowan like that!' Logan glowered. 'Like some sort of mindless slave.' He glanced from Kieran to Maeve, Dante, and Calain.

'We've been waiting for this moment a long time, Logan,' Maeve said. 'You know how she is. She'll find some ridiculous ethical reason to object. This could be our only chance.'

'You're seriously considering this? Remember what he's done to our people?' Logan pointed at Kieran. 'You can't trust him and you can't betray Rowan. Calain? You're her father.'

Calain scrubbed at the back of his neck. 'Aye lad, I am. But I've carried my duty as the *ocair* for longer than I've been a father. I have to do whatever I can to make our people safe.' He glanced at me and pain flashed through his eyes. 'Even if it means overruling Rowan's scruples. She's too young to understand the gravity of this.'

'I don't believe you people,' Logan said. 'I defended you – all of you – when Rowan feared and distrusted you. Looks like I was wrong.' He stalked to the other end of the room and stared out the window onto the street below.

I wanted to hug him, to thank him for standing up for me, pointless though it was. Calain, Dante and Maeve were wavering. I hated them for being willing to use me, but I also understood. All three had given hundreds of years to the pursuit of this one goal. To have it handed to them on a platter must be the deepest temptation.

And part of me wished it were true; wished it could all be that simple.

But a bigger part knew that trusting Kieran was a mistake. I just had no way of warning them.

TWENTY-ONE

Kieran sighed. 'I do understand your hesitation, son. I know you all have doubts. What must I do to convince you all of my sincerity?'

'You could start by returning my wife to me,' Dante said, his voice low and hard.

Kieran blinked at him. 'Your wife? I didn't know I had her. Who, pray tell.'

'Nesrin.'

'Ahhhh.' Kieran gave a satisfied sigh. 'That explains a great deal. Certainly. I'll bring her in. One moment.'

Inside, I groaned. How could Dante make such a stupid error of judgement? Now Kieran had yet another lever to use against us. In my head, I slumped against the door protecting me from Kieran.

You have to let me out.

I gasped. Michael Eisen stood before me, shadowed and insubstantial in the darkness of my innermost sanctum. Beside him hovered the bewildered half-shade of the environmental scientist I'd tucked away just a few days before.

I can't, Michael. I'm as much a prisoner in here as you are. I'm sorry. I have no power.

Yes, you do. He pointed at the environmentalist. *You have him. With the power you took from the others, one soul contains enough energy for you to break out of this. Then you can restore me and show them it works.*

I frowned. *I can't do that. I can't sacrifice him to save myself. I've already killed too many.*

He's already dead, Rowan, Michael said harshly. *And I think, being an environmentalist, he'd be happy to help us do something to save the whole damned planet.*

Us? I gaped at him. *Since when do you care?*

He grimaced. *Since you mucked around with my DNA. Dammit, girl! I can feel the sianfath crying out now. Even from here. As much as I hate to admit it, you were right. We humans have been blind. We need this.*

I buried my head in my hands. *I don't know how, Michael. And how can I trust you? If I restore you and you turn on us, what then?*

Well, you can't be much worse off than you already are, can you? He crouched before me. *I've made a lot of mistakes in my life, Rowan. And I regret many of them, now. I was wrong about Calain.* He pointed at the rows of doors holding Calain's memories. *I've had a bit of time here and I've checked some of those rooms. I found Calain's memory of the period when my parents died. He was telling the truth. Their death wasn't his fault. The Mors ordered it. Dyson...Ivaldison ordered it. Everything I thought was true for the last forty years of my life was a lie.* His bitterness was painful to see. *The only thing I got right was Paul and I have you to thank for his life. I owe you. And your family.* He passed a hand over his face. *And the whole damned sidhe race. Let me make it up to you.*

But I'm not sure even how to go about it.

Like I said. Just use the environmentalist to power your release and get me back to my body. I can distract Ivaldison so you can get free.

But he still has part of me. I'm just a shadow, myself. And if he forces me to draw power for Calain and Dante, I'll have more than enough to return you to your body.

No! Michael tried to grab my arm but his fingers passed through. *Ivaldison won't limit the power you draw. People will die. I won't be able to hang on here. I'll be carried with them into the sianfath in the cycling process. You don't have enough control to stop it. If you're going to convince the others Kieran's lying, you have to return me.*

I regarded him doubtfully. What he said was probably true, but was he just saying it because he didn't want to die? How could I tell? Wait. I straightened. Logan had once told me it was impossible to lie in our form of telepathy. So, assuming that wasn't a lie, Michael must be telling the truth.

Alright. I gestured to the environmentalist. Rico, his name was. My heart hurt as he approached. I took his insubstantial hand and channelled the extra power I'd stolen into him. His *enath* brightened. I turned to Michael. *I'm ready. What do I do?*

Can you duplicate what Ivaldison did and restore my enath?

I nodded.

Michael threw back his shoulders. *Then wait 'til he blends you with the others and starts making you draw power. If we're lucky, he'll be so focussed on supervising that part of your abilities he won't notice if we slip out.*

That's a lot of 'ifs'.

Your other choice is to stay in here and watch your world burn; your people and mine die in a war that will last generations.

His words were a cold slap.

'Come, my friends.' Kieran raised his glass in a silent toast to the sidhe and waved them to the decanter. Calain, after a moment's hesitation, poured himself a drink and swallowed it in one gulp. Dante joined him. Maeve accepted a glass and sipped at it, her gaze flicking between me and Logan. Erin refused. She edged closer and stood next to me, so close the heat of her body warmed my chilled arm.

The door opened and two sidhe entered, carrying Nesrin. They laid her on a leather couch and bowed themselves out. Dante hurried to her side and crouched, stroking her hair back.

'What's the matter with her?' He glowered at Kieran.

Kieran shrugged. 'I had her sedated. When she emerged from the *demenath* she was rather…disorientated and violent.'

'Emerged!' Logan spun from his brooding contemplation of the world outside the window. 'You really can restore an *enath?*'

'I said so before,' Kieran said. 'Once all this is over, I'll restore Rowan, as promised.' He indicated Nes. 'My gesture of good faith should reassure you I'm in earnest.'

With all attention on Dante and Nes, no-one watched me. Could I restore Michael now? I gathered myself.

'Rowan,' Erin whispered into my ear. 'If you can hear me, can you blink once for yes?'

I tried. I focussed all my concentration on the simple act of blinking and failed. Swearing I thumped on the door in my mind, unable to do more than listen.

'I don't trust him,' she continued, watching Kieran and the others. 'And I'm pretty sure you didn't either. I may not like the way you do things, but I know you had good reason not to trust Maeve…' She swallowed hard. 'And my father. You've got an outsider's view of us and it's clearer than ours. If you can hear me, tell me how to stop this.'

I said nothing; unable to respond.

'Child,' Kieran's tone sharpened. 'What are you doing? Leave her be.'

Erin snatched up my right hand and slipped the signet ring onto my middle finger. She raised her chin defiantly.

'Just returning her ring.'

Kieran's expression segued into the thoughtful. 'Ah, so you're Erin? Excellent. Come, child. I have a special task for you.'

Erin hesitated, but followed him to the knickknack-crowded shelf. Kieran picked up a small, ceramic unicorn and studied it.

'You'll need these,' he said, pointing at the shelves.

'What for?' Erin screwed up her nose and touched a broken plastic comb.

'These belong to the sidhe I need you to find first,' he replied, enigmatic. 'They…left our facilities and went their own ways. Each one has a key skill we'll need to help convince other sidhe.'

'What skill?' Calain approached, frowning.

Kieran lifted one shoulder. 'I call them "nodes". I'm not sure if there was a H*enath* word for them. People who are better than most at drawing others into the *lorntinn.*' He nodded at Dante. 'Much like you, but their gifts are less powerful. About two hundred are scattered all over the world and each one will serve as an amplifier and help us draw in others around them.'

Erin examined the bewildering array of things dubiously. 'I can only find one person at a time. How will that help?'

'But Calain, I understand, has the ability to find sidhe by their signature. Between the two of you, in the *lorntinn*, I'm confident you can connect with all these good folk.'

'And once they've connected all the sidhe?' Logan asked. 'What then?'

'Then Calain introduces himself as the *ocair.* Aeona Silverblade's son.'

'What's that going to achieve,' Erin scoffed. 'Most sidhe of my generation have never heard of either of them.'

With an urbane smile, Kieran inclined his head. 'Indeed. So it will be up to all of us to convince them. And to convince them to join with us.'

'How?' Logan asked. 'With the power of scintillating arguments? That seems, unrealistic.'

Kieran's smile widened. 'Leave that to me. I can sway them to our side. Once they are with us, Maeve and Rowan will switch off the Dark gene in those that have it.'

Dante, Maeve and Calain exchanged looks I had no trouble interpreting. Apparently neither did Logan for he growled, low in his throat, and backed away.

'I can't believe you're falling for this bullshit.' He returned to my side and folded his arms, glaring first at Kieran then at Finn. 'You can't trust them, Dante.'

'You're young,' Dante said. 'When you've been doing this as long as we have – seen as many friends die – then you can judge.' When Logan returned no reply, Dante continued, 'Very well, Ivalidison. We will assist. But first...' He pointed to the walking cane, still in Kieran's hands. 'Unless you would like to add piracy to your list of crimes, I'd like my property back. It is an heirloom.'

I started. Piracy? Why not theft? That was an odd phrase and it tweaked an elusive memory.

Kieran caressed the cane's golden length and fiddled with the ornate top, twisting and pulling at it. The cane's silvery celtic decoration gleamed in the dim lights. He slapped the wood twice into his palm, assessing Dante narrowly. Then he passed it back.

'We'll call it another gesture of good will.'

Dante accepted, tucked the cane under one arm and bowed. He extended a hand, which Kieran ignored.

'Let's get started,' Kieran said. He gestured to the couches and seats. 'Please make yourselves comfortable. This could take a while. Excuse me while I arrange for refreshments.' He strode to his desk, pressed a buzzer and spoke in a low tone to someone outside the room.

Dante sauntered over to Logan and me.

'I don't understand you, Dante,' Logan muttered. 'Maeve, I get. But you? How could you betray Rowan and me like this?'

'Shut up, Logan,' Dante snapped. 'Just stay out of this. I know what I'm doing.'

Logan snapped his mouth shut, scowling. Dante squeezed Logan's shoulder. Logan sucked a quick breath, his eyes widening a fraction before he schooled himself to neutrality again.

Dante gripped my arm, though his attention remained on Logan. 'Just keep an eye on her, will you?'

And something knocked on my innermost shield. I hesitated. Dante's hold on my arm tightened.

Kieran ceased talking to his people and stepped to the shelf of knickknacks, waving Erin forward. He gestured to Maeve, Calain and Dante.

The knock on my shield repeated, louder, faster. My hand was numb, so tight was Dante's hold. Piracy. The memory returned. Dante's signal to his team if there was trouble – the pirate flag. Was he trying to let me know he knew Kieran was trouble? Or was this just a test to see if I was truly under Kieran's control.

A third knock.

I opened the shield. Dante's shade thrust through the gap.

Excellent. I hoped you retained some self. We have but a second, sister. I can only hide this from Kieran because I'm touching you. He hasn't yet realised the extent of my abilities.

But I thought you could walk through shields at will?

I lied. I can't get through an inner shield. That is sacrosanct and can only be opened from the inside, by the owner. Though there is an old belief that fam...No, not important now. You must be ready.

For what? I can't do anything. Not while Kieran has my enath.

Leave that to me. If I can lay a hand on him, I can get into his shields unseen and retrieve it – as long as it's not behind his inner shield. Just wait for my signal. At the right moment, we'll distract Kieran.

You aren't going to do what he wants?

Calain and I made plans for many contingencies. His reply was evasive.

What are you going to do?

We'll go along with him to start with. But when the time comes, you'll have to trust me. Our success depends on you.

But even if I am free to act, Kieran will just cut me again.

We'll deal with that if it happens. He's coming. Get ready. Don't fight him.

But I—

And he vanished. His grip on my arm relaxed. With a nod for Logan he strolled to a seat next to his wife's prone form, sitting with elegantly-crossed ankles and a faintly-amused expression. Maeve and Calain took seats, dragging them closer to Dante and Nes until they formed a semi-circle facing me. They left a single chair, two paces in front of me, empty. Erin sent Logan a questioning look. He responded with a quick nod at the shelves. With a swift, puzzled frown, Erin took up a position standing near the shelves.

Logan shifted his position so he faced his father. Their eyes locked and Finn straightened, something akin to doubt flickering across his face.

I could do nothing but watch. Was Dante telling me everything? He couldn't lie, that was true, but he hadn't outright declared himself against Kieran, either. He'd dodged my question about what he planned to do. Was he just playing me to get my co-operation until it was too late? And how would he stop Kieran's *torryl?* I hadn't had a chance to tell him Tom's message. Riposte. What did that even mean?

Sardonic, Kieran surveyed the group. He sank into the seat and threw his arms wide.

'Let us begin.'

TWENTY-TWO

Now! Michael's shade reappeared at my shoulder. *You must return me now, before it's too late. He's going to use you to draw power.*

I swore then sent a silent apology to the environmentalist and gathered his power, a glowing orange non-light.

In the study, Kieran's voice droned on, giving Erin instructions on how to connect with the objects and their owners en masse. How he knew anything about psychometry I had no idea, but he had been around a long time.

I waited for the right moment. If I extended what was left of me into the *sianfath* too early Kieran would detect me. If I waited too long the power draw would swamp Michael.

'Rowan,' Kieran said. 'If you will, please?'

Logan took two steps away. Probably wise.

Involuntarily, my powers engaged and I siphoned energy from humans outside the building. I slipped free of my imprisonment, dragging Michael with me. I stepped into the *sianfath,* leaving my body with a single, molecule-thin anchor – something Aeona's book warned never to do. But I didn't have enough of me left to anchor more securely.

I looked back. Finding myself might not be so difficult after all. In the *sianfath's* greenish non-light, I was a beacon of power. Orange energy, drawn from humans, swirled and pulsed in me, swelling my otherworld form into enormity and frightening potential.

I ran, pulling Michael, using the energy from the environmentalist to push us against the drag in the opposite direction. Every step sucked at my feet. Every inch forward was a struggle against a tide of molasses pulling me back as power swirled past us.

I don't think I can get you there!

You can, Michael cried. *We're close. Let the enath go and that will give you the boost.*

Reluctantly, I released the environmentalist. His laughing wail – half fear, half relief – twisted a dagger into my heart. But Michael was right. Empowered, I snagged a tendril into Michael's body and forced myself into his darkened mind. He had no mental shields barring the deepest one set by Dyson. I thrust his soul into the depths of the darkness and his mind lit up, sparkling and exquisite with his return home.

In one shadowed corner stood the block set by Dyson. I paused, uncertain. Then I pushed my hands into the thick concrete. Using techniques Maeve taught me, I concentrated.

What are you doing?

I have a feeling you need to see whatever's behind this. How's your body?

I thinned the concrete to steel-studded oak.

I think I'm sedated. I my arms and legs are too heavy to lift and I can barely open my eyes.

Crap! The oak softened to pine. My energy level was almost to zero. I had to get back to my body or I risked being permanently separated, lost in the *sianfath*.

Draw from me, Michael said. *You're more important than me.*

I hesitated, then complied, drawing just enough from his body to power the final change from pine to cloth, to web. I tore the web aside and cleared the path into his memories.

I can't stay. I'll try to burn off the sedative, but it won't be much. I'm too weak.

Go. I'll be fine. Good luck.

You too. And thanks.

I released the hook in his form and let the tide of energy haul me back to myself.

Energy bloated me, crackling from my fingertips and hair, swelling and pulsing through my body. The taste of ozone was strong enough to be bitter and unpleasant. I raged within the confines of my shield. Death for Kieran lay, literally, in my hands but I was unable to wield it.

His mind brushed mine and I cowered behind the shield, hating myself and him. Who did I trust? I had no idea what memories I'd released for Michael. What if he betrayed me, influenced by whatever had been hidden? And Dante. What was his angle? Was he really going to sabotage Kieran's plans? Or did Dante just my inner shield open because that would allow *him* control of me, instead?

'Now...' Kieran said, triumph ringing in his voice. 'Dante. Bring Erin, Calain and Maeve into the *lorntinn*. Erin will find the nodes. I'll convince them to work with us. Maeve will use their connections to begin switching off the Dark gene.'

'How,' Maeve asked. 'I'm only one telekinetic. I can change maybe two or three an hour. That would take forever.'

Kieran oozed smugness. He pointed at the shelves full of trinkets. 'I chose each *lorntinn* node because they're also telekinetics. They will assist you with the gene manipulation. Using Rowan's power, and the *lorntinn's* cohesive effect, they'll also amplify Calain's ability to detect sidhe with the Dark gene. So you see?' He spread his arms and encompassed his audience in one sweeping motion. 'All is in place. It wants only your co-operation to begin the greatest step forward in sidhe history.'

'Oh, stop making speeches and get on with it,' Erin snapped. 'You're worse than my father was.'

Beside me, Logan smothered a laugh. Dante's lips twitched into a smile. He rose and tugged at his jacket. The others rose, too, Maeve watching Dante uncertainly; Calain watching Kieran with unwavering, unreadable intensity.

'The *lorntinn* is easier to maintain at deep levels if we are in physical contact,' Dante said. 'If you would?' He slid his cane through a loop in his belt, like a sword, and extended one hand to Kieran.

The small muscles in Kieran's jaw worked. He hesitated, then clasped Dante's hand.

I waited, but Dante didn't appear. Didn't restore my *enath*. There was nothing I could do until he did. Why did he wait?

'We'll need Rowan and Logan in the circle, as well,' Dante said. 'It will be far easier for Calain and I if Logan assists in controlling the flow of her powers in the *lorntinn*. She trusts him.'

'Very well. Come here.'

My legs moved without my willing them. My body felt five sizes too large, swollen with unreleased power, the floor unfelt beneath my feet. Logan grasped my hand on one side, Dante on the other. Power arced into them and they gasped but didn't release me. Erin stood opposite me in the circle, one hand lying in Kieran's, the other touching several objects on the shelves. Maeve gripped Erin's shoulder.

One by one, the others dropped into the *lorntinn* under Dante's direction. I seethed, still under Kieran's control, held apart from the others by him. Kieran also held himself back, merely skirting around the outside of the entangled, intertwining of the others.

'Erin,' he said. 'Find them. Rowan feed power to Calain and Erin to assist them in the search.'

He spoke aloud. Most likely to allow for lies and deceit that could not be uttered within the *lorntinn* connection.

Dutifully, I fed power to the others, relishing the light brush of Logan's mind as he helped channel and control the feed. He probably couldn't sense me, weak as I was, but the touch was enough. Erin, Dante and Calain dropped deeper into collusion, their thoughts drifting far through the *sianfath,* drawn by Erin's psychometry and Calain's ability to find sidhe. As Erin moved from one object to the next, ghost-faces appeared before us. Transparent, oblivious, engrossed in their own lives: laughing, sleeping, working, eating.

'Excellent,' Kieran said. 'Now, Dante, bring them into the *lorntinn.* Calain, you'll find each one will lead you to hundreds more. When they are all connected...' He sucked a deep breath and a satisfied smile pulled at the corner of his mouth. 'Then we can proceed to the next step. Rowan, you'll need to draw more power. This will require a great deal to maintain the connection for so many.'

'You're not trying to convince every single sidhe on the planet, are you?' Erin asked.

'No, indeed,' Kieran returned. 'Just a few...key individuals. Perhaps four thousand. Once their Dark gene is switched off, they will influence others to join our cause.'

I drew more power, following Kieran's instructions to spread the pull thin to minimise the damage. At this time of day Florence seethed and swarmed with tourists so there was no shortage of humanity.

Straining at my peripheral vision gave me a view of Michael's still-prone form off to one side of the room, and Nesrin's on the other. Nesrin shifted, the leather creaking beneath her. Kieran's eyes narrowed. Behind me, the door opened and one of his pet sidhe entered. He joined Finn and both stood over Nesrin, hands resting on holstered guns.

Michael still hadn't moved.

I was conscious of the karambit blade, nestled beneath my breast, and the katar punch-blade, which Kieran had laid on his desk six steps away. But even had I had been able to move, I couldn't reach both a knife and Kieran's neck before someone stopped me.

Tension twisted its blade through my stomach as I waited. But for what? Dante drew more and more sidhe into the *lorntinn*, gathering them like a dragon hoarding gold. A thousand whispered voices teased the edges of my mind. Why was Dante still waiting to release me? Was he not able to manage the *lorntinn* and get through Kieran's shields at the same time? Or was he stalling for some other reason?

Erin paled, and whimpered. Logan's grip on me tightened. Even Maeve and Calain grew rigid as the strain of finding and holding the sidhe increased. Only Kieran and Dante seemed unaffected; Kieran because he remained outside and Dante presumably because his strength came from the *lorntinn*.

Erin trembled as she swept her fingertips across the last few items on the bottom shelf. She groaned and sagged against Maeve's chair. The final few hag-ridden faces appeared and were absorbed into the maelstrom of green, shifting lights inside the circle.

'Yes,' Kieran murmured. 'Well done, child. That's all of them. Dante, extend through the nodes and draw in those they're attached to. Rowan. More!'

Outside in the piazza, two people collapsed. Their souls swept through me, into the *sianfath*, wailing. I railed against my helplessness. Where was Dante? Had he betrayed me?

Dante's hand tightened on mine. His jaw worked as he drew thousands of minds into deeper rapport.

'I don't know...' he grated, 'how long I can keep them all together. Many are...resisting. If you're going to speak to them, Kieran, do it now before this falls apart.'

'Yes,' Kieran hissed, triumphant. He flicked a glance at one of his pet sidhe, who nodded and left the room. Before the door to the outer office closed, the sidhe's two-word command drifted through the gap: 'Activate now.'

Kieran dropped into the *lorntinn,* but shallow, withholding his inner self from the group mind, as I had. I could do no more than watch from outside. He disseminated himself through the network, touching every mind. And, in every mind he touched, a deep-held, thick barrier dissolved as he spoke those same two words: 'Activate now.'

TWENTY-THREE

Dante's knock rapped on my inner shield. I forced the door open against the pressure of the energy swirling in me. He slipped inside.

What's happening? What's Kieran doing?

I don't know yet. Here.

He thrust something at me; a tiny kernel of brilliant green energy, so bright I couldn't look at it.

Your enath. I just stole it back from Kieran. Take it.

Won't he notice?

He seems to be preoccupied

But what's he doing?

Your guess is as good as mine. Don't waste time bickering with me. This is our only chance – while he's busy. Make it good.

What do I do?

We still don't know what his game is. For now, pretend nothing's changed.

With my enath back I can drain him in a few seconds. Why wait?

We can't risk it. If your timing was off by even a second he would cut your soul again and my gift would be revealed. We'll get only this one chance to destroy the Ferrum for good. We can't waste it on revenge.

So, what, then? Just wait for you to tell me what to do?

You must, sister. Shelve your ego for once. We must work together.

He turned away.

Dante, wait!

He paused.

'Riposte' is a fencing term, isn't it? What does it mean?

Frustration. Effort. Anger, even. Then his terse reply. *A quick thrust, immediately after parrying an attack.* And he vanished again, leaving me seething.

I released my *enath* into the deepest recesses of myself and bathed in the exquisite sensation of being back in control of my own body and gifts. Relief flooded in along with the full awareness of the sheer power at my disposal. The temptation to drain Kieran teased me. But I was already so engorged I couldn't. I had no choice but to wait.

I checked on Michael, still lying on the stretcher, drip in his arm. If that drip carried a sedative my feeble effort to burn the drug out of him may not have helped. There was nothing I could without alerting Kieran. His distraction wouldn't last if I moved or did anything too obvious. Michael would have to find his own way back.

Doubt assailed me. What if he couldn't? What if returning his *enath* wasn't enough and my attempt to alter his DNA to sense the *sianfath* had caused permanent damage? I had no way of knowing. Should I check?

The office door opened again and admitted a heightened burble of voices from the other room. Commands and chatter intertwined into meaningless noise. Nothing more than the occasional 'Affirmative', or 'negative' or 'abort' came through clearly. Whatever Kieran's people were doing, though, it involved a lot of action. All at once.

There was one thing I could do. Two, actually. Slowly, unobtrusively, I squeezed Logan's fingers. He stiffened but didn't turn. He squeezed back. I sharpened my focus on Erin. Her restless gaze caught mine, passed on and snapped back, widening. I blinked once, slowly. She caught her lower lip in her teeth and looked away.

Then her gaze shifted, wide and stark, to Kieran. 'Oh my God!' She tried to tear free but his lean fingers tightened and she gasped a whimper of pain. His eyes remained closed, a feral grin thinned his lips.

'All those people I led him to,' she choked. 'They were sidhe he'd caught, tortured and released.' She spoke directly at me, filling me in verbally because we couldn't speak telepathically without being heard.

A low chuckle growled from Kieran's throat but he said nothing.

'Shit.' That was Logan. 'You're right, Erin. They had those deep-seated shields, but he's removed it in all of them.'

I forced back the questions burning on my tongue and held Erin's gaze.

'There are thousands of them, Logan,' she added, but her attention never strayed from me. 'All over the world. There must have been some sort of post-hypnotic suggestion.' She swallowed, grabbing at Maeve now as though for support. Tears streaked Maeve's cheeks and her mouth worked.

Erin's eyes bored into mine. 'Those thousands of sidhe. They're all Dark and all *demenath*. He's been holding *all* their souls – some for years. He's insane. He's ordered them to kill the Light sidhe. Even their own families. They're just mindlessly murdering their own kind.'

Kieran's smirk curved into certainty.

She broke into sobs and wrenched free of Kieran's grasp, covering her mouth.

I swallowed sickening guilt. There was little I could do to stop the *demenath* sidhe. We had to stop Kieran and it didn't look like Dante and the others even could. I studied my companions. Dante's brow furrowed. Calain's lips drew back into a snarl and the muscles in his neck corded. Maeve was pale, swaying. Whatever they did, it took all of their concentration and effort. They sucked power from me as fast as I could deliver it.

So maybe I could just cut the power?

No. Kieran would work out I'd been released.

There was one other thing I could do. Possibly a delaying tactic; possibly essential. Hard to be sure at the moment. I slipped one, microscopic tendril of thought into the *sianfath*. A sliver of silver, it twisted and slid along secret byways, avoiding Kieran's brilliance and the chaos in which those around me were embroiled. The tendril faltered. Praying Kieran wouldn't notice, I diverted more power, thickening, strengthening, killing another two tourists in the piazza.

The thought drove onwards, across seas and lands, although distance meant nothing in the *sianfath*.

Jen, can you hear me?

A sense of startled hope. *~Rowan? Wow. You really can reach around the world.~*

I need your help. Did you get hold of the people I asked you to?

~Y-yes. Kind of.~

How many? Where?

~Only about a hundred responded. A lot of people don't like my mother.~ Her mental tone carried hints of defensive anger, guilt and satisfaction. *~But they agreed to help. What do I do?~*

All telekinetics?

~Yes. And all over the world, like you asked.~

Give me their details; their mental signatures so I can find them. She did. *~What are you doing?~*

This. I dumped a quick series of images. *Tell them to choose wisely and work fast. Tell them to expect to hear from me but don't let anyone else contact them. And to watch their backs. Something else is happening and I have a feeling it's going to balloon fast.*

~Will it work?~ Doubt; fear.

No idea. But it's the only thing we can do. I have to go. Be ready.

I pulled away before she could question me further, since I didn't have any ready answers, anyway.

In Kieran's office, Calain, Dante and Maeve were swaying and ashen. Was there some way I could help them that wouldn't reveal myself? No. The only way to find out what was happening was to join Dante and the others in the *lorntinn*; to connect with them. Risk Kieran cutting at me again

I shuddered and swallowed my reluctance.

My heartrate doubled. I fought to stay still and calm. My hands trembled and I anchored myself on Logan's steadiness. I dove into the *lorntinn*, trying not to drown in its seductive depths. Logan's brilliant strength orientated me and I clung to him while I tried to make sense of the swirling green chaos.

Calain, Dante and Maeve are trying to undo what he's done. Logan's bitterness did nothing to ease my fear. *But they left it too late. They kept hoping he was for real. I couldn't convince them. I'm sorry.*

I get it. They wanted it to be real. They wanted it so much they were blind to anything wrong. We have to stop him.

How? He's already cut away a chunk of Maeve's enath, and Calain's. The only thing stopping him from using the torryl *on all of us is that he still needs us to co-ordinate the attacks. Almost all his* Dark sidhe *are activated. His telekinetics are switching on Dark genes all over the place. In a few seconds he'll be free to kill us all. Can't you just drain him?*

The second I try he'll cut me dead. He's too fast.

So what then?

You get out of the lorntinn *and arm yourself. My katar blade is on his desk behind Erin. Kill him or kill me. Either one. And watch*

Finn and Michael. Michael's alive but I don't know where his loyalties lie.

Kill you? No!

Logan, you promised you wouldn't let me become a monster. I'm calling in that promise now. Kieran has me under his thumb with the torryl. If I can't beat that, then I'm the biggest threat to the world you'll ever see. Kill me.

He swore and pulled out of the *lorntinn*. I was bereft, unable to even sense his hand in mine any longer. Surrounded by the faint screams of thousands of dying sidhe. Their faces swept through, then into, the *sianfath's* churning, swirling green non-light; absorbed, dead, gone. This couldn't go on.

I steeled myself and sank further into the circle of minds, seeking Dante.

His thought-house appeared as an architectural nightmare now; enmeshed with Calain's medieval castle and Maeve's Georgian mansion. Their combined minds so deeply intertwined in the *lorntinn* it was difficult to see where Dante began or how to reach him.

Drawing a metaphorical breath, I plunged through the jumble of shields and into the blended-minds beyond.

Sister!

Dante. We need to act now. We need to stop him. He's activated the Dark sidhe and they're killing our kind all over the world.

We know. Your power is feeding us, but it's feeding him and them, too. You must stop the flow.

He'll cut me. You know he will. If he has me under complete control, I can't stop him.

Then join us wholly in the lorntinn. Perhaps your strength, added to ours in the blending will be enough.**

...

I froze, undecided. "Perhaps" wasn't enough assurance. Still separated from their deep connection, I had no way of being certain they worked against Kieran and not with him. Yet why would they work with him to kill sidhe? Unless all three had been brainwashed, or Dante's Dark gene activated. That was distinctly possible. I couldn't take the risk. Joining them in the blending was something Dante pushed for every time we spoke. Yet it could be the thing that gave Kieran ultimate victory. Perhaps he'd known I'd held back some of my soul; resisted him. Perhaps Dante returning it was just a trick to gain my trust.

I backed away.

Sister! Dante's ephemeral image stretched out a hand. *You must open to us. Join us. You must help me save my people.* My people, he'd said, not our people. Did he mean Dark sidhe, or all sidhe?

I can't. I fled.

There was no way of knowing. And only one way of stopping this. Kieran was the source and instigator of everything. I couldn't trust anyone else to help, except perhaps Logan.

I withdrew to the *lorntinn's* shallower levels and sought the familiarity of Logan's thoughts.

Rage and pain cloaked his mind, obscuring rationality.

I opened my eyes.

Near the door, Logan fought with Finn, both men grimly silent and equally-matched for strength and speed. Finn's gun lay halfway across the room. The two sidhe guarding Nes lay on the floor, blood pooling beneath them. Nes was sprawled, limp, nearby. But her chest rose and fell regularly. A bruise darkened her temple.

Logan struck with stiffened fingers at Finn's throat. Finn slapped his blow aside and sliced a blade-hand at Logan's jaw. Logan blocked. Finn drove an elbow into his cheek. Logan staggered back, eyes glazed. Nes stirred, groaned and sat up. She saw Finn and scrambled towards the gun.

Finn uttered a low growl, spun on his heel and bolted through the door.

Logan followed.

'Logan!' The shout escaped me before I could stop myself.

'You leave this room and Rowan dies,' Kieran's voice cut through the chatter from the outer room.

Logan froze, his hand on the door. He looked back at me. Then he stared into the other room.

TWENTY-FOUR

'Logan?' Nes held the gun, the muzzle aimed at Kieran. 'What the hell is going on? Who are these people?'

'Throw the gun away, Nes,' Kieran said. 'Or Dante dies also.'

'Do it, Nes,' Logan said. 'He's not bluffing.' He closed the door and returned to my side. But he glanced once more at the door through which his father had vanished.

Kieran focussed his attention on me. 'So, you found a way to steal your *enath* back, did you, girl? Impressive.'

I straightened, chin raised.

'I suspect,' Kieran said conversationally, 'by that militant sparkle, you intend to cut the flow of power to your friends and thence to my operatives. But I'd advise against that.' The door opened and eight more sidhe appeared, all armed, weapons aimed at my companions. 'After all, I do have the advantage of numbers. I'm sure we could kill a few before you managed anything terribly damaging.'

I froze, allowing the flow of power to continue.

'Very good.' Kieran nodded. 'Won't be much longer.' He considered Calain and Dante. 'They are trying hard, but they're up against four thousand of my best sleepers. They don't stand a chance. But it keeps them occupied, which is good.'

He released Dante's hand. Erin shrank back against her chair, arms wrapped around her waist. Kieran strolled over and stood before me, staring into my soul.

'Do tell how you returned. I'm most interested.'

'Fluke,' I said with a shrug. 'No idea. Just woke up.'

Flint sparked in his eyes. 'Liar. Never mind. I shall find out soon enough.' He circled the room, stroking his jaw. 'It's almost over. A few more hours and most sidhe in the world will be either my activated Dark warriors, or dead. The few remaining will be hunted down.'

'Why?' I grated. 'Why are you doing this?'

Kieran raised a cool brow and strolled to the window. 'You know why. We've been feared, hunted, and burnt for over two thousand years. As has our world. It's time we emerged from the shadows of the forests and took control of things. Before it's too late. We need to be of one mind and this the only way to achieve it.'

'We can work with the humans and bring both sides of the sidhe together.'

He cast me a pitying look. 'Aeona was an idealist like you. It took a century or so, but she saw the truth, too.'

'No. She didn't turn against humans, did she? You lied.' I took a step towards Kieran.

A soft, metallic click made me glance around. A sidhe had his gun muzzle pressed against the back of Dante's head, but his focus was on me. Dante's rowan-wood cane hung loosely in the hand I'd released. His fingertip tapped repeatedly on the fern carving's tight-curled centre, as if he debated an action, impatient. What was he thinking? He was quick, but not fast enough to use it as a weapon against a bullet from close range.

Dante's face was a mask of concentration, but a frown gathered. The fern head inched towards my left hand. His lips moved, forming a silent word.

I almost laughed aloud.

Kieran spun and stalked towards me. He passed Michael, still prone on the stretcher.

Michael leapt up and staggered. He regained his balance and looped his dripline around Kieran's thin neck. He placed a knee in Kieran's back and hauled, his mouth contorting into a snarl.

I snatched Dante's cane, slammed it across his captor's arm, and released myself into the *sianfath*. Eight tendrils stabbed into the eight sidhe guarding us. Their attention rested on the struggle between Kieran and Michael. My body overflowed with power. I couldn't take much; just a few drams from each. Enough to make them slow-blink and sag on their feet. Enough to give my companions time to fight back.

Erin snatched up Kieran's cat and threw it at her guard. It yowled, claws scoring deep red welts on legs, arms and face as the man shrieked and flailed madly at the animal. Maeve's first attacker collapsed, blood pouring from his eyes and nose. Logan swept the leg of a nearby sidhe and brought him to ground. Logan grimly snapped the sidhe's neck. Nes grabbed a fallen nine-mil and coolly shot one through the head. Another man tried to wrench the gun from her but their combined grip crushed the steel into uselessness. The pair fell to the floor, scrabbling for dominance in a brutal groundfight.

I ran towards Kieran, cane in my hand, thumb on the leaf-carving.

A small dagger appeared in Kieran's hand. He sliced through the plastic tube around his throat. With a swift backward kick, he propelled Michael across the room. Michael crashed against a tapestry, which tore and folded over him.

Kieran straightened. His eyes narrowed.

I was within striking distance. I raised the cane.

Then he cut at me with the *torryl* and I screamed. He sliced first through the ties connecting me to Logan and the others. Each cut hacked at a piece of me, leaving gaps in my soul and eating at my will to resist him.

Then he cut at the threads drawing power from the people outside. Agony paralysed me and I curled around it, gasping. If he was willing to cut my power draw, he didn't need the continuous flow any more. He cut again. Breathless, I almost dropped the cane as pain lanced through my chest and head. He wouldn't stop this time. I would be *demenath*. He would ensure every last thread was cut and I was utterly his. Then the world would be his as well.

I would be unstoppable.

'Logan,' I whispered and collapsed to my knees on the hard floor.

'He won't help you now, my dear,' Kieran said, brushing his hands together. 'None of them will. My people have prevailed. Yours will be dead momentarily. You lose.'

I couldn't turn my head to even see if he spoke truth. I could see only him. Only his amused certainty. I drew more power in a desperate attempt to counter him. But I was already engorged.

He cut one more thread and I could do no more than whimper. My hand convulsed around the cane knob, pressing, prodding, desperate.

Kieran gasped and the pain eased for a moment. His polished shoes shifted in a staggering step.

'Damn you, boy!' Kieran's words came out wet and muffled. I squinted up. Blood frothed at his lips. He turned and confronted Logan. My katar blade protruded from Kieran's back. He yanked it free and threw it aside. He swung a fist with casual speed and slammed it into Logan's chest. Logan's feet flew from the ground. He hit the polished floor and slid to a stop against the wall, limp, eyes closed.

The hole in Kieran's back knitted, slowly.

I managed to push the right spot on the cane.

I anchored the last thread of myself to my convulsing body and launched into the *sianfath*. If he cut that filament, I was done.

Kieran appeared before me. His image in the *sianfath* was taller, broader, more handsome. His ideal, presumably.

Unwise, child. His green-wraith face twisted into a wry smile. *You expose yourself to me. Had you remained in your body, I couldn't have done this.*

His arm turned blade-like and he sliced at the glittering thread anchoring me to my body.

I know. I lunged forward. My blade connected with his and both felt solid. But I knew nothing of fencing. My surprise counter gave me one chance. He blinked, his ghost-mouth falling open. I twisted his arm aside with the glowing blade in my hand. And drove the point through, into where his heart would be in his real body.

Kieran gargled and staggered back, his arms flailing. I yanked the greenish blade free and cut again. A slice at his arm hacked his blade free. Whether it was real or only symbolic of his *torryl* ability, I had no idea. Hopefully removing the symbol would remove the gift as well.

He gaped at me and at the shining stump of his ethereal arm.

In sweeping strokes, I chopped through the ties holding him to his earthly body.

Kieran's body-image dwindled into a brilliant green, floating speck. I cupped it in my hands, unable to cry, wishing I could.

And released it into the *sianfath*.

With a faint, wailing protest Kieran Ivaldison vanished into the green-wild.

I dropped back into my body, still curled on the floor, still only half-alive. Kieran's body folded onto the floor beside me, his eyes glassy though a pulse beat in his throat. My *enath* was still splintered into fragments, contained in Kieran's soulless living form. I hadn't the control to go through his shields and retrieve it. Or release the thousands of others he still held captive.

No wonder he was insane.

Someone grasped my arm. Sparks flew and Dante jumped backward, swearing.

'Don't touch me,' I gasped. 'Too full of power. I need...to get the rest of my *enath* back. And release all the others he holds. Only way to stop all this.'

'Kieran?' Dante spoke. The others crowded around, pale, anxious, bloodied. But all alive.

'He is *demenath*. Gone. Help me get through...' I sucked a painful breath. '...his shields. I can't control this power much longer. He's cut away too much of me.'

'Very well.' Dante glanced up. 'Logan. You take Michael, Nes and Erin and get down to those labs. Release any prisoners. Then get everyone back to the safe house.'

'The outer room's full of Dark sidhe, Dante,' Logan said, pressing at his bloodied head.

Michael appeared at his side, limping and cradling his left arm. 'There's a hidden elevator in this room.' He jerked his thumb at the massive Ottoman empire tapestry I'd admired.

Logan hesitated. I managed to speak through the pain and convulsions wracking my body.

'Go, Logan. I'd rather you weren't here anyway. Save as many as you can. If I can't control this...'

He kissed me, ignoring the sparks, his lips warm. He stroked my hair, matted and damp with sweat.

'You can, Ruadhán. I know you can.' He kissed my forehead again. 'Please.'

He rose and yanked the tapestry aside. Michael pressed one of the stones and the rest slid away to reveal the metal doors. Erin cast a worried look over her shoulder as she vanished into the elevator.

'Do we all need to be here?' Maeve asked, eyeing the elevator.

'Merda!' Dante glared at her. 'I did not think you such a coward, Madre. You helped bring us to this point. You will see it through. She cannot release four thousand some souls on her own.'

Calain switched his solemn gaze to me. 'He's correct. We have failed her too often, Maeve. We'll not abandon her now. This is what the prophecy meant us to do, I'm certain.'

I kept my thoughts on that to myself.

She drew herself up and swept her skirts close. 'Then I know I'm not needed. In fact I may be a hindrance. The prophecy calls for only you three. A fourth will wreck it.'

Dante growled, low in his throat.

'No, she's right,' I said painfully. 'Mairi made no mention of her. Let her go. Help the others to release the captives. Besides, someone has to keep the rebellion going if…this goes pearshaped.'

Maeve fled into the elevator when it returned, her final glance at me filled with guilt and self-hatred.

I struggled to sit up, fending off Calain when he would have helped me. The power engorging my body strained, pushing at me, unbinding my very molecules and cells. I needed to use it. Soon.

'Sorry Dante, this is going to hurt.' I gripped his wrist. He winced and clenched his jaw. I grabbed Calain's and both men took hold of Kieran's limp hands.

The three of us stepped into the *sianfath*. My form was a mere whisper of its usual solid shape, my connection to my glowing body the veriest silken thread. It would yet take very little to unmake me.

Lead on, brother.

Very well. Have care, though.

We stepped into Kieran's French palace, following Dante's lead. We separated and hurried from room to room, each one empty, echoing. Ghostly winds bemoaned the loss of its occupant. It seemed to take days to search the whole castle, but time was irrelevant. We met again at the final door.

This must be the place he's holding them all.

It's the only door left. Dante grimaced. *His innermost shield. We can't get through. I tried before you arrived. Unless he opens it, nothing can get through.*

TWENTY-FIVE

-I don't believe that's quite true- Calain touched the thick door. *-Rowan. Aeona's message. In Mairi's book. What did it say?-*

I gasped. *How?*

-She mentioned it on her death. But I didn't know where the book was. Not until Maeve said you had it in Brisbane. Did you find the message?-

Yes. It just said 'Riposte. Inner cannot stand against blood'. But what does it mean? The second half, that is. I'll explain the first later.

Calain's hand curled into a fist. *-She's right. The taboo against opening an innermost shield is deeply ingrained. Most think it's impossible. But the truth is that blood-family, bonded in the* lorintinn *do have the power to force an inner shield open.-*

An expression of revulsion flickered over Dante's mobile face. He made a negatory gesture then drew his shoulders back and raised his chin.

We cannot afford to be squeamish. Not while Kieran's thousands of demenath are slaughtering our people. We must help them. He stretched out a transparent hand. **Come sister, you must join with us or this won't work.**

Still I hesitated, staring at the door. I swallowed, shivering though it was impossible to be cold here. I backed away, hating myself, hating my father and brother.

-What is it, Ruadhán?-

The gentle question almost broke my control and the thread back to my body tightened, thrumming with power desperate to be released. A few moments more and I'd have no choice; I'd have to release the power or die trying to hold it in.

But doing this meant opening the deepest parts of myself to people I barely knew and hardly trusted. Under their power and influence; open to their scorn; their love – and its withdrawal.

Outside, in the real world, my body shuddered. The thread connecting me thinned to near-invisibility. If it snapped I would vanish and my body would release the power like an explosion, killing Calain and Dante, if not destroying the building.

I gripped Dante's ghost-hand, and Calain's, and blended my thoughts with theirs.

For a long moment we struggled, fighting for leadership. Then our minds merged and I saw into the darkest corners of their souls. Calain's worst moments I knew from my nightmares, already. But I saw also the things Dante had done to get to this point – deaths, painful choices, destruction – and recoiled in horror. A quick taste of hurt from him brought me to my senses. Wasn't that reaction exactly what I'd feared from them?

I opened my inner shield and let them in.

Their warmth, their love, their imperfections entwined with mine. Their fears echoed mine. Their hopes; their losses were mine a thousandfold for they'd lived so much longer and borne so much more. My hurt was nothing to theirs. My self-centred fears a scratch on what they had endured for so many centuries.

I reached out, aching with their pain, seeking to ease. For the first time, I let go of the fear of who I might become. Released the tight restraints I placed around my inner demons. Focussed wholly on someone else's hurts.

And, in doing so, the monster in me was diminished; pale in comparison. A small, wrinkled, powerless thing, deprived of the fear giving it strength. In our shared self-doubt and self-awareness, we three grew in power and wonder until the *sianfath* shuddered with our arrival.

We felt the world pause and watch us, wary. We felt the fighting sidhe cease. We held them immobile, effortless.

Now. We spoke and thought as one. Kieran's inner shield opened without resistance. The thousands of *enath* imprisoned within swarmed out, radiating fear and bewildered loss.

Enfold them, Dante. Make them understand. Then guide them home, Calain. Mine will be the power to return them.

Dante's gift drew the thousands into the *lorntinn* with us. The blended minds swelled in a disharmonious whole of unhappy Dark and brainwashed souls. Dante and Calain whispered, cajoled, convinced, and cleansed until the voices sang in one liquid harmony of exquisite connection.

Then Dante released them, Calain directed their paths back to their bodies and I pushed them home. Faintly, I sensed my own *enath* return to me, my body gasp and straighten.

I turned my attention to the next task. Kieran had used telekinetics. I used them now, leveraging their newly-altered allegiances to correct Dark genes once and for all. I fed them power, drawing without hesitation and without mercy on the city of Florence. People died, but many thousands more lived because of my work.

I could live with that. I would live with that.

Finally, we released them and withdrew, basking in the deep bond of our threeway merging.

We must return. There is more to do.

Wait. There's one more thing.

-What, daughter?-

Trust me. There was no irony in my thought and they acceded without hesitation.

I extended everything I was into the *sianfath*, trusting my anchor to Calain and Dante to help me find my way home. This would take nothing less than all of me.

Jen. Now.

~I understand.~

I drew her into the *lorntinn*. At my instruction, Dante did the same with the hundred other trusted women, scattered around the world. Lastly, I contacted Maeve and showed her my intent. She hesitated, searching my mind for truths. I held nothing back.

Will you help? I can't do this without your expertise.

<You trust me to do this?>

Jen and I stepped through her shields and I knocked on Maeve's inner shield. It opened and I drew her in, merging her with us in the deepest levels of the *lorntinn*. Maeve's distance collapsed and I sensed she sobbed.

We are your family, Maeve. I gave her gentle encouragement. *You've lost many children, I know. But don't push away the ones who remain because you're afraid to lose them, too. That's the mistake I made and I almost lost everyone because of it.*

She said nothing but threw herself into the task with a fervour and enthusiasm that both worried and pleased me. She demanded more power. I gave it, using my body as nothing more than a conduit while she, and the other women worked. Calain and Dante, their chief task completed, could do little but watch with me, supporting and holding the *lorntinn* together.

There was no way of knowing how long it took but it seemed like hours.

When, at last, the work was completed, a sense of hope swept through the combined thoughts of our little group. One by one, the threads of connection fell away. Last to leave was Jen, who blew me and her mother an ethereal kiss before the left. Then Maeve vanished, leaving only Calain, Dante and I still blended.

I lingered, reluctant now to leave the womb-like security of their all-encompassing thoughts and minds. With a sense of wry amusement, Dante untwisted us and we fell back into our bodies, gasping, smaller. Heavier with solitude, lighter with shared experience.

My legs gave way and Calain and Dante hauled me back to my feet. I still throbbed with power for I had one more job to do. One I hadn't let myself think about while we were still blended. While my father and brother headed for the elevator and spoke telepathically with the others for an update, I knelt before Kieran's body. He stared blindly back at me. The pulse in his throat still beat. Without the force of his personality, his body seemed thinner, paler, almost translucent. Hardly the bogeyman to be afraid of.

Dante's hand came to rest on my shoulder.

'We must go,' he said. 'Logan and the others have released the sidhe being held hostage. They're outside the building.'

'What about the rest of them?' I gestured to the outer room, hidden behind the closed door.

Calain's eyes lost focus. 'Those that were *demenath* are doing battle with those who are loyal to the Mors. The true sidhe are prevailing by sheer force of numbers. Kieran was arrogant to surround himself with so many *demenath*. I've told them to evacuate. There are few of Kieran's people left alive.'

'We must go,' Dante repeated. Sirens wailed in the distance. 'The polezia are coming. We cannot be found here.'

'I can't leave him like this,' I said, indicating Kieran. 'His body is still alive.'

'But his soul is gone. He cannot harm us any longer.'

'But he could return.' I groaned, knowing what I had to do, hating it. 'Aeona's book said a lost soul could find its way home. We can't risk it.'

I reached beneath my shirt and tugged the karambit blade free of its hidden sheath. I lay the gleaming steel against my grandfather's thin throat. My hand trembled.

Calain crouched and gripped my wrist. 'A blade will not work, daughter. Even with his soul fled, his body will heal itself.'

'Oh, God.' I dropped my head. 'Then stand back.'

Calain released me and moved away, holding Dante back.

'Do what you must, daughter.' His face was set in stone, pale.

I extended my hands towards Kieran. A pulse of white-hot energy arced from my palms to Kieran's body. His clothes burst into flames. I poured more and his body smouldered, flaring into fire. The stench was horrific, overpowering the taste of warm lightning on my tongue. I staggered backward, gagging.

I fell into Calain's arms, crying in earnest. Calain held me, his tears falling to mingle with mine, his body shaking.

'I'm sorry. I'm sorry.' I trembled, unable to stop, stammering my regret. His memories of Mairi's fiery death lurked close to the surface of my mind.

'It's alright, Ruadhán,' he murmured. 'It's alright.'

Dante appeared at our side, mouth and nose covered with the hem of his shirt.

'Elevator's not functioning. Power's been cut to the building. Either the remaining Mors or the police. No. Logan says it's not the police, though they aren't far away. We need another way out.'

I straightened, aching. 'Can we go down the elevator shaft to the basement? The escape tunnels?'

Dante shook his head. 'Nes tells me some Mors members escaped through them and collapsed them behind. They're impassable now. And the elevator is blocking the shaft'

Calain put me aside. 'The front room is empty. Our people have left. We can go that way.'

The men headed for the door. I began to follow, then returned to Kieran's desk. I yanked his laptop free of its cables and grabbed an external harddrive sitting nearby. A jacket, stripped from a fallen Mors, provided a wrap for the electronics. I tied the sleeves around my shoulders like a backpack. Dante raised his brows.

'Evidence,' I said. 'There are more cells around the world, aren't there? You may need this.'

He nodded wearily. 'A wise thought, if a depressing one.'

We crept through the darkened operations room, encountering no resistance. Our steps left bloody prints behind as we trod through the carnage left by the battle. I pressed fought the urge to throw up. Bodies lay everywhere, broken, bloodied, limp. Impossible to tell friend from foe.

The spiral staircase was mercifully empty, as was the whole lower half of the building. We followed a trail of blood and bootmarks. Our people or Mors?

Logan?

Rowan? Thank God. You're alright?

Yes. Basically. Not injured, anyway. Do we have a clear run out of here? Are the cops here yet?

You've got about five minutes before they show up in force. There's a crowd gathering. It's not going to be easy to get away unseen.

Figured. Get our people as far away as you can. I'm going to provide…a distraction.

What are you—

I cut the connection.

Dante led us through a back room to a small exit onto Via Orsanmichele between the Mors headquarters and the Orsanmichele church behind. We stepped outside, into the curious gaze of dozens of tourists lining the nearby streets.

Calain and Dante paused, surveying the onlookers.

'Come, daughter,' Calain murmured, grabbing my wrist. Energy sparked and he released me with a surprised oath. 'We must leave. Dante and I will provide glamour that we may pass unnoticed.'

'Wait,' I said. 'We can't leave this much evidence for the police. Remember the parcel? If any of that information is still in there, we'll be on the net so fast you won't know what hit us. It has to be destroyed.'

'We can't… You cannot mean to!' He glanced wildly around at the crowd. 'You would kill these people.'

'Not if you and the others clear space. Go!' I shoved him away. 'Get everyone back. Use telepathy if you must. Go.'

'Rowan!' Logan appeared at the corner of the building, running towards us.

I turned to Calain with a silent plea. He threw one strong arm across Logan's waist, holding him back. I handed Dante the jacket containing the laptop. He grasped Logan's other arm, talking to him in an urgent undertone.

Logan paled, his eyes darting back to me. His mouth formed a denial lost in the crowd's murmur as Calain and Dante dragged him away. The crowd, looking bewildered, shuffled awkwardly backward in an ever-increasing, ragged circle. When I judged them far enough away, I drew most of their energy, leaving just enough to keep them alive. Like cut marionettes they crumpled to the cobbles, leaving me in the centre of a ring of eerie silence.

TWENTY-SIX

You can't let her do this!

-She's the only one who can, Logan. And she's right. We can't let the information in there fall into government control.-

I drew more power from further afield until my body once again filled to aching.

Then I touched the ancient blocks at the building's base. It took several long moments until I found the right resonance and matched the green *sianfath* and orange human energy to the stones' dull brown. Energy sparked, arcing from my hands in a hazy shimmer that distorted the stones and set them atremble. The shuddering spread until the very stones underfoot shook.

Glass shattered in the windows overhead. Inside, electronics exploded, setting fires ablaze. Rooftiles slipped and smashed to the road all around, sending fragments flying. More and more until the sky rained glass and ceramic and my legs and arms bled in a dozen places. I ignored the pain and drew more power, from further and further afield. More people died, the elderly, the sick. Tears coursed a river of guilt down my dusty cheeks but I didn't stop.

The building foundations gave way; the ancient cellars imploded; the mortar between bricks dissolved into sand and dust. It all needed to come down. Every cell in my body vibrated in perfect harmony with the stones and grains themselves and I found an even deeper connection to the *sianfath* than I believed possible. A connection to the Earth herself; the rocks, the pulse of the whole planet.

And I laughed and gave myself up to the Earth.

Then the building collapsed and dropped tonnes of stone onto the street where I stood.

Granddaughter? Prithee speak. Ist thee, indeed? I can hardly make out thy countenance. Come closer, child.

Aeona? I spun in circles, lost, grasping at nothing for I could see nothing but darkness and flashes of non-light.

Indeed. Tis I, child. Come to me.

A faint beacon of greenish light drew me and I drifted towards it.

In a rush I drew breath into lungs not my own and felt a bone-weary pain so deep I cried out. I pushed free of the body and stood aside, looking back in bewilderment.

Aeona? She lay on a vast, tapestried bed in a grey-stone room decorated with heavy timber furniture and thick furs. A fire crackled in a huge stone hearth nearby.

She reached out a thin arm and beckoned. I gaped, shocked at the change. Last time I'd seen her she'd seemed not much older than I. The time before, a woman in perhaps her late forties, though both appearances were deceptive for sidhe. Now her hair was white, her skin parchment-pale and her brilliant eyes faded to dull grey. She gestured me closer, a faint, wry smile pulling at her lips.

'Let me look at you, child,' she whispered, coughing. 'Still wearing immodest clothing, I see.'

Aeona, I don't understand. Where am I? My transparent hand passed through hers. *Am I dead?*

'Nay, child,' she said. 'Hast but slipped again.' A frown creased her wrinkled forehead. 'But I sense thou art not far from death. Hast expended too much power. Didst thou forget thine infirmity?' She touched her own throat.

I copied the gesture and shrugged. *I figured it was a one-way trip so it didn't matter anyway. Expending power was the least of my worries. I'm buried under a tonne of rubble. Will be buried...oh, I don't know. I'm dying.*

She chuckled. 'Nay, child. That's my line, not thine.'

You don't understand. I had to destroy all the evidence in the Mors headquarters. The only way was to level the building and I had to be touching it. My body must be crushed by now. I don't understand how I'm even here.

'Foolish child,' Aeona said fondly. 'Art here because, noble as thy sacrifice was, thy time is not yet over. Though 'twill be soon if thou returnst not to thy form anon. E'en now thy companions search for thee.'

They'll never reach me in time. I felt little more than vague sorrow. Mostly for Logan and my mother. Jen, too. The rest would mourn me a little. Erin would probably dance on my grave in glee.

'Go back, Ruadhán,' Aeona said. 'Thy time is not done. Thou hast work to do yet. Many more sidhe need thy help, as do many humans. Go back. And upon thy return to Lothien, seek out the hidden space behind this room's mantle. Thou'lt find a parting gift awaiting thee. Go with my love, little light-bringer. And know I'm proud of thee, now and always.'

She flicked a hand at me, like swatting away an irritating bug.

I careened back into the *sianfath,* freewheeling, directionless, nauseated.

A voice called. Logan? How was that possible? I orientated on his words. My name, over and over, his voice breaking, pleading, begging.

I fell back into my body and it hurt exactly as if I had fallen from two stories up. My limbs and body were weighted by more than mortality. I seemed unable to control them. It was too much effort. I wanted only to be back in the *sianfath*, where I truly was safe and loved. A tonne of guilt pressed my eyelids closed. My chest struggled to rise and pain slipped along every nerve with excruciating precision.

'Rowan?' Logan's voice.

I dragged a breath. Then another.

'She's alive.' Logan gathered me against his chest and pressed a hand to my stomach. Warmth spread from his palm as he poured energy into my depleted body. I batted his arm aside.

'Stop. I'll do it.' I whispered. I reached out and found…nothing. I was trapped in my body. I could sense the *sianfath* all around, but I couldn't step free and slide into it, draw power.

'No,' Logan whispered. 'Don't try. You overstretched yourself. You won't be able to use the *skath-sheel*.' The warmth from his skin started up again. 'Let me help until you're stronger.'

'How long?' I managed.

He shook his head, horror lingering in his expression. 'I don't know, Rowan. Maeve says she's never heard of this. All she can tell is that you depleted yourself so far you almost died and the part of your mind that works the *skath-sheel* has shut down. Maybe for good.'

I couldn't deal with that so I pushed it aside. 'Where are we? Why aren't I buried under the building?'

We seemed to be in some sort of van; white interior, dented walls. I lay on the floor, wrapped in grey felt removalist blankets, my head in Logan's lap. Calain and Dante sat beside us, clinging to straps attached to the van's wall as we lurched around corners.

'We're headed to one of Dante's safe houses.' Logan kissed my forehead. 'Go to sleep. We'll talk later. You're alive and that's all that matters.'

His words made both a great deal of sense and none at all. I was powerless to resist, anyway. Sleep dragged my eyelids shut, content with the warmth of his shared power and the secure touch of his mind. As an afterthought, I opened my inner shield.

He drew a sobbing gasp and kissed my lips. 'Thank you.' He twined his thoughts intimately with mine and cradled me close as the van's movements jolted us.

You stayed, I said. *You wanted to chase down Finn, but you stayed.*

I made the mistake of chasing him in the museum and Kieran captured you. I wasn't going to abandon you again.

Thank you.

I love you, you idiot. Just stop trying to get yourself killed!

I smiled and drifted into sleep.

'But *how?*' Calain said, frowning at me. 'We saw the entire wall collapse on you. No-one could have escaped. Yet we found you lying half a block away.'

I shrugged and pulled the woollen blanket closer around my shoulders. A fire blazed in the hearth but I couldn't seem to get warm. Logan drew me under his arm and I leaned into his warmth.

A circle of eyes watched me with unrelenting curiosity. Seated in a ring of overstuffed, plush armchairs, my companions awaited my reply. Erin and Mia sat close together on a twin couch opposite. Nesrin curled against Dante in another, her head on his shoulder. Michael leaned against a wall, arms folded, legs crossed at the ankles, lips pressed. Calain had taken the largest, central chair, dominating the group like a king holding court. Maeve sat apart, her back straight and ankles crossed, methodically smoothing the blue silk of her trousers over her knees.

'I want to know how you stopped Kieran's *torryl*,' Logan murmured.

I sucked a deep breath and stared into the leaping fire. 'Aeona left me that note, in the back of Mairi's book. I'd asked her for a way of countering Kieran's gift. She just said "riposte". It made no sense. Until I remembered Dante had skill similar to the *torryl*. And he'd used what looked like a sword of light.' I quirked a smile. 'A lightsabre that seemed to only exist in the *sianfath.*'

Dante caressed the rowan-wood cane lying on his lap.

I continued. 'Calain had said Aeona gave that cane to him and I guessed it must be a sword-stick. And since rowan-wood used to be associated with fending off the faery folk, I assumed it had some connection with the *sianfath,* which enabled Dante to use it as a weapon there.'

Dante nodded and pressed the leaf-fern. A faint click sounded and the stick and knob separated, revealing a slim, silvery blade. 'Steel and silver alloy. Both metals reputed to kill fae.' He inspected it with bemusement. 'But I had no idea it could exist in the *sianfath* until I used it against you in the beach house. It just appeared.'

I pulled the blanket closer and shivered. 'Putting that together with Aeona's message, I figured it must be the way to stop Kieran.'

'But how did you know it would work?' That was Maeve, her voice cool and curious, like the scientist she was.

'I didn't. But given I'm Kieran's descendant as much as Dante is, it was a strong possibility I'd be able to use the sword and counter Kieran.'

Admiration glittered in Dante's eyes. 'You took a big risk, sister.' He stroked Nesrin's hair and kissed the top of her head. 'But

I am grateful. But Calain's question: how did you escape the building's collapse?'

'It's something I've done a few times before,' I said. 'But only in life and death situations. I can't control it.' Under the blanket, my fingers locked together so tightly my knuckles ached. 'Aeona's book calls it translocation'.

Maeve gasped. Calain reared back, his mouth falling open.

'Teleportation!' Dante breathed. 'I thought that gift had long since died out. Merda.'

There followed a long, speculative silence in which the fire crackled and an owl hooted in the garden outside. The safe house was a renovated ten-bedroom villa, up in the Tuscan hills, surrounded by autumn-barren trees and overlooking the glittering city lights. Dante had twenty guards posted on the perimeter.

A sidhe man entered, carrying a tray of steaming mugs of tea and coffee. I cradled mine, absorbing the heat, breathing in the scent of camomile. Late though it was, sleep held no draw for me. Nightmares lay there, waiting. Nightmares of burning bodies and falling stone. I shivered and Logan pressed his lips to my temple.

I held nothing back from him, now. My inner shields were open to him without reservation. The connection's intimacy no longer frightened me and my reward was a depth of closeness I'd never imagined possible.

'So, what now?' Michael spoke from near the door. He sipped at his coffee and watched me over the rim.

'You go home and make amends with Paul. Run your company. Use your research department to find ways to…I don't know…prevent global warming or something.'

He quirked a grin. 'Use my power for good instead of evil?'

'Something like that.'

The grin fell away and his gaze slid into the flames, brooding. He had his own battle to fight against his own demons and knowledge of how many people he'd hurt. The shield I'd removed had hidden his memories of his parents' deaths, and other atrocities he'd witnessed as a child. Nothing I could say would make it easier and I felt no need to make it worse for him.

'That's it?' Erin scowled at him and at me. 'After everything he did, you're just going to send him home?'

I shrugged one shoulder. 'If he's the man I think he is...' I cast him a look beneath my lashes. 'I suspect he'll spend the rest of his life – and his fortune – trying to make up for...everything. I'd rather have him working with us than sitting in jail.'

'And you trust him not to betray us again?' Erin blinked at me but her voice held none of the old belligerence.

I studied Michael. He raised his chin, his expression a mix of guilt and determination.

'Yes,' I said. 'I do, actually. He is, after all, part sidhe. He can sense the *sianfath* more strongly than the other humans. He'll do the right thing.'

Michael's cheeks flushed. Then his brows drew together. 'Wait. What do you mean I can sense it more strongly than the other humans? What did you do?'

TWENTY-SEVEN

Do we tell him?

-I believe the time for secrets is long past, daughter. We need men like him to help us, as you said.-

Calain swept a hand over his face, half a millennia of life shadowing his expression. 'First we switched off all the Dark genes we could reach and reversed the brainwashing Kieran had done. Then, with the help of Maeve, Jen, and Maeve's other daughters, we altered about five thousand key humans around the world. Leaders, activists, businessmen. People with power both economic and military.' He lifted his grey eyes to Michael. 'Not enough, but all we could do with the time and resources we had.'

Michael sank onto a straight wooden chair. 'So five thousand humans are like me? They can sense...' He gestured vaguely at the dark window.

Calain nodded. 'We'll continue to alter more over time.'

'And they'll need your help,' I put in.

Michael cocked his head.

I smiled. 'You're the only one who knows what's happened. I've asked Jen to email Paul a list of everyone we changed. You're going to need all your business savvy and contacts. You'll have to get to them before they think they've gone mad. We're trusting you to be the liaison between sidhe and humans. If we're going to fix the hot mess humans have created on this world, we need to work together.'

Excitement displaced confusion in Michael's expression and he shot to his feet. Unspeaking, he strode from the room. The door to his bedroom slammed.

'Is that wise?' Maeve stared after him, her lips pursed.

Calain grimaced. 'Impossible to be certain.'

'We altered Paul, too, but his name's not on Jen's list,' I said, sending Maeve a cool look. 'Him, I trust. He knows to watch Michael. He'll let us know if anything underhanded is happening.' I gazed after Michael. 'But I think Michael will be fine. He has everything he wanted now: a monumental goal and the power to achieve it. And his son.'

I sipped my cooling tea and leaned into Logan's shoulder.

Soon people dispersed. We would go our separate ways in the morning and my throat tightened at the thought of losing them.

'You won't,' Logan murmured. 'When your gift returns, you'll be able to connect with them anytime, anywhere. They're your family.'

'If it returns,' I said, without bitterness.

He gave a low chuckle, but said nothing.

We were the last to leave the room, barring Erin. She hesitated in the doorway and came back. Logan, after a quick look at her, left us alone.

Erin clasped her hands together and bowed her dark head like a guilty schoolgirl. Then she flicked her hair back, jutting her chin out.

'I'm...I'm sorry, ok?'

A small part of me bridled at her tone. I let it go. If nothing else, being blended into the *lorntinn* with Dante and thousands of other sidhe had shown me the depths of hurt we all carried. We were all broken. All monsters to ourselves. All, nevertheless, worth loving.

'I just...' She swallowed. 'You had everything I wanted. You were free. You had a mother who loved you. Gifts I couldn't dream of. And Logan. I hated you – and Ian. Then Ian died and I felt so guilty for hating him that I wanted to blame you, instead.'

I closed the distance between us and wrapped my arms around her. She held herself stiff for a moment, then her arms encircled me and her body shook with long-suppressed grief. Tears soaked my shirt.

We stayed that way a long time, until her sobs became sniffles. She backed away, laughing sheepishly. I passed her a tissue box and she blew her nose.

'Thanks,' she said, shrugging one shoulder.

'You're welcome. And I'm sorry, too. I was a bitch and you were scared.'

Her lips lifted in a rueful smile. 'So was I and so were you. We just handle it differently. You run in with guns blazing. I run away.'

I chuckled. 'Before I met Logan I spent my whole life running away. When I stopped, all this started. There's a time and place for both, I've discovered.'

Erin frowned. 'I think you're right. I've spent most of my life hiding, too. Behind my father. Behind my work.' Her chin rose. 'Maybe it's time I found my own path.'

'Maybe,' I said gently, 'now Ian's not calling the shots, you can do what you always wanted to? What he wouldn't let you.'

Her eyes flew to mine, startled, shadowed with guilt, lit with tentative hope. She chewed her lip.

I smiled. 'You know what else occurred to me?'

She shook her head.

'We're both Silverblades. We're cousins.' I shrugged, feeling awkward. 'I've never had a cousin.'

Erin stilled, then she gave a tentative smile. 'Me neither.'

Mia peered around the corner. 'Coming to bed?'

Erin flushed and hurried to her side, glancing back at me with quick wave.

I spent a few minutes aimlessly tidying the room, not ready to sleep, still savouring the comforting remnants of connection. The house resonated with warmth from more than the fireplaces. In their bedroom, Nes and Dante renewed their love. Mia and Erin lay together, wrapped in each other. Logan waited patiently for me. Calain's thoughts drifted to Anna in Lothien. I felt no embarrassment in being aware of their intimacies. It felt normal; like I belonged for the first time in my life; like I was part of something bigger.

'You know it's not over, don't you?' Maeve's low words from the doorway broke the spell and I sighed.

'I know.' I faced her and threw back my shoulders. 'But you could let me enjoy it for just a few minutes, couldn't you?'

'I'm sorry.' She sank onto a leather couch and gazed into the dying fire. 'I never used to be such a…'

'Cold-hearted bitch?' I said, laughing.

She flicked a bitter smile. 'Yes. You were right.' Her hands twisted together on her lap. 'I didn't realise how much I'd cut myself off from loving my children. It happened in tiny increments, over such a long time. I guess it crept up on me. It hurt too much to lose them, you see. Jen…Logan…they were just the next set of tools for the job. Now…' She spread her hands. 'What do I do?'

I sat beside her. 'As you said, we're not done. We have a lot more humans to change and a lot of lost ground to make up if we're going to save our people. I don't know if my gift will return so you and the other telekinetics have a long, slow job ahead. You'll have to change people one at a time.'

I hesitated, then touched her wrist. 'It's a task you're well suited to, if you want it, Maeve? We need someone to co-ordinate the changes. To work out who the key influencers are. You won't be training Hunters any more. We need facilitators now. People who are willing to help change the world in a good way. Are you up for that?'

'What about Dante?'

'He'll still be needed as Hunter for a while, I suspect. There are Mors cells all over the world. It'll take time to mop up and release any remaining sidhe. Dante can handle that side of things.'

Maeve cast me a quizzical look that held more than a hint of trepidation. 'How did you end up being the mature one in all this?'

I laughed and stood. 'I have a thousand years of parent and grandparent memories rammed into my brain. Some of it had to rub off sooner or later.'

She rose and brushed at her pants in quick, sharp motions. 'Very well. I'll return to Australia with Michael to make sure he's under control. Then I'll start things moving. And you? What are you going to do?'

I tried, automatically, to send a tendril of self into the *sianfath*; to reach out to my mother in Ireland. Nothing happened. I screwed up my nose.

'I'll take your advice and rest up awhile in Ireland. Get to know Calain. Plan the next few years. We need to find Finn, I think. He's the one most likely to regather the Mors against us or try to continue Kieran's work.'

She frowned. 'True. I'll put you in touch with Torin O'Connor of O'Connor Inc in the USA. They're an excellent firm of private investigators in New York. If anyone can find Finn, it's Torin's people.'

'Thanks,' I said. 'We'll keep you posted.'

'You'd better,' she said. 'I'm not shouldering this on my own.' She nodded sharply and turned away, then paused, her expression softening. 'Will you do something for me?'

'What?'

She hesitated, her cheeks flushing. 'Keep Jen with you for a while. Teach her…' Her hands fluttered. 'What I can't…won't. She needs you.'

I have her a swift hug. She didn't return it but didn't pull away, either.

'She needs you, too, Maeve,' I said. 'I'm happy to have her in Lothien, but only if you promise to visit.'

She hesitated, nodded, then vanished down the corridor to her room.

'Rowan!' Jen threw herself into my arms, bawling and laughing at the same time. She babbled into my chest about genes and humans and the *sianfath* until I laughed and pushed her back so I could see her.

'Stop, Jen. I can't understand a word you're saying. Let's get inside. It's freezing.'

She mopped her cheeks with her sleeve and grinned.

The massive oaken doors of Lothien castle stood ajar. My mother waited in the doorway, looking like home, her red hair gleaming in the pale wintersun. She held out her arms and I fell into them, inclined to emulate Jen's outpouring. But I held myself together and we shuffled aside as Logan and Calain hauled our meagre possessions in.

Calain stopped on the threshold and sucked a sharp breath. He let it out with a sigh and scrubbed at the back of his neck.

'Tis an age since I've been here. Seems naught has changed.'

Anna kissed my forehead. 'You're wrong, there. A lot has changed.'

He pulled us both close. I breathed in the warm scent of my parents and fought back tears that seemed always close to the surface these days.

'Is it true?' Jen's excited question broke into our hug and we drew apart. 'Is it true Mother said I can stay?' She glanced back and forth between Logan and me, hands wringing in a gesture that echoed her mother's.

I nodded. She squeaked and threw her arms around Anna and I, squeezing the breath out of me. Anna gargled and Jen let go.

'Sorry. I forget you're not as strong as me.' She turned an eager expression on me. 'Rowan, you *have* to see the things I found here. So much cool stuff! You won't believe it.'

I chuckled and resisted the urge to tell her I'd seen it all. 'Sure, Jen. But give me a minute. There's something I need to do, first.'

Logan looked askance at me. I waved him aside and headed up the great stone staircase that led off the main hall to the first floor. I followed the hall to the right and all the way to the end. There, in the largest corner room of this wing, I halted before a massive bed. The tapestries were faded and the stone walls had been rendered to hide modern piping and insulation, but it was still the room Aeona had occupied; died in. I smoothed the bedlinen and sighed.

I strode over to the mantle and pushed and prodded at the stones; pulled at the candle sconces embedded in the stone. Nothing. No secret hidey-hole. What had Aeona left me?

'They found it during the renovations.' Calain's deep voice startled me.

I spun, blushing like a child caught in wrongdoing. He stood in the doorway, a bundle of faded green velvet in his hands.

'When I renovated the castle before you were born, the workmen found this.' He stroked a green ribbon that tied it shut. 'Your name is embroidered in the ribbon. It's from Aeona.'

I took it from him. 'But you haven't opened it.'

'I…' He sighed. 'You weren't even born yet. I hadn't met Anna. It sounds mad, but it felt wrong to open it. I guess, when you've been around awhile, waiting isn't so difficult.'

I tugged gently at the ancient ribbon. My name was picked out in tiny, faded-red stitches. The silk frayed and disintegrated. I cried out in dismay.

Calain laid an arm around my shoulder. 'It's alright, Ruadhán.'

'But…' I sniffed. 'But she stitched it for me. It had my name.'

He chuckled, deep in his chest. 'Aeona hated sewing. She always had the maids do her needlework.'

I laughed and unwrapped the crumbling velvet with a clear heart. The cloth fell away and revealed a leatherbound book with thick cream pages. Inside the cover, an inscription bore Aeona's name in flowing script. Each crackling page was covered in close-written lines, the ink faded with age but still legible.

'It's her journal,' Calain murmured. 'She kept it after she came here to live with me and Fionn.' His voice cracked. 'Memories. Things not in the other book she wrote about sidhe gifts. Things only you would understand about the *skath-sheel*.'

I closed the book, my heart too full to read it. I didn't want my tears to mar the ink and erase precious words. I hugged it to my chest.

'I can take you to her grave, later, if you like,' Calain said.

'I'd appreciate that. I wish I'd known her more.' I sank onto the bed, sweeping a hand over the rich quilt.

Silence lay heavy between us. The silence of too many years missing and the awkwardness of how to forge a new relationship.

'You have the journal. And Aeona's memories.' He sat beside me, his weight pulling at the mattress. 'You can visit her.'

'I suppose. If my gifts ever return.' The ache in my chest sharpened. At first I'd been almost glad to have the burden of my stronger gifts lifted. Now I was afraid. Without them I was…ordinary. Too normal when I was used to being different and special, even amongst my own people. Where once I'd wanted invisibility, now I wanted my uniqueness back.

Calain sucked a slow breath and released it, his shoulders slumping. 'There's something I've been debating whether to tell you. About your gifts. You will get them back.'

I eyed him askance.

He hunched a shoulder. 'How many times do you remember slipping into my past?'

'Just twice,' I said. 'Once when you were a kid and you ran away. Once when Aeona and Fionn drew me back and told me I had to release your memories. Why?'

His jaw worked and he rubbed the back of his neck. 'I'm sorry, then. There's one more time. And I believe one more visit to Aeona, also.'

'Why are you sorry? What time?' The fear lifted from my shoulders. I would get my gifts back.

He looked away. 'You came to me about fifteen years ago. When you were just four.'

'Why?'

Calain pressed his lips together. 'You came and told me…' He sighed. 'You said I had to leave my family. That the Mors were close on our trail and my departure would keep you and Anna safe.' He pointed to the ring I wore; his signet ring. 'You showed me that as proof. But I knew who you were the minute I saw you. I'd seen you before.'

'No!' The journal slipped from my grasp and fell to the bed. I jumped up, arms wrapped around my stomach, trembling. 'No. It wasn't me. It can't be me.'

He rose and moved closer.

I backed away, shaking my head. 'Don't make me the one that starts all of this. Don't make it my fault.'

His arms encircled me, holding me close as I cried tears of frustration, guilt and, finally acceptance into his shoulder.

'You must, Ruadhán,' he murmured. 'You also told me to download my memories, and asked me to keep secret the fact that Dyson and Kieran were the same person – and my father. You needed to find out for yourself what sort of person he was in order to learn to trust Dante and I.'

'But I almost chose wrong!' I pushed ineffectively at him. 'I almost betrayed you because you'd all lied to me so often.'

'You didn't, though,' he murmured. 'And I knew our only hope of success lay in those falsehoods.'

'So now I have to go back and tell you to lie to me,' I said bitterly. 'And inflict the pain of that corrupted version of you and your memories on myself.'

'And you must go to Aeona, in 1405, when she was staying with Mairi.'

'No.' I wept, not wanting to hear what must be coming.

'The prophecy. It wasn't from Mairi. She couldn't see beyond her own life. The words came from you.'

'No,' I repeated, but inevitability weighted my tongue and my heart.

'I'm sorry.' Calain sighed. 'You must go back or none of this will happen. The world will fall to the Mors. Our people will die.'

He was right. We both knew I would complete the circle and set his footsteps on the path that pulled us apart then brought us back together, here. I nodded, drawing strength from the slow heartbeat in his chest.

I was the light.

And, when the time came, I would once again awaken the shadows.

THE END

If you enjoyed this novel, please leave a review on Amazon and Goodreads. Reviews help other people find good books.

Other books by Aiki Flinthart

Discover other titles by Aiki Flinthart at:
www.aikiflinthart.com

The Ruadhán Sidhe Novels
(YA Urban Fantasy)
Shadows Wake (#1)
Shadows Bane (#2)
Shadows Fate (#3)

The 80AD series
(YA Adventure/Fantasy)
80AD Book 1: *The Jewel of Asgard*
80AD Book 2: *The Hammer of Thor*

80AD Book 3: *The Tekhen of Anuket*
80AD Book 4: *The Sudarshana*
80AD Book 5: *The Yu Dragon*

The Kalima Chronicles (YA Adventure/Fantasy)
IRON (#1)
FIRE (#2)
STEEL (#3)

Romance/Adventure stories
Sold!

Short Story Anthologies
Return
Like a Woman

Connect with me on Facebook
Twitter: @aikiflinthart
Instagram: Aikiflinthart

Healing Heather

Book 4 of the Ruadhán Sidhe Novels

ONE

(Author's note: This is a stand-alone story about new sidhe
characters.
Rowan and Logan feature briefly)

'So you'll take the case?'

The heavily accented voice made Torin O'Connor glance up from
his perusal of the document. In his doorway stood a tall, swarthy
man of Middle-eastern origin. His dark blue suit, though perfectly
tailored, couldn't entirely disguise a thickened middle, just as a
gleaming Rolex and several large, gold rings didn't distract from
fingers swollen with rich living. Flanked by flat-eyed bodyguards,
Prince Ahmed seated himself opposite Torin without awaiting an
invitation. The leather creaked beneath his bulk.

He pulled a cigar from his pocket, bit off the end and spat onto
the polished timber floor. His dark eyes, calculating beneath thick
brows, watched Torin. Leaning back, he pincered the cigar and
pointed it at Torin. A guard produced a lighter and stepped forward.

Torin controlled his annoyance and leaned back as well, lifting a
brow lazily. 'Light that, your Highness, and you can leave now.'

Ahmed's eyes narrowed briefly, then he rolled his wrist, inscribing a circle in the air with the cigar. 'As you wish. You read the file?'

Torin nodded, lifting one corner of the grey suede folder in front of him. 'I've read it.' He waited a moment to see if the Prince would speak and continued when he didn't. 'Why do you need to find her?'

The Prince smiled, his teeth white against dark skin. He shrugged and waved the cigar dismissively. 'I don't think that's really relevant, is it?'

Torin leaned forward again, allowing his heels to hit the wooden floor sharply.

'Yes.' He clasped his hands on top of the folder. 'With fifteen branches around the world, O'Connor Inc. has a reputation to maintain. We certainly don't kidnap young women with no reason given.' He stared into the Prince's black eyes, allowing ice into his own, unintimidated by Ahmed's sneer.

'So, I repeat,' he said evenly, 'what do you need her for?'

Ahmed shrugged. His expensive Armani jacket rucked up around his ears until his head appeared to grow straight from his chest.

'She's connected the death of my youngest daughter. I want…information. I need to know how and why my daughter died, and where her husband is now.'

Torin stilled, sensing something more; something withheld. It was what made him good at this job; he had a sixth sense for when people lied to him. 'Surely that's a matter for the police?'

Ahmed sniffed. 'I do not want the authorities involved. This is a purely personal matter.'

'But if your daughter's dead...'

'They are aware of it. They believe it was natural causes. But my daughter, and her husband...' For a moment the Prince's eyes hardened and his jaw worked. '...are *my* affair.' He regained control and relaxed his mouth into a white smile. 'I simply wish to ask the lady what Amali's last words and wishes were. And to extend my condolences to my daughter's husband. I'm hoping this woman can tell me where to find him.' He lifted an open hand, supplicating. 'Please. Indulge a grieving father and find her? Surely, you understand how important family is.' He nodded towards the picture Torin kept on his desk: a twenty year old photo of Torin's parents and his sister.

'I will pay extremely well,' the Prince said, smiling.

Torin hesitated, still not liking the feel of this interview. He'd learned to trust his feelings over the last thirty-three years and something about the Prince just didn't sit right. Still.... He glanced down at the file on his desk. The young woman in question, if the prince's information was true, was dangerous. Someone needed to rein her in, preferably before she killed anyone else.

'I'll put my best man on it,' he conceded, standing up to shake the Prince's hand.

'I trust so,' Ahmed murmured. 'When he finds her, please have them meet me here, in New York. Here is my card.' He handed over a gold-embossed business card and swept regally from the office without a backward glance.

Torin texted his partner.

Twenty minutes later Kael swung into the room, energetic, careless, carrying a laughing rejoinder to Torin's secretary on his lips as he flicked the door shut. He sauntered across the timber floor, his sneakers soundless, hands jammed into the pockets of faded jeans, plain grey tshirt hanging loose across his lean shoulders. He looked comfortable. Relaxed. A lopsided smile was echoed by ironic humour in his grey eyes.

Torin eyed him speculatively, debating the wisdom of handing him this case. It had taken years for the bitter withdrawal to fade into acceptance and for Kael's natural humour to resurface. Was Kael ready to take on something that hit so close to the bone? There was really no one else available, and something about the case made Torin uneasy. He wanted it in the hands of someone he trusted.

Settling into a chair, Kael put his feet up on the desk and stifled a yawn. 'What's up, oh great leader?'

With a sigh, Torin sat down, his hand on the folder. 'We're equal partners, Kae.'

Kael's grin twisted into smugness. 'But you *like* the leader thing. I much prefer the road.' He swept a hand around the leather-and-timber office with its dark timber furniture and colours. 'You get off on running this place. And you're good at it. Let me do what I'm good at.'

'And that is?' Torin raised a brow, tapping one finger on the folder. He knew what the answer would be.

'Finding people for money,' Kael replied promptly. 'Isn't that why you called me? What've you got?'

Sliding his fingers over the folder, Torin grimaced. 'Not sure it's a good idea to give you this one. I just don't have anyone else available.'

Kael leaned forward, twitched the folder out from under his fingers and opened it. 'Reverse psychology? Bit obvious for you. What's so…' He flipped a page. 'Ah. Not reverse psychology. You were serious. Shit, Tor. You know how I feel about people like this woman.' He blew a thick breath and the humour fell away from his mobile face, leaving it blank. He finished skimming the written file and closed it, staring at the grey suede. The eyes he raised to Torin's were haunted by old pain and Torin cursed his own stupidity. He should have turned the job down rather than inflict it on Kael.

'No one else at all?' Kael's voice was flat.

'Sorry. I should have backed out. It's just…' Torin glanced down at the grainy photo, still under his own hand. He spun it and slid it across the desk. 'There's something about this girl. She seemed familiar. And something about the client. I don't know, Kae. I think we need to take this job. I just don't know why.'

Picking up the photo, Kael's eyes widened. He blinked and frowned, his whole body stilling as he inspected it minutely. Slowly, he lowered it, looked at it again, then back at Torin. Nodding, he stood. There was a hint of bewilderment in his eyes as he slid the photo slowly into the folder and patted it.

'Alright,' he said quietly, 'I'll do it. You've always had good instincts about people. It's how we're still alive, after all. So set me up a meeting with this prince. I have a few questions.'

Slightly taken aback by his ready acquiescence, Torin could do no more than nod and agree. Kael, holding the folder tightly in one hand, left.

Torin watched him leave, noting the lack of spring in his step, and cursed himself again. Something stank about this case, he just knew it. He only hoped he wasn't putting Kael in danger.

End of Chapter 1

Healing Heather will be released in mid 2019

www.aikiflinthart.com

www.ingramcontent.com/pod-product-compliance
Lightning Source LLC
Chambersburg PA
CBHW030630110726
47901CB00002B/396